REA

Reinventing Olivia

Reinventing Olivia

Nancy Robards Thompson

Five Star • Waterville, Maine

First Edition
First Printing: July 2003

Set in 11 pt. Plantin by Liana M. Walker.

Printed in the United States on permanent paper.

Library of Congress Cataloging-in-Publication Data

Thompson, Nancy Robards, 1964–
    Reinventing Olivia / by Nancy Robards Thompson.—1st ed.
        p. cm.
    ISBN 0-7862-5536-6 (hc : alk. paper)
    1. Rejection (Psychology)—Fiction. 2. Self-realization—
Fiction. 3. Young women—Fiction. I. Title.

PS3620.H684R45 2003
813′.6—dc21   2003052925

This book is dedicated to Michael and Jennifer for your love, patience and faith.

Acknowledgments

Undying gratitude to Teresa Brown, Kathy Garbera, Elizabeth Grainger, Catherine Kean and Mary Louise Wells—the best friends and critique partners a writer could wish for. I truly couldn't have done this without you; to my agent Michelle Grajkowski for taking a chance on me; to my editor, Russell Davis, for taking a chance on this book; to Matt Brown for unlocking the secrets of the music industry; to Juanita Eitreim, Christina Mancia, Robin Tremble, Joanne Maio and Jay Robards for cheering me on and understanding when I had to retreat into my cave; to Susan and Pete Pettegrew for all the celebrations (even before we really had anything to celebrate); to Lynn Robards and Wiladean Barnett for reading my manuscripts and being unfailingly enthusiastic; and finally, to Jim Robards and Barbara Robards for raising me to believe I could do anything I set my mind to.

Chapter One

You don't have to be Einstein to figure out certain women get way ahead in life merely because they've deemed themselves *entitled*. You know the type. The ones with attitude. The rule-breakers.

The poor saps who haven't mastered the art of entitlement, the rule-followers, end up holding the door for the sisters of the "I deserve the flawless three-karat diamond."

Some call it the natural order of the singles' food chain. Others call it a personal problem.

I'm a rule-follower and I'm not ashamed to admit it. Always have been. It's just who I am, part of my genetic makeup. I don't like calling attention to myself. I don't believe in throwing fits to get what I want. I'm not bucking for the three-karat marquise. I'm perfectly happy contributing my fifty percent to the simple life my boyfriend Richard and I have made together.

On the other hand, my best friend Karen is a total rule-breaker.

"Liv," Karen said to me, "attitude isn't genetic like, like— Cindy Crawford's mole. It's a state of mind."

It was Friday night at Hue. The bar was packed, and a Euro-disco mix blared from the sound system. Combined with the din, it stirred up a frenetic energy that rained down like a tropical storm. Karen had taken me out for a bon voyage party because I was leaving the next day to visit Rich in Paris. We'd been together for three years, but he'd been working in France for the past six months.

I waved away a stream of cigarette smoke trailing from the

woman sitting on the barstool next to me. As a tall guy with spiky two-toned hair and tattoos on both forearms tried to squeeze his way up to the bar, he knocked my arm and red wine sloshed onto the blue silk pants I'd just gotten from the dry cleaners.

Great.

I dabbed at the stain with a napkin. That's why I hated going out. I hate crowds. I hate the predatory nature of the dating jungle. I didn't need this because I had a boyfriend, who might very well become my fiancé within the week if he'd managed to conquer his fatal fear of commitment.

Karen flipped her long blonde hair over her shoulder. "Attitude's just like Pamela Anderson's boobs."

What? I stopped mid-dab and stared at her, sure I'd heard her say something about Pamela Anderson's boobs. But I must have heard her wrong over the noise.

She repeated herself.

Ugggh, I'd heard her right. I should have known because it was such a Karenism.

Karen Denton looks like Jerry Hall in her prime, only prettier, and is perfectly at home in her own gorgeous skin. Despite her personal motto—*attach yourself to no man as you would have no man attach himself to you*—she's never wanted for male attention. Thank God she was my best friend. Otherwise, I'd have to hate her, which wouldn't be hard since the closest I come to resembling a star was maybe Sandra Bullock with boobs and a butt on a humidity-induced bad hair day. And that would only be plausible if you squinted your eyes and stretched your imagination really far.

Anyway, I digress. I was telling you about how Karen had latched onto the idea that all I needed to do to get Rich to put a ring on my finger was to act as if it were a given.

"Think about it," Karen said over Hue's rising din. "Attitude is so like a boob-job. It can be acquired and overinflated to ungodly proportions."

She crossed her arms so they cradled her own manufactured C-cups and smiled down at them like they were exhibit A. A guy sitting across the bar who'd been eyeing her all evening nearly snorted his drink.

It's always amazed and baffled me how women with implants can show off their breasts like they were a new pair of shoes or some equally detached possession. As if by virtue of paying for what nature didn't install, they could bypass the modesty that burdened those of us who'd been saddled with big ones since puberty. I'd tried to minimize my D-cups since middle school.

I knew Karen was fully aware of the choking man at the bar. I felt myself flush for her, because I knew darn well she wouldn't blush on her own.

"Any woman with enough self-esteem can cop an attitude," Karen said. "Even you, Liv."

I frowned, then sipped my wine. "From my perspective, attitude looks more like Cindy's mole. When isolated and studied, it's really ugly."

Karen quirked a knowing brow and leaned in. "Sure, but use it right and men will fall flat at your feet." She pointed a touché finger at me and settled back into her seat to nurse her Madras as the bartender set another round in front of us.

"We didn't order these," I said.

He smirked. "Compliments of Romeo, across the bar."

We looked over. The guy, whom Karen's bosom-showcasing antics nearly knocked off his stool, raised his glass. Simultaneously, his eyes fell to her breasts, then slid to mine, all for the bargain price of a couple of drinks. Karen swiveled her stool so her back was to him and she faced me.

"A good-looking guy friend of mine used to say all the

women he was attracted to were 'Three Bs.' " She paused for effect, then ticked them off on her fingers. "Blonde, Buxom and *Bitchy.*"

I laughed. "Another of your deep, meaningful relationships?"

Karen smiled, then leveled me with her knowing gaze.

"You need to get a little bitchy with Rich. Quit accommodatin' him." Her southern accent shaved the edges off the words, but the seriousness of her tone was still 100 percent intact. "When you get home tonight, hon, you call him and tell him when you get to France you're draggin' him to the top of the Eiffel Tower, where he'd better put a ring on your finger. Then he'd better get his cute ass back to Florida and marry you. And if he's a good boy, tell him he just might get lucky."

I shifted on the black leather barstool and imagined myself saying that to Rich. I almost laughed out loud.

God love her. Karen meant well, because she thought I wanted marriage. I thought I wanted marriage. I did. I do, but . . . I was probably just nervous. It had been a long, dry season since the last time I'd seen him.

"That's not very romantic," I muttered. "I shouldn't have to drag Rich into a proposal."

"Well, hon, don't think of it as draggin' him. Think of it as helping him make up his mind. I mean, he owes it to you after all this time."

"Owes it to me? What? Like paying off a debt he's racked up?" I made a face. "Uh-uh."

She stared at me. "Don't you want to marry him?"

I shrugged, swirled my merlot, sniffed it and took a sip. It tasted like blackberries and oak. I vaguely remembered the way Rich's kisses tasted. The memory, like my burning desire for him to demonstrate some form of commitment, had grown dimmer as each day passed.

He'd asked me to move to France with him since he had to be there for six months. I chose not to go. I didn't want to give up everything to follow him, since he was so hesitant about the ultimate destination of our relationship. Instead, we agreed to give it six months and revisit "our future" when I met him in Paris.

Then he left.

Without me.

I hadn't given up *my* life. I'd stayed behind to maintain ours. Our home. Our yard. Our phone number. *Our* life.

"Do you really think *forever* happens?" I mused, staring into my wine. My father left before I was born. I'd never known him. I had no proof *forever* wasn't just the ultimate urban legend. "I mean, two people loving each other forever?"

"Of course," Karen assured. "When it's right."

Profound words, coming from a woman who went through men like paper plates. I bit my lip and surveyed all the people crammed into the bar. Men and women all searching for the same elusive ardor.

"Don't tell me you're having second thoughts?" Karen said.

"I'm not. It's just *'til death do us part* is a really, really long time. . . . I shouldn't have to coerce Rich into marrying me. I shouldn't have to drag him to the gates of that long road to eternity."

Karen's mouth fell open, but she didn't say anything.

I swallowed. Hoping she couldn't see down into the raw, exposed roots of my fear, I leaned in and exchanged my empty wineglass for the full one Karen's admirer sent over.

"I knew it." She shook her head. "He was an idiot to go off and leave you."

I waved off her new tirade.

"Serves him right." She slumped back in her chair. "You could have your pick of any man here."

I rolled my eyes, sorry I'd opened Pandora's box. "Enough, okay?"

"I'm serious. Liv. Look. Look. Over there." Karen grabbed my arm and nodded at a guy across the bar. "He's checking you out."

Oh, great. I glanced over his head, because knowing he might have been looking at me, I *couldn't* look at him.

"He's not looking at *me*," I said.

Karen laughed. "He *is*."

Unwittingly, my gaze connected with his. Ohmigod. "Okay, so he's looking at me," I said to Karen without breaking the eye contact spell.

"Cute, too," Karen said. "If you liked the dark, artsy, bad boy type."

I tried not to fidget. He looked a little like the singer from Matchbox Twenty. He smiled and I tried to smile back, but my face felt stiff. Out of practice.

The guy mouthed something. I didn't understand, but I finally managed a smile and nodded like I got it because he was grinning at me and I felt stupid. He raised his glass and maintained eye contact. I even counted to ten and, God love him, his gaze didn't meander to my boobs.

I could be a slave to a guy who looked me in the eye. A strange sort of awkward thrill reverberated through my body and my heart chided, *well, Rich, I've still got it.*

Then the bartender rang the tip bell and reality crashed down around me. What the hell was I doing? I looked away. Rich might be half a world away. In France. Without me. And the intimate portion of our relationship might have been on intermission, but tomorrow I was flying out to be with him. It felt strange, like we'd have to get reacquainted. Even so, I was committed.

I'd better be if we'd be talking *'til death do us part.*

Oh, God.

I swilled my wine then turned back to Karen, who was talking to the guy standing next to her.

I took a deep breath of smoky bar air and tried to quiet the alarm buzzing in my head—*'til death do us part.* It was a very, very long time. I darted a glance at Mr. Matchbox. But he was gone.

For some odd reason, my stomach sank. I was tired and hungry. The sum of these two parts always added up to funk.

I caught Karen's eye and leaned over and said, "Why don't we get out of here and go to Dexter's? I'm supposed to write a review of their new menu when I get back from vacation and I need to eat there at least a couple of times. Come on, the newspaper will take us out to dinner."

"I'm starving. You must have read my mind."

She pulled a wad of cash out of her jeans pocket and counted out enough for the bill. As she tossed them on the bar, the guy next to her said something in her ear and handed her a business card. She smiled and shoved it in her hip pocket. I envied her unself-conscious ease.

We worked our way through the crowd to the fifteen-foot shimmery-gray chiffon sheer suspended by a wrought iron rod that covered the entrance. Before I passed through, a hand touched my shoulder.

"You're leaving?"

I turned around and stood nose-to-nose with Mr. Matchbox. He had longish light brown hair and up close, I realized he might have been a few years younger than me. He was kind of pale, like an artist who slept all day and stayed up all night. Rich was always asleep by ten.

My mind searched the dusty archives for a witty response. But I couldn't think over the damn "emergency warning" that started buzzing in my head.

This is a test, I repeat this is just a test of the "emergency reality-check system." If this were an actual emergency you would find yourself attracted to the male-who-is-not-Richard in question. In an actual emergency, keep your hands to yourself and your pants on and everything will be fine. This concludes our test.

I worried he'd think I was mute, so I said the only thing I could think of besides *danger, Liv Logan.*

"We're leaving."

Smooth, Liv.

"Too bad. I wanted to buy you a drink."

Two glasses of merlot on an empty stomach and my face was really numb. So was my brain because I said to him, "Maybe another time?" Yeah, right. Like when?

It was a rhetorical question. You know, like when people say, "Hey, how ya doin'?" They don't really care and they certainly don't want you to unload. Could you imagine? "Thanks for asking. I'm not doing so good. I haven't had sex in six months. Do you know what it's like to go without sex for *six months?*"

"Yeah, sure," said Mr. Matchbox.

"What?!" I blinked. Ohmigod. He was reading my mind. Then I realized he was talking about the drink.

He shrugged. "Maybe another time." And gave me this sexy half-smile. Our gazes held for a second too long. All of a sudden my heart thumped and the emergency alarm in my brain warned of imminent danger. A little devil who sat on my shoulder whispered, "Go for it, Liv. Rich'll never know."

I shot Mr. Matchbox a shaky smile and made a break for the door. Two drinks and I couldn't trust myself. It was worse than I thought. When did I lose my edge? Not that I ever had an *edge*. Well, not a Ginsu-sharp edge, anyway.

I never used to worry about making a fool of myself or watching my willpower melt to the consistency of putty. I always sat back, content in my ineligibility, and reaped the benefits of being Karen's friend. Karen was the woman the men wanted. I was on my way to Paris.

As I made my getaway, the little shoulder demon shouted, "You dig him. He digs you. Go for him. Rich'll never know. 'Til death do us part is a long, long time."

I knocked the devil off his perch and joined Karen outside. She was talking to a couple of guys dressed in black. One had a shaved head and a goatee. The other had longish hair and was a little too perfect to be straight.

It was warm for late January, and I was glad to be outside. Free from the confines of the bar. The scene was just a little too predatory. And it was only Friday. Still early in the weekend. What was it like Saturday come midnight when the players only had a couple hours left to score or strike out? Who were those desperate souls who hooked up in the eleventh hour? Where would Mr. Matchbox be tomorrow come midnight?

Outside Hue there was room for the sexual energy to disperse. A definite absence of clashing libidos and colliding attitudes. Quite a place. Though I'd always thought Hue was a funny name for it, an oxymoron, because everyone who worked there wore black. As you drove by, you could see people sipping drinks as they lounged on white couches artfully arranged on the terrace. A definite absence of color. Or maybe a lack of soul. So many people searching. I should be happy with the safe, quiet life Rich and I had built together, with or without talk of the future.

I stood back and looked up at the condominiums that sat high atop the bar. There was a party in full swing on the top floor. I heard laughing and loud industrial-sounding music, but all I saw were hands holding drinks over the balcony.

The condos were part of a new development in the Thornton Park neighborhood of downtown Orlando. Part of the redevelopment that was breathing new urbanized life into the area. I'd always wondered who lived in the lofts.

The "About Town" reporter for the *Orlando Daily*, the paper where I worked as the restaurant critic, wrote that some Arabian prince owned one of the condos for the occasional weekend he spent in Orlando. Supposedly, he owned the top unit on the northwest corner that overlooked Lake Eola, Orlando's answer to Central Park.

The prince rumor was surprising because from what I understood, the lofts weren't palatial. For that matter, not even that expensive. But it drew a colorful crowd. Supposedly, the place was crawling with a mix of artists, filmmakers, actors and *real* writers (unlike me, who took the safe route of journalism school and became a critic). Free spirits who would view moving to France as an opportunity to nurture their creative souls, steady job and engagement ring be damned.

I suddenly felt way out of my league. The place reeked of cutting edge, of individuals who were born with the natural ability to *live*. To want for nothing. If they had an ache, they'd just paint it a brighter shade or write it out of the script and move on to something more exciting.

Rich and I lived in a little bungalow about ten blocks east on Washington Street. He'd bought the house for a steal fifteen years ago. He once said when I'd moved in was when it became a home. Our home.

"Liv, this is Juan," said Karen, motioning me over. "He does my hair and this is his friend, Ron. Juan lives on the third floor." She pointed up at the lofts. "Juan and Ron." Karen beamed at them. "That's adorable."

"Nice to meet you, 'Livia," said Juan. Traces of a proper Spanish accent made him sound genteel. "We were on our way up to the party. Would you like to join us?"

I glanced at Ron to get a read, to make sure we wouldn't be crashing their own little private party, but he'd all but turned his back on us watching the Hue crowd.

My curiosity out-voted my growling stomach. How cool to be a fly on the wall and see how people with *real* lives lived. We followed Juan and Ron into the lobby, done in shades of pumpkin, ocher, chartreuse and chrome.

An unconscious part of me nagged that I should be home waiting for Rich's call, but I reminded myself he was *traveling*. He said he wouldn't call tonight. He'd see me at the airport when I got there.

An unwelcome, wine-inspired voice wondered why it was any different for him to call from Florence or wherever he was than from Paris. No matter where you were in Europe, it was all long distance to the States. But the practical strong-woman part of me chimed in that Rich had his reasons for not calling. For God's sake, I'd see him the day after tomorrow.

We stepped into the elevator. When the doors closed, gay man's cologne filled the close space. Karen chattered with the guys. I watched them in the elevator mirrors. Juan exuded confidence in his black turtleneck and leather pants. He stopped checking himself out for a moment to explain, "This guy, Bob, who's having the party, is one of my clients."

Giving the host a name made me feel like a party crasher. I envisioned Bob putting on a gracious face, making us feel absolutely welcome while underneath he'd be saying, "Who the hell are these people?"

As the elevator rose, my thumb automatically rubbed the wine spot on my pants. It had dried, but it felt conspicuous. I felt conspicuous—conspicuously frumpy—big as a house conspicuous—conspicuously out of place.

I glanced at Juan's reptile-skin boots, then at my plain pumps, which seemed so sophisticated when I got them to go with the silk pants. Now they seemed—well, sensible.

I curled my toes and noticed Ron's nails, buffed to an immaculate shine. I couldn't remember the last time I'd had a manicure. Even an artist couldn't work much magic on chewed cuticles. Ron wore a thumb ring and two silver hoops in each ear. He even had better jewelry than I did.

"Are you sure Bob won't mind us dropping in?" I asked.

A patronizing smile tugged at the corners of Ron's mouth. "Honey, the more the merrier."

My gut tightened. I felt like a woman venturing into the gay man's world. Probably how Dorothy felt when she realized she'd landed in munchkin land. I just hoped my big clunky house wouldn't kill anyone.

The elevator dinged a final time, and the doors opened into a crowded party. Actually, it was the hallway, but two apartment doors were open and people had spilled out into the extra space. An industrial mix of Depeche Mode's *Master and Servant* blared. The bass thumped through my bone marrow. But I felt smug that I recognized the music. Maybe I wasn't as far gone as I thought.

A crowd that looked a lot like the Hue horde stood shoulder to shoulder smoking, sipping drinks, and talking over the music. I wondered how many of them heard the party from the street and decided to wander up to check it out.

Party crashers.

Ron took off in one direction. Juan motioned with his head for us to follow in another. As we squeezed through the crowd, Juan stopped every few feet to talk to people.

As I waited, I watched a rail-thin girl with spiky, clown-red hair and several visible piercings dance by herself. She seemed oblivious to the crowd, to people's personal space. And to the heat, though sweat glistened on her forehead and her mascara was smudged under her eyes like a football player's grease paint.

No windows, cigarette smoke and too many people jammed together—Ugggh, it was hot.

My head swam. Oh, God. I wished people would quit bumping into me. I needed to get out of there before I had a claustrophobic episode.

Chill. Just chill.

Watching the dancing girl made me feel 100 years old. I was born old. Old and content in my safe little sheltered world.

I glanced back where Juan had stood talking. But he wasn't there. Neither was Karen. Gone. Great. They'd left me watching the freak show.

I pushed through the crowd, my senses assaulted by the various aromas and textures of intimate contact with strangers. Ow! Someone stepped on my foot.

Did the words personal space mean anything to anyone? This was a party? This was supposed to be fun—

Oh, yuck! Somebody's deodorant quit working. Ewww. Either that or the guy who'd just squeezed himself in front of me had smuggled a bag of tacos into the party. And he wasn't carrying anything. No, he was using both arms to shove his way through the crowd.

Well, at least he had been doing that until we'd come to a gridlocked halt.

Oh, God, gross. Can't people smell themselves? Obviously not. Maybe he thought it made him smell manly? A manly man. Maybe he couldn't smell his own stink because the chicky-babe next to me had bathed in perfume—Calvin

Klein Eternity, to be exact. The air smelled like smoky, perfumed BO.

Eww!

Not a good place to be.

I tried not to breathe.

Okay, if I didn't get out of here fast, I was going to gag or pass out.

This called for some serious elbow work.

"Excuse me." I elbowed my way past the ripe man. "Oops, sorry." He shot me a dirty look. Listen, stinky dude, if you could smell you, you wouldn't want to be downwind, either. Go home and take a shower.

A few more strategic bumps and maneuvers and I was closer to the two open apartments.

It was still too crowded to see more than eight feet ahead, but still no sign of Karen and Juan. Which apartment had they gone in?

I chose the closer of the two and pushed and elbowed my way to the door. The music was a bit muffled in there and at least the bottleneck of people gave way once I got inside.

I scanned the room for Juan and Karen. No luck. I would've even settled for finding Ron. Well, maybe not. He wasn't very friendly.

A small pixieish woman blew smoke in my face as I shouldered my way past her. My eyes burned. Ahead I could see what looked like the door to the balcony.

I gave a final push for freedom and on the balcony, I ran headlong into Mr. Matchbox, looking oh-so-fine in his crisp white T-shirt and faded jeans. For about a second, he looked as surprised as I felt.

"Hey," he said. "How 'bout that drink?"

Chapter Two

I felt like I'd slid into heaven through hell's back door, after spending the rest of the evening on the balcony with Hunter, formerly known as Mr. Matchbox. A banjo-playing philosopher, with rock and roll dreams.

As I unlocked my front door, I succumbed to the giddy urge I'd suppressed all night and laughed out loud—for all of about two seconds, until I heard the phone ringing.

My heart lurched, and I struggled to get the key out of the lock. Rich? Who else would call me at two in the morning? I hadn't given Hunter my telephone number.

By the time I got inside and turned on the lights, the machine had picked up, and I couldn't find the damn receiver. I dropped my purse and keys on the floor.

"I *hate* cordless phones."

Frantically, I upended couch cushions, tossed throw pillows to the floor and turned around in circles like a circus dog, trying to find the receiver. *Dammit!*

"Wait, Rich! Don't hang up."

Just as I spied the phone on the kitchen table, partially hidden by a mess of newspapers, I realized not only had Rich hung up, but he hadn't even left a message.

I flung the papers to the floor, then grabbed the receiver and pressed the caller ID button, hoping there was a number. I don't know why I did that. All his overseas calls came through as "Unknown Caller." I stared at the useless receiver and willed it to ring, willed Rich to call back. But he didn't, of course.

I stalked across the floor and slammed the phone down in

its cradle. That's when I noticed I had five messages waiting on the machine. My stomach flipped.

Oh, God! Had he been calling me all night? Well, it was only two. Not like I was slinking home with the sunrise. I had *nothing* to feel guilty about, despite my hammering pulse and the very vivid memory of Hunter's intense indigo eyes.

Hunter and I had just . . . talked.

And flirted.

Okay, so some serious sexual vibes were binging back and forth between us. But *binging* and *banging* were two entirely different things, even if a single letter and a very fine line was all that differentiated them.

I'd told him I was going to Paris and would probably come back engaged. He said he was happy for me. We spent a lot of time talking about Carl Jung's theories on synchronicity. Don't ask me how we got on that subject, but we did and it was kind of cool. He's pretty deep for a guy who plays the banjo at Disney by day and sings in a band by night. But don't get me wrong, he wasn't pretentious. He was about as far from being an intellectual snob as a gorgeous, interesting man could be.

I punched the rewind button. While the tape scraped and hissed its way back to the beginning, I ran into the bedroom and grabbed Rich's big flannel button-down and my old gray sweatpants off the hardwood floor. I guess I should have been tidier, but I was alone, why bother?

I got back to the living room just as Rich's voice came over the tape.

"Liv, it's me. Are you there? I thought you'd be home from work by now. Guess not. Uh . . . listen . . . um . . . I need to talk to you. Um . . . Well . . . guess I'll call you later."

I draped the clothes on the back of the couch since the cushions were still in a heap. He sounded disappointed, even a little dejected. Needles of guilt prickled my skin, and I rubbed my arms to quiet them.

Why should I feel bad for going out with Karen and not being at home waiting for Rich to call when he'd said he wouldn't? For having a drink with a guy?

Hmmm, was Rich checking up on me?

I unbuttoned my pants, tugged them down over my hips and let them fall to the floor. Tomorrow before my flight, I'd have to take them to the one-hour dry cleaners to get out the wine stain. I added my silk blouse and bra to the pile and pulled his flannel shirt over my head. The downy softness swept over my cheeks. Instinctively, I breathed in, but his scent had long ago surrendered to a mix of perfume and laundry detergent.

I made a mental note to bring the shirt to France, to reactivate the scent. Flannel wasn't very sexy, I know. But one of the things I loved most about being together as long as Rich and I had was that we could ditch the uncomfortable formalities and be real with each other. I held the shirttail up to my face and inhaled deeply.

Nope, no trace of Rich.

The machine voice announced, "Call received at 5:32 p.m." That would have made it 11:32 p.m. in Italy. Since he'd been gone, I thought in two time zones. Rich-time and Liv-time.

Hopefully, nothing had happened to keep him in Italy while I arrived in Paris. Since I was supposed to fly out in a few hours, it would be hell to change the ticket at this late date. He probably just wanted to go over specifics, where he'd meet me, and what we were going to do while I was there.

I pulled on my gray sweatpants. Comfortable at last. While Rich's second message played, I put the cushions back on the couch, then padded barefoot into the kitchen to make a cup of Sleepy Time tea.

"Hey. Me again. Are you there? Liv? Guess not. Well . . . um . . . I'll try later." His deep voice sounded a little shaky, and a spiral of tenderness uncoiled in my heart.

He missed me.

As I put my cup of water and tea bag in the microwave and punched the buttons, I let the thought wash through me like nourishment. And the cranky, hungry child in me wanted to snuggle up to the idea that he missed me and nurse on it until I got my fill of the emotional sustenance I'd been lacking over the past six months.

So, Rich, had your lover's radar sounded crazy warnings tonight? *Danger! Danger! Alien forces invading sacred territory.* Are we so tightly connected that bells and whistles were tugging at your intuition, warning you of a poacher on the home front?

I tried to take pleasure in making him wonder. It was good for him. But it felt hollow and shallow. Hearing his voice on the machine filled in the cracks of doubt that had tried to shatter me earlier. He missed me. We'd be fine once we were together.

"Call received at 5:59."

Not even thirty minutes after the first call.

After that message, two hang-ups. One at 6:30, the other at 7:30.

Next call 9:30. "You're obviously out for the evening." Uh-oh. He sounded annoyed. I heard him take a deep breath, and I missed him so much it was almost a physical pain, until he said, "I tried your cell phone, but you're not picking up. Hot date?" He loosed a dry, unenthusiastic laugh that struck me deep in the murky hollow where my insecurities feed. The battery on my cell phone was low. I don't know what it was about his tone, but unease wove its way through my body. Oh, for God's sake, he had no right to get annoyed just because I was out.

The microwave beeped.

If he'd called at 9:30 Florida time, it was three-thirty in the morning over there. He was probably tired. I was on my way into the living room with my tea when the phone rang again. As I scrambled to answer it, I nearly scalded myself.

"Hello?"

"Olivia? God! Where have you been?" It was Rich and he sounded pissed. I set my tea on the coffee table.

"Hey! I just got home. What's going on?"

"Did you have a good night?"

Hunter's half-smile flashed in my mind.

"It was okay. I was out with Karen. Were you missing me?"

There was a beat of silence that lasted a little too long.

"Listen, Liv. . . ." His tone made me picture him rubbing his temples. I sucked in a quick breath and held it. It seemed like hours before he continued, but I waited, not wanting to break the thin veil of silence that hid whatever he was having such a hard time telling me.

"God, Liv, I really think the world of you. I'm sorry. I'm really sorry."

"What, Rich? What's happened?"

I felt the blood drain from my body. A slow, sickening process. First from my head, then from my limbs. I half-expected to look down and see my feet planted in a crimson pool. I squeezed my eyes tight because I knew the instant before he answered me that if I looked down it wouldn't be just blood I'd see. My heart would be on the floor, too, all battered and beaten because he was about to rip it out and stomp on it.

27

He sighed. "I don't know how to say this, so I'll just say it."

"Rich, whatever it is we can fix it."

"No, Liv, we can't. I got married last night."

The room spun and his words knocked me down onto the couch. I swore I was imagining things when I heard a French-woman's voice ask, *"A qui tu parles?"*

Who the hell was *that?*

"À personne," Rich said quickly. His reply sounded muf-fled, as if he'd shoved his hand over the receiver. But I could still hear him.

A molten liquid rushed through my veins. I sat up on the edge of the couch. Ohmigod. *She* was there. And I could still remember the basics of college French 101.

"Nobody? You told her you're talking to *nobody?"* My voice sounded shrill and thin, like it didn't come from me. "Tell her who I am. Tell her you made a mistake. You love *me.*"

Suddenly, I was floating above myself, watching the whole scenario like a scene from a heart-wrenching, melodramatic soap opera.

This wasn't real. It wasn't happening. I would wake up and realize I'd just had a nightmare and everything would be fine.

"Ree-shard?" In the background, her sultry French accent drew out his name and pulled sobs from somewhere deep in my gut.

"I've got to go, Liv. I'll call you another time, when I can talk."

And just like that, the line went dead.

"What the hell is left to talk about?" Karen plucked a doughnut from the box on my kitchen table and nudged the Krispy Kremes toward me. It was three-thirty in the morning, and we were sitting across from each other devouring a box of doughnuts like they would save our lives. Before she'd arrived I'd managed to shove my hysteria behind a paper-thin shield that felt like it would hold as long as I didn't say too much. If I didn't think about Rich, didn't talk about him, I'd be okay.

"I mean he's not even speaking your language anymore," she said around a mouthful. Her southern accent always got thicker when she was mad. "Seems to me *Rich-urd* ended the dialogue when he said 'I do.' *Rich-urd. Bast-urd.*"

I felt my bravado slip a notch and tried to regroup by focusing on the box of doughnuts Karen brought over after I'd called her cell phone, hysterical, tangled in the barbed wire of post-breakup delirium.

"He probably wants to talk about the house," she continued, waving the uneaten portion of her doughnut at me, "and how you're going to divide up the CDs. *Bast-urd.*"

I tried to let her words roll off me, but fresh tears welled in my eyes. One brimmed and rolled.

Karen sighed and called Rich everything from asshole to son-of-a-bitch, while I did my best to resurrect my flimsy wall of composure.

I stared at the doughnut on the napkin in front of me, at the place where the tear had slid off my face and splattered onto the hardened glaze, reconstituting it, giving it new life.

New life.

If I hadn't been so numb, the mere idea would have terrified me. But at the time, I couldn't think of anything else beyond living comfortably numb and existing on nothing but Krispy Kremes.

"*Dick!*" Karen shouted.

I tore my gaze from the table to her.

"*Rich-urd,* my ass." She pulled the box back into her zone

and tucked into an éclair. "The guy's always been a dick. Now, he's living up to his name. The two-timing Dick marries The French Tart."

It was classic. Tragic, but classic. And I couldn't help it. It was so perfect I laughed. No, I guffawed. So hard the layer of ice frozen over my hurt melted, and I started to feel again.

Oh, not good.

I shouldn't have done that. Because along with the feeling came the tears. Big, fat, bossy, unwelcome tears with a mind of their own. They broke loose and streamed down my cheeks.

This go-round, they wouldn't be dammed. They dragged me right along over the edge until I had no choice but to jump off into sheer misery. I buried my face in my hands and sobbed.

I'd loved a *Dick*.

The Dick didn't love me.

The Dick loved a French Tart.

My life was shit. Small. Stinky. Meaningless. Insignificant.

Right there at the kitchen table, I cried a million tears for every wrong I'd ever suffered in my miserable thirty-two years. A million for my mother dying before we'd had a chance to be friends. A million for being a poor judge of character, for being such a *fool*. A million for this house that, until midnight, used to be *Olivia and Rich's* house, but it was never really *my* house. I'd just paid rent. A million for being such an unlovable sap who'd deluded herself into believing in the farce of *'til death do us part*.

My mother was dead and The French Tart got to be Rich's bride. That was the sum total of my worthless life.

I didn't realize Karen had stopped laughing until she was at my side, cradling my head against her stomach.

30

There was no such thing as loving one person for eternity. That's why my father left my mother. 'Til death do us part meant staying together until the relationship died a slow, painful death.

The thought sobered me into dry hiccuping sobs.

For the first time, I realized Karen had been patting my back the way my mother used to when I was upset. With her free hand, she handed me a napkin.

The phone rang. She gently squeezed my shoulder.

"You okay?"

I sniffed and nodded and swiped at my eyes. They felt red and puffy. And my throat hurt from crying. She gently pulled away and walked toward the phone.

"No! Don't answer it," I said, sure it was Rich. Karen looked at the caller ID and snatched up the receiver.

Uggggh!

"Hello?" she said in a hushed voice, then turned her back to me.

I watched her and tried to hear what she was saying. All the while refusing to let myself believe Rich might be calling to say he'd made a terrible mistake. "I'm getting on the first flight home so we can talk about this." Then he'd say words like divorce or annulment. Maybe The French Tart wedding was never legal in the first place. Did a foreigner need a special permit or was there such a thing as wedding remorse? You had three days to change your mind and run for your life.

"It's Abby," Karen said.

Oh. Abby. Karen's roommate. The three of us used to go out until Abby met Chaz.

I felt myself start to slide off the razor-thin edge of stoicism. How Persephone must have felt when Hades grabbed her and dragged her into the underworld. But unlike

31

Persephone, I didn't have a mother to do my bidding, to bring me back from the gates of hell.

I closed my eyes and dangled over composure's edge, hanging on by my fingernails. I was determined not to fall through the open floor of my life, no matter how hard it pulled and tried to suck me under.

All for the love of The Dick.

I had a sudden moment of quiet clarity. Richard *was* a dick to do this to me. He didn't deserve this much emotion. He didn't deserve *me*.

I could commit emotional suicide or pull myself up and out of the underworld before the earth closed over me and I drowned in my grief.

An ambitious thought for someone who felt like a tired swimmer about to go under.

"Abby's sister is leaving tomorrow to go out of town," Karen said. "Abs says you can stay at her house while she's away, if you want to get away."

I took a deep breath and opened my eyes.

"Hold on," Karen said to Abby, then turned to me. "Talk to her. It'd be good for you to have a change of scenery."

I shook my head. I was in no mood to talk to anyone.

Karen sighed.

"Abs, I'm putting you on speakerphone."

She walked over and pushed the speaker button, hung up the handset and dropped down in the overstuffed chair.

"Hey," I croaked.

"Hey yourself," Abby said, her voice husky over the phone line.

There was an awkward pause.

"Liv, Karen called and told me what happened. I'm so sorry. Are you okay?"

"I'm fine, Abby. Or at least I will be fine. Sooner or later."

Keep it together. Don't fall apart.

"Want me to come over?"

"No. Thanks. Aren't you with Chaz?"

"He's sleeping."

Nausea crested and taunted that Abby had someone sleeping beside her who loved her.

I didn't.

But just because Rich bagged out didn't mean the end of all Coupledom. Though, suddenly finding myself exiled in Singledom felt kind of like I'd had the rug pulled out from under me. Or you know that feeling when you start to sit in a chair you think is there, only to fall on your ass because someone's moved the seat without warning? That's exactly where I was. Flat on my ass, feeling like an idiot.

"Why don't you stay at my sister's house this week while she's gone?"

Hmmm, well, maybe. If I stayed there, I wouldn't be here sitting around pretending I wasn't waiting for the phone to ring. Because if Rich called it would only be to soothe his dog-guilty conscience. Or to tell me not to take the Don Henley–autographed *When Hell Freezes Over* Eagles CD.

Well, he could go to hell until it froze over for all I cared.

But I did care.

And that's what sucked.

"That way you can have a little vacation," Abby coaxed. "You're still taking vacation, aren't you? Or are you going back to work on Monday?"

Oh, God. I hadn't even thought about it. The week I was supposed to spend in Paris with Rich still loomed ahead. But I wouldn't be flying out. I mean, I'm *not* Meg Ryan. I'm not about to go rushing over to Paris to fight for a louse who dumped me, like she did in *French Kiss*. What was the point? At least, Timothy Hutton gave Meg a chance to talk him out

33

of the marriage. The Dick didn't leave me an option.

"I don't know what I'm going to do. All I know is I'm . . . not going to Paris." I made a little half-laugh that sounded really thin and forced. "Guess I'll just hang out around here. You know, look for a new place." My high-pitched voice sounded like it could break glass.

If I stayed at Abby's sister's and found a place quickly, I might never even have to talk to Rich again and he wouldn't get a chance to ask me to move. My stomach ached dull and deep. A less rational part of me tried to take issue with the avoidance idea. The "Liv's big move" talk would probably be one of the last "we" talks Richard and I would have.

But if I never talked to him again I could pretend that Rich had died and The Evil Dick—a man I didn't know—was masquerading in his place.

"Juan's looking for a roommate," Karen said as she thumbed through my *Real Simple* magazine. "He lives one floor down from where the party was tonight. I could call him and see if he's found someone."

My stomach flipped and for the first time since Rich had dropped the bomb, I sensed a ray of light trying to penetrate the miserable gloom. But, God, living with *Juan?*

"I don't know. I mean he's—you know—he's a *guy*."

"Oh, go for it." Abby's voice echoed from the speaker.

"He's gay," said Karen.

Oh. Right. I wasn't sure if that made it better or worse. I sighed.

"You sure know a lot of gay guys," I said.

Karen smiled coyly. "I know a lot of *guys*."

"That's right," said Abby. "So it's your job to fix up Liv now that she's in the market."

I leaned back and rested my head on the cushion.

"I don't want to be fixed up." God, I was tired and my

stomach hurt from too much sugar, too much emotion.

"You don't need to be fixed up, judging from the way that hot guy was after you tonight," Karen said.

Hot guy? "Oh! Hunter?"

"What hot guy?" Abby said.

"Liv met a guy tonight."

I waved off the comment. "I just talked to him. It was very innocent."

I didn't want to talk about Hunter or being fixed up. Hunter was yet another missed opportunity. It just made me feel worse, because it underscored how needy and pathetic I felt.

"I'll call Juan later," said Karen. "We'll go look at the place and then tomorrow night—or I guess it's tomorrow already—tonight we're going back to Hue to hunt down Hunter."

My gut knotted.

"I don't even know his last name."

"You can ask him after you buy him a drink," said Abby.

I shook my head. "Can't."

"Yes, you can," they said in unison.

"Don't want to."

Karen pinned me with her I-won't-take-no-for-an-answer look. "Being around a hot guy who worships the ground you walk on is exactly what you need right now."

I had no idea why my stomach was tied in knots. Karen and I were just walking over to look at Juan's condo.

It was like I'd been pressing my nose against the candy store window of the lofts and had just been handed the keys. It wasn't exactly my dream house. But it suddenly stood for everything my life lacked.

Maybe that's why I was so nervous. That and because

after Karen finally crashed on my couch around four o'clock, I'd tossed and turned until dawn, mentally moving in with Juan, planning my new life *sans* Rich.

I'd take everything I could fit in my car. Leave all the furniture and memories attached to them for The Dick and The French Tart to sort out. I wouldn't even give him a say in the CDs. Just take what I wanted, leave the rest.

But was the loft really where I wanted to be? I didn't have to jump at the first opportunity that materialized.

I took a deep breath. I didn't have to decide right now. If I didn't like it, I could always move. It certainly wasn't the last place on Earth. It wasn't like marriage. In France.

We rounded the corner from Washington Street onto Summerlin. The building loomed ahead like a gleaming ivory tower. The bare metal balcony rails glinted in the sun. My heart beat faster with every step closer. I had the same out-of-kilter feeling I'd had last night right before we crashed the party.

I don't belong here.

I was a poser trying to pass myself off as someone desirable. Rich found me out and escaped in the nick of time.

"That's pathetic," I murmured, as we stopped and waited for the light to cross the street.

"What's pathetic?" Karen asked, and I realized I'd said it out loud.

"Nothing."

Actually, it was something. Something *major*. But nothing I could share. Not even with Karen.

It was hard enough to admit to myself how easy it was to hate myself. To let Rich rob me of the only thing I had left. My self-respect.

I refused to be pathetic, but I couldn't tell Karen. Nope, instead I'd start doing affirmations. *I am not pathetic* would be at the top of my list. I'd look in the bathroom mirror every morning and say it until I believed it, until I wore the notion like a jeweled crown. Wasn't that how affirmations worked their magic? Keep repeating them until the reality manifested and it oozed out of your pores?

As we turned the corner I noticed a tall guy dressed in solid black walking a good twelve yards ahead of us. From the back he looked like Hunter. Long, lean, bed-head longish light brown hair. A sexy, self-assured saunter that oozed, well . . . sex.

Oh, jeez.

I am not pathetic.

The guy turned the corner.

"Oh, my God!" Karen shrieked and stopped in front of Starbucks. "It's *him.*"

She grabbed my arm and squeezed and pointed straight ahead. I looked around for Antonio Banderas or some other celebrity worthy of a woman's frenzy, but all I saw were people reading newspapers at the crowded outdoor café. Laughing, talking couples shared coffee and morning pastries and other intimacies that came with the comfort of years or contented morning-after satisfaction. A twinge of envy tweaked the lonely realization that I was on the outside looking in.

Karen pointed toward the now-empty corner of Hue. "Hunter!"

Coffee smells wafted out to the street. I breathed in deeper. "Hunter?"

Ohmigod! *That* was him? It *was* him. I couldn't talk to him. Not now. I just wasn't up to it. I wanted to flatten myself up against the coffee shop wall or hide under one of the tables, even though he was gone.

Calm down.

He'd already turned the corner. I couldn't see him anymore. He couldn't see me.

Karen grabbed my hand and tried to pull me along, "Come on, go talk to him."

I dug in and stood my ground.

"No. We have to meet Juan. Besides, Hunter looked like he was on his way . . . somewhere."

Had he spent the night here? After I'd left had he picked up some bimbo at the party who lived in the lofts and slept with her? Probably hooked up with The Loft Slut.

Of course.

There was one in every building.

I couldn't quite tell if the strange sense that snaked through me was disappointment or relief that I could cross Hunter off my list. He was probably no better than The Dick. Made you feel like the only woman in the world when you were with him, but the minute you were gone he hooks up with The French Tart or The Loft Slut—same difference.

"Come on, Liv. Go say hi."

I yanked my hand out of Karen's. "I'm *not* going to say *hi*."

Karen looked at me like I had two heads.

"Why not? Maybe he'll ask you out."

"And why would *that* be a good thing?"

Karen sighed. "Because he likes you. And did I mention he's hot?"

Did she have to say that so loud?

A middle-aged guy in a baggy jogging suit stared at us. His sad-eyed dog slobbered and panted at his feet. And two women in scarves and coats at the table next to him had stopped in mid-conversation. Their chic-radar, no doubt, homing in on the words *hot guy*.

I pointedly turned my back on all of them and lowered my voice.

"It's been less than twelve hours since my boyfriend of three years announced he'd gotten married. I still haven't canceled my ticket for the flight that's supposed to take me to Paris to see him. And I need to find a place to live before he asks me to move. With all of this looming over me, I'm not quite in the mood for a date, okay?"

Karen's face fell. She glanced at the vacant corner where Hunter had disappeared.

"You're right," Karen whispered. She ran her hand through her silky blonde hair. "I'm sorry. Let's go see Juan."

Sure, now that the whole neighborhood knew my business, I'd go see if I could move in. I avoided looking at the café audience as we walked away.

I am not pathetic.

We passed the soap shop, the pottery painting place and the funky clothing boutiques that shared the first floor of the building with Hue and turned down the narrow hall that led to the lofts' lobby.

The decor looked austere in the light of day. The ocher and pumpkin didn't seem quite so warm, the chrome colder and harder. Isn't it funny how things can look totally different in a new light?

Unlike last night when we simply got in the elevator and shot up to the party, we had to buzz Juan before the elevator would take us up. How *did* we get up there last night? Juan, of course. Duh. He lived there.

Karen pushed the intercom.

"Yeah?" said a sleepy-sounding, Spanish-tinged voice.

"Hey honey, it's Karen and Liv. Are ya decent?"

"I'm never decent. So enter at your own risk." I couldn't decide if Juan's mumbled accent gave his voice a lazy quality or if we'd actually woken him up.

"Get in the elevator and hit one, three, four, three and the

39

chariot will carry you up to my lair."

At least he had a sense of humor. Lord knows I needed a little levity. Rich was always so serious, sometimes he seemed like he didn't even have a sense of humor.

Troll.

Big, fat, boring troll.

"See ya in a sec," Karen said.

I pushed the elevator button and the doors opened like a mouth ready to devour us.

We stepped inside, willing victims.

Karen hit the code and we were off to Juan's lair. Glancing at my distorted image in the metal walls, I remembered the way Ron had scrutinized us in this same elevator last night.

"Ron doesn't live there, does he?"

"Hell, no. That would be much too confining."

"Confining?"

Great, just what I needed, a promiscuous roommate parading a steady stream of unattainable men in front of me. It was like inviting someone on a hunger strike to a dinner party. I just needed to focus on the three words *unattainable gay men*.

"Ron's pretty much a free spirit. Doesn't want to make a commitment. Juan's always whining about him when he does my hair."

Oh, so it was the other way around?

Hmmm. Another commitment-phob. It figured someone as beautiful as Ron would keep his options open. The image I had of the parade of gorgeous, unattainable men melted into a sad picture of two old maids sitting home watching *Survivor*, pretending to have fun.

The Loft Slut probably had enough fun for all of us. I wondered which floor she lived on and if Hunter would see her again.

Please let it be a one-night stand. Please let him just go away. I'd only spent an evening talking to the guy. So, why did I feel like I'd been dumped twice in less than twenty-four hours?

That was pitiful, bordering on pathetic. I silently said my little affirmation.

I refuse to be pathetic.

I would forget Hunter who would forever remain last-nameless. May he and The Loft Slut live happily ever after. I shoved them into the compartment of forgotten memories, right next door to The Dick and The French Tart.

The elevator stopped on the third floor and doors opened into a hallway identical to the party floor, one level up, we'd visited last night. The hall looked much bigger without wall-to-wall bodies. Karen led the way to door 3-A and knocked.

A shirtless Juan in low-slung Levi 501s answered the door. Nice body. His shaved head gleamed to beat the chrome in the lobby. He smoothed his goatee before he kissed Karen on the cheek. Then he turned to me.

"Man trouble, hon?"

I half-nodded, half-shrugged.

"Bastards," he said. "They're all bastards. Are we ever going to have some good girl talk."

I didn't quite know what to say. I mean, Juan was a man. Technically. Oh, God. This was too weird.

"Make yourselves at home. Look around," he said with a wave of his hand. "I'm just going to go put on a shirt. Oh, wait. Kare, doll, come here. I must show you something."

Juan motioned Karen into the bedroom. She smiled at me and rolled her eyes.

"You okay?" she mouthed.

I gave her an *of course* expression and shooed her off.

Alone in the entryway, I could finally take in the place—

the high ceilings, exposed ductwork. I realized it was probably the same layout as the condo we were in last night, though I hadn't noticed the details because of all the people. I walked into the center of the living room. The same raw brick walls and painted concrete floors as the party apartment. But Juan's walls were done in different primary shades—each wall boasted a block of bright color and hosted humongous abstract paintings on unframed canvases.

Everything was neat as a pin. The place even smelled good. Like a mixture of morning coffee and remnants of the man's cologne I'd smelled in the elevator last night. Was that Juan's or Ron's scent?

The sleek furniture was simple—deceptively so, I was sure. Probably the kind that looked unassuming, but cost a fortune. The kind you had to pay them to take the frills off.

I blew out a breath as I looked around this *Architectural Digest* model apartment.

Did Karen say how much he was asking the roommate to pay? What was wrong with me? In the heat of the moment I'd totally forgotten the most important question. Money.

This was a showplace. No way could I afford it on my restaurant critic's salary.

The winter sun streamed in through the oversized windows and sliding glass doors. I walked over and pushed aside the sheers to take in the view. At least it didn't cost anything to look.

I heard Juan and Karen laughing.

I slid open the door and stepped out onto the balcony. It wrapped around two sides of the building. As I walked to the rail, the cool morning breeze whipped my hair and tingled my skin. I pulled my jacket shut. Winters in Florida tended to be like spring in any other state. The only difference was once your blood thinned, you thought you were freezing when the temperature fell below seventy degrees. The radio had said it was supposed to be in the lower sixties today. Brrrr.

I leaned over the rail and looked down onto Summerlin Avenue. The weekend morning traffic was light compared to the hustle of the night before. The view from three stories above downtown Orlando didn't quite miniaturize the scene, but compacted it, rounded off the intimidating edges.

I could live here. God, would this be sweet. As I glanced at a muscular guy in a white T-shirt that said *freedom,* I suddenly remembered that last night Hunter was wearing a white shirt and faded jeans. The guy we saw this morning was dressed all in black.

If it was Hunter, either he'd planned ahead and brought a change of clothes or—maybe he hung out in Thornton Park. Maybe he lived around here and had just come for his morning coffee.

The stone in my stomach shrank a bit. But it didn't completely go away.

I walked around the corner of the balcony and looked out over the tops of the trees that bordered Lake Eola Park. In the distance I saw Robinson Street. The post office. Following the line of the street up to Orange Avenue, I looked at the various storefronts and if I wasn't mistaken, two doors to the left of the wig shop was the place where my mom and I used to dream of opening our own bakery.

In better days.

Before Mom got so sick and the cancer started to ravage her body and drain her spirit. After she was gone I'd lost that dream. I still had every cent of the money she'd saved to make the dream come true. The money was in the bank right where she'd left it, but she was gone.

Eleven years now.

When was the last time we'd stood with our noses pressed

against the window of that place? I couldn't remember. My life had become a series of little milestones that had slipped by unnoticed because I'd been too busy worrying about the ridiculous, like how much better my life would be if I'd lose ten pounds or got promoted. I worked long days, weekends. No wonder Rich was hesitant to commit.

No, wait. This breakup was not my fault. He was the one who was wrong.

Standing high above Summerlin with the wind blowing on my face, it became devastatingly clear that I'd been so obsessed about when Rich was going to put a ring on my finger that I'd quit living in the moment.

Even before he came into my life, I'd zoned on the important things. Like what was the last real conversation I'd had with my mother? After eleven years I'd just realized I had no memory of the last words she'd said to me.

I know what I said to her. But that's not surprising, seeing how it was always all about me when I was with her.

I was too busy trying to make her see how senseless the whole notion of dying was. How could she just give up? How could she leave me? You'd think I'd have accepted the truth by now. People *always* left, eventually.

"There you are." Karen's voice cut through my melancholy. I blinked back the moisture the wind had whipped into my eyes and turned to face her. She took my hand and pulled me toward the open sliding doors, where the pearly sheers billowed in and out.

"You've got to come in here and look at Juan's penis."

Chapter Three

"It's huge," I blurted as I stared at the six-foot-by-eight-foot painting that hung on Juan's bedroom wall. What could I say? The title alone spoke volumes: *Phallic Phenomenon.*

He clapped his hands like a child who'd just cranked free a jack-in-the-box. "Isn't it beautiful?"

"It's quite *comely,*" said Karen. She and Juan pointed at each other and booed over the bad pun.

I rolled my eyes. "Please."

"Cut to the chase," Karen said. "Who's the model and when can I meet him?"

"Don't I wish I knew, girlfriend?" Juan turned to me. "So what do you think, 'Livia?"

What did I think? I was standing in a guy's bedroom in front of a painting of a penis. The corners of my mouth twitched.

"Well, it's not the *biggest* dick I've ever seen."

Juan's expression changed to one of near reverence.

"Actually, Richard is the biggest dick."

Karen shrieked. "That's my girl!"

"Oh, I love you!" Juan pulled me into a tight hug and nearly knocked the wind out of me. "We're going to have so much fun being roommates. When would you like to move in?"

I laughed. "I haven't even seen my room."

Juan gasped, stepped back and held me at arm's length. "Forgive me. I get ahead of myself sometimes. Allow me to give you the grand tour. Next, we'll have a nice little espresso. *Then* we'll talk business."

He turned and started out the door, but paused in the threshold. "It's just that I *knew* you'd be my new flatmate as soon as you stepped into the hall this morning. Call it intuition. I go by my gut and my gut says go for it, Juan."

Go for it? Oh, to be so free. I suddenly felt like I was on a big roller coaster, and it had lurched forward on its mad course before I'd fastened my seat belt. It was great Juan was so gung ho to take me in by virtue of our mutual friendship with Karen. But, the more I looked around at the huge cherry-wood sleigh bed set atop an Oriental rug and the little designer touches that certainly didn't come from Target, I couldn't help but wonder if he was desperate for a roommate to support his taste for life's finer things. Tastes my conservative pocketbook couldn't afford.

As we followed him down the hall away from his bedroom, I breathed in deep and savored the smell of the place, a combination of rich, freshly brewed coffee, cologne and clean. I glanced through open doors at a guest room and a bathroom. We paused in the living room, and I drank in the perfect details of the immaculate condo. It didn't exactly smell like home. It smelled new, exotic.

Like a fresh start.

A brand-new life.

Juan pointed to the ultra-modern kitchen, separated from the living and dining areas by a short wall, and designed for entertaining.

I sighed and stepped inside. A cook's dream. Stainless steel appliances, porcelain sink, gas range. My heart beat a little faster. Okay, so I was in love with the place. I didn't even need to see my bedroom. I could live happily in a small corner of the humongous pantry.

Juan smiled at me. "Karen tells me you're a gourmand?"

Gourmand? "Karen has a tendency to embellish." I

46

glanced at her, but she'd busied herself inspecting the contents of the refrigerator. From where I stood, it looked nearly empty except for several bottles of micro-brew and some fancy condiment jars. "I'm the food critic for the paper."

"Oh, drop the modest act, Liv." Karen shut the fridge door and started opening the glass-paneled cabinets. "She could be a chef. She'll have ten pounds on your bones in no time."

Juan's eyes widened. "The kitchen will be all yours, honey. When I designed it, I fully intended to *learn* to cook. You know what they say about the path to a man's heart. But I've since come to terms with the fact that I'm no domestic goddess." He stroked his goatee and smiled a wicked little grin. "And I've discovered other paths that may not lead to the heart, but certainly get me where I want to go."

Yeah, the heart's way overrated. Wistfully, I ran my hand over the granite-topped chopping island and added another $100 to my half of the rent. If the lofts were a haven for creative sorts, how in the world could they afford such luxury? "Are all the lofts like this?"

"Hell no." Juan planted his fists on his hips. "They start out just a big cavernous space. Each unit is what the owner makes it. Come see your bedroom."

With all Juan had done to the place, there was probably no way I could afford it. Sure, I'd paid half the mortgage on Rich's house, but the bungalow and Juan's place were like night and day. The loft was one of those places that magazines photographed.

Suddenly, it was hard to breathe. I didn't belong here. Then again, I'd always been adaptable.

Juan paused in front of the room at the end of the hall. His hand was on the doorknob. An excited little grin played across his face. As he flung open the door and gestured into the room with a flourish, he reminded me of Carol Merrill re-vealing the grand prize behind door number two on *Let's Make a Deal*. Carol Merrill with a goatee. Well, maybe not.

"May I present the gypsy room. You, my dear, should feel right at home."

I inhaled sharply. I couldn't help it. The room was exqui-site. Decorated in shades of rich maroons, purples, and teals. An eclectic mix of paisleys, velvets and deep woods. The lamps had beaded fringe, and the poster bed was covered by at least fifteen pillows made of satins, raw silks and other luxe fabrics.

Karen nudged me. She crossed her arms and looked smug, like a satisfied cat.

"Of course, you're free to change it," said Juan. "If you want to move in your own things, we can figure something out."

Was he crazy? He obviously hadn't seen the early Rooms to Go décor Rich and I had picked out together. "No, it's beautiful just the way it is."

Juan smiled. "I'm glad you like it. Espresso, everyone?"

"I'll help you," Karen offered. "Liv, why don't you look around a bit more. Okay, Juan?"

"But of course."

My head spun as I did one last cursory tour of the condo. Here I was, standing on freedom's threshold with a splinter in my self-esteem. I'd once read that freedom's a bigger oppres-sion than attachment because we have no one to blame but ourselves if we mess up.

Right now, I blamed Richard for screwing up my life. And I was allowed. I wasn't quite unnumbed enough to be able to hate him, but I could blame him. As if that mattered.

What left me even more unsettled was from here on out my life was totally up to me. My mind jumped to the synchronicity conversation I'd had with Hunter last night, just one floor up from where I stood now. I clung to the small consolation that supposedly, when you're on the right path, the right choices present themselves in an effortless flow, like riding a river's current. Maybe so, but so soon after weathering Hurricane Dick, my river felt much more conducive to level four white-water rafting than a leisurely float downstream.

And that gypsy bedroom. My stomach fluttered. Carefree, bohemian, gypsy was a tall image to live up to, but what a cool thought.

Finally, I'd come full circle back to the balcony. I leaned against the rail and squeezed the cold metal bar, the thin line that kept me from free falling to the street below. Into a new life.

A life on my own.

Was this synchronicity at work? I'd have to really stretch to see the crap that had redefined my life over the past twelve hours as a fortuitous intertwining of events, as Hunter had put it. My recent turn of events seemed more snarled than intertwined, a heavy shroud-like chain mail on my heart. Was it all part of a serendipitous plan for making over my gray, flabby life?

Because I liked my life—or at least I thought I did. It wasn't the Garden of Eden, but now that my eyes had been opened I could never go back again.

I leaned a little farther forward over the balcony rail, glanced down at the corner where Hunter had disappeared earlier, and reminded myself of the consequences of feeling. God, I didn't want to feel anything, for anyone, ever again.

It was time to look out for myself. Time to take a blind leap of faith into living.

On my own.

Oh, God. I squeezed my eyes shut until I felt a presence at my side.

Juan smiled and handed me a blood-red demitasse.

The aroma of rich coffee wafted up. He'd sprinkled a dash of cinnamon and other spices on top. I sipped the hot liquid. Umm, heaven. The mingling scents drew my mind to the bohemian bedroom—its lush tapestries and exotic colors. A whole new world. A far cry from the life I'd known with Richard.

For a moment I had an image of myself, dancing around a fire with a band of gypsies. With Hunter, dark and shirtless, glistening with primal life.

Juan stirred his coffee. The spoon clanked as he set it on his saucer. "Ready to talk business, *amiga?*"

Around noon, I pulled into Rich's driveway. Not my driveway anymore. I sat there for a few minutes, staring at the old bungalow's teal and white front porch.

The ghosts of my now-dead relationship lurked in the bushes, around the corners, beneath every blade of grass. I could see Rich and me performing domestic duties like painting the front porch and cleaning the oak leaves out of the gutters. And there was that time we tried to carry our new overstuffed couch in, only to realize it was too overstuffed to fit through the front door. So, we'd set it on the lawn, while we tried to figure out what to do.

"God, what if it doesn't fit?" I'd said. "Our neighbors are going to love this." I'd plopped down, giving the cushions the bounce test.

"I'm going to hate this if it kills my grass, or if it rains and ruins my new couch."

Mine, mine, mine. My grass. My couch. My way or no way.

"I knew I should have paid extra for delivery."

Cheap bastard. But at the time, I'd probably praised his frugality and tried to lighten the mood.

"Everyone's going to think we've been influenced by those college guys who were renting the brown duplex down the street last year. Remember? They used to drag their Salvation Army living room set out in the driveway and drink beer."

I'd laughed. Rich had furrowed his brow, intensely focusing on a way to dismantle the offending couch so he could get it off his precious lawn.

"Maybe trailer trash and frat boys are onto something," I'd said, stretching out on the sofa. "I mean functional lawn furniture is so uncomfortable. Why not drag a big, comfy couch outside and really enjoy the day?"

Again, Rich grunted. "Get up and help me turn this thing over. If I take off the legs, I think we can squeeze it through."

I vividly remember gazing up through the mammoth oaks. The sky had looked so blue that day. I'd always loved those trees. They made me feel safe and sheltered. But in the loft, I would live above the trees, floating on their lush canopies. Now, sitting beneath them felt smothering, stifling.

I guess everything changes. Since then, someone had bulldozed the duplex and replaced it with one of those new houses that looks old. They'd done a good job of making it seem like it had been there for decades.

Is anything ever what it seems?

I swallowed past the heavy knot in my throat, took a deep breath, opened the car door and prepared to walk into the house of shadows.

The place felt cold and distant, like I'd already been evicted. No, moving was *my* choice. The rent Juan was asking was reasonable—more than I was used to paying, but a small price for my salvation.

I could move in today.

As I slid the key into the lock, I felt like an intruder sneaking into an enemy camp. I just wanted to pack my things and get the hell out.

Heart thudding, I pushed open the front door. My gaze was drawn to the answering machine's blinking light.

My stomach clenched.

"Ohmigod! Richard?"

Had he called back? The possibility tore at my insides, and I dashed for the machine. In my flight, I nearly tripped over my own two feet. Midway, I stopped to steady myself.

Don't even. I pressed my hands to my face, my purse dangled at my elbow. This was ridiculous. I was ridiculous. Richard refused to commit to me after consuming three years of my life. He married someone else days before I was supposed to fly in, and I was still falling all over myself to see if he'd tossed me some crumbs?

Get a life, Liv.

Or at least get some self-respect.

Just to prove how strong I was, I put down my purse and decided I'd pack before I checked the messages. I walked into the bedroom and pointedly ignored the anxious whirlwind brewing in my gut and denied how I felt like a piece of steel drawn by the answering machine magnet.

I forced myself to walk into the bedroom and surveyed the slightly unkempt area. Screw him, I was going to leave everything exactly the way it was and let him know what it felt like to clean up a mess after being abandoned. Especially all the personal stuff I planned to leave for him and The French Tart to deal with.

Automatically, I glanced at the photo of Rich and me on the nightstand. The self-satisfied grin on his smug face struck a nerve. I hit the frame so it fell forward and landed with a thud. Then yanked the corner of the bedspread so hard it sent the covers askew.

What if Karen had called? What if the message was from her or Juan?

So, what if it was? I'd just seen them ten minutes ago. They'd have called my cell phone if it were urgent.

I knelt down and pulled a suitcase from under the bed. A new one Rich bought me the week before he left so I'd have a decent suitcase to take to Paris. On sale, of course. Gee, how gallant of the cheap bastard.

I picked up the case and heaved it onto the bed.

Abby! The thought made me draw in a sudden, victorious breath. I *had* to check messages. What if Abby had left a message about me staying at her sister's house? I needed to call and tell her I was moving in with Juan today instead.

As I started for the machine, reason settled in. If she didn't have my cell number, she could get it from Karen. Besides, she said she'd drop the key in the mailbox before noon.

I paused at the bedroom threshold. Rich knew my cell phone number, too. If he'd desperately needed to beg my forgiveness because he'd made the mistake of a lifetime after getting drunk on European wine and women, he could have gotten me. I shuddered. The thought sucker punched me between the eyes, shattering the remaining shards of my rose-colored glasses.

Sucking in deep breaths, I walked into the living room, out onto the porch and peered into the mailbox. Sure enough, there was Abby's sister's key. I held it for a minute, the metal cool in my palm.

Why did I feel like some higher power was practicing tough love on me? Leaving this house, my home, made me feel sick, but staying made me feel damaged and abused.

I put my hand on the doorknob. Even if Rich had called me and left a message, what did I expect? Could we really get past this? A horrifying vision of the two of us, old and gray, talking to our grandkids popped into my head.

"Yep, your grammy and me had a fine life together. Smooth sailing on the Sea of Love."

"Well, except for The French Tart era."

I squeezed my hand shut over the key.

Nope. No way. Not a chance in hell. There was no getting past this.

I'd spent years contorting myself, forcing my ten tons of life into Richard's five-pound bag. And dammit, now that I had a chance to stand up and stretch, I didn't feel like bending over and balling myself up again in hopes that he'd change his mind.

I slammed the door behind me and walked back into the living room, straight over to the caller ID. Grabbing it up from its place on the table, I checked the call log.

One stinking message.

From a bastard named *unknown caller*.

My stomach whirled. Was it him?

Before I could change my mind, before I could listen to the recording, I punched the erase message button.

Poof, just like that, the blinking light stopped winking at me. I stood and listened to the machine rasping and grating as it rewound. I'd always hated that sound, but the eighties-era antiquated model was Rich's. "Good enough," he'd always said. Now, I'd never again have to settle for "good enough" when I craved superb.

And I'd never know if he'd called or not. No more need to worry or wonder.

I held my breath until the machine finished its job. Then, I reached down and unplugged it and the caller ID, too.

If Rich called back, he'd get exactly the response he deserved. A ringing line with no one home to answer it. For once, he could wonder about me.

With tears streaming down my cheeks, I laughed and walked back into the bedroom to finish packing my things.

I will never be predictable again.

This was my newest affirmation, born earlier in the day, the instant I decided to lock my house key in Richard's bungalow and not look back. As far as I was concerned I'd never see or speak to The Dick again.

Closure.

I repeated the vow over and over in my head as Karen and I walked through Hue's sparse Saturday night crowd.

I really didn't want to be there, but I'd weighed my options and in a weak moment decided being out was better than staying home alone in my new bedroom. I wasn't quite up to gypsy standards yet. Juan had a date, and Karen had a stubborn streak. No matter how many lame excuses I came up with, she wasn't buying any of them.

So there I was, back at Hue, on a recognizance mission to find and talk to Hunter. If I'd felt conspicuously frumpy last night, I felt ridiculously overdone tonight in a pair of stilettos I'd borrowed from Karen and a short skirt I now remembered why I never wore. Juan had painted my face and twisted my curly brown hair into an up-do that felt more like a *don't do*. All because earlier I'd wanted to be *unpredictable*.

But if you purposely tried to be unpredictable, did it cancel out the effort, making you predictable by default? Who knows? Frankly, I didn't really care. Unpredictable sounded so much better than *not being pathetic*. Because that was a pretty pathetic affirmation.

I'd come a long way in just a few short hours. In fact, I was a new woman. It would just take a little getting used to the new me. Call it phase one of my reinvention.

Some of the numbness and shock was starting to wear off. Leaving me . . . well, let's just say I was pretty pissed off at The Dick. But I also realized the space I found myself in now wasn't as dank and dark as I'd feared. It was more like an illuminated hall of brightly lit mirrors, and I was forced to take a good, hard look at myself from every angle. Whoa, did my life ever need a major overhaul.

It wasn't such an epiphany, really. Subconsciously, I guess I'd known I'd been so *complacent* during my time with Rich that the better part of my thirty-two years had eroded into a vast sea of nothingness. But it wasn't too late to reshape my life. Was it?

I smoothed my skirt and scanned the bar for Hunter. I saw lots of nice-looking men, but not him. Oh, well, it was only eight o'clock, early by nightlife standards. Things didn't even get rolling until after ten.

"What do you want to drink?" Karen called over her shoulder from the bar.

I started to say merlot but changed my mind.

"A Cosmopolitan." Perfect. I smiled to myself and looked around. That's when I noticed a short, middle-aged guy next to me grinning back.

I looked away. Ohmigod. Did he think I was smiling at him? Please, no. Nothing against him, I just wasn't ready to have my new-woman bluff called. Though better he call it than Hunter.

I looked at Karen, but her back was to me as she ordered our drinks. *Calm down.* This was no different than last night when I was out on the town, secure in my *I'm someone's girl-friend* armor.

"You have lovely eyes," the guy murmured.

I slanted him a glance. He was a good two inches shorter than me in my stilettos and his thinning hair looked as if he'd used that Grecian Formula stuff. He smiled expectantly. Panic twisted my insides.

"Thank you," I said and forced a smile back. I angled myself away from him, toward Karen.

I didn't want to be rude and certainly not mean, but I didn't feel like making small talk with a stranger. Grecian god or Grecian Formula, it didn't matter. I couldn't do this. I doubted I could even talk to Hunter if he showed. I felt ridiculous and I just didn't have it in me. Maybe we should go after we finished our drinks.

The couple who'd been sitting at the bar next to where Karen had ordered, stood. She planted her leather purse on one stool and her butt on the other, and motioned for me to sit in the one saved by her bag.

I slid onto the chair without looking at the guy. To my relief, he melted into the background.

I felt kind of bad for coming off as a snob. So the guy had paid me a compliment—be it sincere or pickup line. It didn't make him a criminal. Still, it didn't mean I had to talk to him, either.

Good God, I was so defensive. That's what I hated about the whole bar scene. It put me on edge. It just flat out drained my energy, sucked the lifeblood from my system. I had a terrible vision of me settling into a new barfly hobby. Comfortably making small talk with the bartenders, exchanging one-liners with kindred lounge-dwelling spirits.

I contemplated telling Karen I wanted to go home, which was just a quick elevator ride upstairs, but stopped short because that would have been so predictable. I wasn't predictable. So I sucked it up and prepared for a long, long, energy-zapping evening.

The bartender set our drinks in front of us. I reached for my purse, but Karen waved me off.

"Tonight's on me," she said. "My treat."

"Last night was your treat," I said. "Bon Voyage for the ship that never sailed. Let me get this."

"Absolutely not."

She had her credit card out and had handed it to the bartender by the time I unzipped my purse. I'd find some way to make it up to her—maybe dinner later at Dexter's since we didn't get to go last night.

As I sipped my drink, I glanced at the spot across the bar where Hunter stood last night. He wasn't there. Tonight a pale blonde who looked to be in her early twenties occupied that station. She sipped a frozen drink, engrossed in conversation with another equally pale blonde.

A bartender friend of mine once said men can sum up a woman's personality from the type of drink she ordered. Frozen drinks, the kind with the little umbrella in them, signaled a high-maintenance woman. Red wine drinkers, on the other hand, were the epitome of class.

Why didn't I order merlot like I started to?

What did Cosmopolitans signify? I couldn't remember. Oh, for God's sake, it didn't matter.

I noted with relief that our drinks came *sans* umbrellas. I picked up my Cosmo and pressed my back into the stool. Maybe it was the bartender's duty to stick little umbrellas in the drinks of the women he either knew or suspected of being high-maintenance pains in the asses. Then again, maybe high-maintenance was just another name for *attitude?* Based on last night's conversation, Karen and I had drawn the conclusion that women with attitude ruled the world.

I, on the other hand, was heading for a painful crash and burn if I didn't toughen up. Okay, think moles—Cindy

Crawford's mole. I checked my posture and held my drink up like I didn't have a care in the world. No, wait, attitude wasn't like Cindy's mole, attitude was like Pamela Anderson's boobs. Oh, hell. Yuck, I did not want to think about boobs or moles. Forget it.

"So, how does it feel to live three floors up?" Karen said. "You're practically at home. You could come here every night if you wanted."

"Oh, goody." I sipped my drink and watched a tall, thin, dark-haired man walk up to the blondes and greet each with a kiss on the cheek. He looked vaguely familiar, but I couldn't place him. Maybe he was a local news anchor or weather guy. Talking heads came through the Central Florida market in a steady stream. It was hard to keep track of them.

The blondes laughed and draped themselves over him, obviously delighted with his company. The woman with the frozen drink coyly twirled the umbrella between her thumb and index finger and smiled up at him. Even from my seat across the bar, her interest was blatant.

The guy looked to be in his mid-forties. I wondered if one was his girlfriend or wife. He wore a glittering pinkie ring. Must have been a diamond from the way it sparkled, but he wasn't wearing a wedding ring. Neither woman kept her hands still long enough for me to see whether they wore rings. Nothing that caught the light anyway.

The bartender greeted the guy and placed a napkin on the bar in front of him. Ah, he must be a Saturday night regular. His dark sports coat and open collar button-down screamed money. Probably a good tipper, hence the good service.

As Karen made small talk, I half-listened and kept my gaze pinned on the man and the blondes. At regular intervals various men and women approached. He greeted each with handshakes or pecks on the cheek, respectively. A small crowd formed.

Something about him seemed weaselish. I didn't even know the guy. Who was I to judge him? He was obviously out to have fun. What was wrong with that?

I glanced around the bar. It had a different feel than last night. For one, it was much less crowded and hosted a more mature crowd. The energy wasn't as frenetic as last night.

I wondered where Hunter was tonight. What were his plans? It didn't feel like his kind of crowd. Like I knew him after talking to him for a few hours on a balcony, even if the conversation ran deep.

This wasn't really my kind of crowd either, but having settled at the bar, with no one bothering me, I was beginning to relax. If I could sit back and observe and not have to fend off unwanted advances, going out might be fun—every once in a while.

"If nothing else," I said to Karen, "watching a live performance of the human mating ritual almost makes the bar scene worth it."

"At least you're not at home brooding over The Dick."

Oh, right. "Thanks for reminding me. I hadn't thought about him for at least five minutes." Huh, I really hadn't.

"See, you're practically over him already. Soon you'll be saying, 'Dick, who?' "

I swallowed past rising despair. I wasn't quite there yet, and the mention of The Dick sparked a primitive anguish that grew and spread like wildfire.

Karen must have sensed my pain, because she smiled reassuringly and changed the subject. "I don't usually come here on Saturday nights. But I was so hoping your lover boy would show. Well, the night's still young," she consoled. "Wait until we go out for ladies' night next Thursday. You'll have a blast."

The thought sent shivers of dread spiraling through my body. "Ladies' night." I rolled my eyes.

"Oh, come on. Just when I thought you were starting to loosen up. You need to get out a little."

The bartender set two more Cosmopolitans in front of us. "Compliments of Jimbo Giani," he said.

Karen and I exchanged puzzled glances, then stared blankly at the bartender. My gaze skittered back to the man with the blondes. *Jimbo Giani.* Of course.

"Him." I nodded across the way. Luckily he was so engrossed in his entourage he didn't seem to notice. "No wonder he looked familiar. We've done stories on him at the paper."

"Really?" Karen seemed impressed. "Smart man. Probably knows who he's dealing with, wants some good press."

"Um-hm, I'm sure. A few years ago, he made a fortune with a dot com business and got out right before the bottom fell out."

"Here, this is for you." The bartender pressed a business card into my hand. Upon closer inspection, it was actually more of a calling card since it only bore the name James "Jimbo" Giani and three phone numbers: Florida residence, New York residence, cell phone.

"Turn it over," Karen said. "There's something written on the back." She leaned in and read aloud over my shoulder.

"Would you please do me the honor of dining with me?"

This was a joke. "He's kidding, right?"

Karen nudged my arm. "Ooo! You go, girl. I should take lessons from *you.*"

My body buzzed with a mixture of dread and panic.

I'd rather be subjected to ladies' night torture every

Thursday night for the rest of my life than go out with a grown man who called himself *Jimbo*.

"How the hell was he able to write me a love note with those blondes draped all over him? He hasn't even looked over here."

Karen studied the card, first the engraved front, then she turned it over and reread the message on the back.

"He probably had it prewritten," I said. "Probably has a whole stack of them in his pocket."

"Oh, Liv, go out with him. You might have fun. Plus if he has as much money as you say he does, I'm sure he'll take you somewhere nice. You've got to do it."

"Ew! No." I shook my head. "Not just *no*. *Hell* no!"

Karen rummaged around her purse and pulled out a piece of paper and a pen. She angled herself away from me and wrote something on the paper, then motioned for the bartender to come over.

"What are you doing?" I asked.

The bartender approached. "Would you please deliver this?" She nodded in Giani's direction.

"What did you just do?" My voice was hoarse with frustration. Karen smiled and shrugged.

"Wait! Come back here." I tried to get the bartender's attention, but he was already in the process of making the discreet delivery. The blondes were oblivious. Giani didn't even glance our way.

"What did that note say?"

"That you'd love to have dinner with him," Karen preened. "I wrote your work number and signed your name."

I slammed my drink down on the bar. "How could you do that to me?"

"Because I'm your friend. I have your best interest at heart, even if you don't. Someday you'll thank me."

I'd like to think I had it in me to get up and go over and tell Giani the truth, that the note was from Karen. But in reality, the part of me that made my legs work was too stunned to take action.

"You know, even if he calls me I don't have to accept. I'll just tell him you answered the note. You're the one he should have dinner with."

"He doesn't want me." Karen raised her chin. "He wants you."

A hint of envy flickered in Karen's pretty blue eyes. Oh, I don't know, maybe it wasn't jealousy, maybe it was just a reflection of my own feelings of inadequacy. I mean, Karen was beautiful. I was just plain old Olivia. Plain brown hair, plain brown eyes. A plain brown wrapper next to Karen's beautiful, shiny package.

We stared at each other for a moment.

Finally I said, "I'll make a bet with you. We'll sit here for another hour. If *Jimbo* gets up and comes over and introduces himself properly, I'll go out with him. If not, he's toast."

Karen smiled and held out her hand. "Liv, you've got yourself a deal."

I shook her hand knowing damn well I had this one in the bag.

Chapter Four

One of the benefits of working for a large company like the *Daily* was how easy it was to disappear. So simple to feel anonymous, to just blend into the background, since I didn't make waves or draw attention to myself. I simply reported for duty, wrote a decent restaurant review, and it would run in the paper under the fictitious byline of "Starvin' Marvin, restaurant critic."

Starvin' Marvin had been my alter ego for the seven years I'd worked at the paper. Honestly, I didn't mind being a faceless name or, for that matter, a name that didn't even exist. As the restaurant critic, I had to be anonymous or the restaurateurs would have spotted me coming a mile away and made a fuss. I guess it was just natural that the anonymity spilled over into the rest of my life. Seemed the longer I wrote under a pen name, the easier it was to fade into life's woodwork.

But invisible or not, I had to go back to work sometime. After spending an aimless Sunday trying to make the gypsy room my own, I decided I'd be better off diving back into reality, rather than postponing the inevitable questions about my aborted trip to France.

Being alone with myself for the rest of my vacation didn't seem like the way I wanted to spend my time off. Plus, you know how when there's an unpleasant issue hanging over your head and the longer you stew over it, the bigger it gets? After stewing over my breakup all weekend, I'd managed to turn going back to work into a mammoth ordeal.

As it turned out, going back to the paper really wasn't that bad at all. No, really. The newsroom was quiet for a Monday morning and that suited me just fine. As I made my way through the sea of mostly empty cubicles and dark computers, only three people even realized I was supposed to be on vacation—the receptionist, Donna Cox; official office busybody and general assignment reporter, Zoe Wood, who happened to be my next-door cubicle neighbor; and my boss, Nolan Rivers. Thank God, they had the good grace not to ask questions. Even Zoe, God love her.

I guess when a woman shows up at work on the day she was supposed to be strolling the Champs Elysées with her soon-to-be-fiancé and stows all pictures of him in a desk drawer, it's kind of a no-brainer she might not be in the mood to talk about particulars.

As I flipped on my computer and sat down, my gaze surveyed the various Richard memorabilia littering my desk and walls. The photos, the dead roses he'd sent me for our three-year anniversary—since he was in France and couldn't deliver them himself, and was probably with The French Tart.

I took a deep breath and stayed the urge to sweep my hand across my desk and knock everything that had anything to do with The Dick to the floor. But if I did that, I'd only call attention to the fact that I was at work and not in France. Since the office was nearly deserted, maybe no one would notice if I just threw one of Rich's pictures against the wall and stomped on it after it fell to the floor.

But I sensed someone was behind me. I turned and saw Zoe peering around the gray fabric-covered wall that separated her office nook from mine. It only took a glance to see how her thick glasses magnified the fire that danced in her small brown eyes.

Had she smelled grade-A gossip in the cubicle right next to hers like a hunting dog hot on the trail of a kill?

I was glad I hadn't thrown Rich's photo, but the longer I watched her craning her neck, the more I regretted it because Zoe needed little encouragement to take full license.

I turned back to my notes and feigned busy, but I could still feel her gaze burning a hole in my back.

Shoo.

Go away.

I was not about to spill the intimate details of how The Dick dumped me to marry The French Tart.

I heard the zip of her chair wheels along the plastic chair runner and in a matter of seconds she'd wheeled her seat into my cubicle. I didn't have to turn around to know she was primed to dish.

Shit.

I kept my gaze glued to my Daytimer and pretended to make notes.

Maybe if I ignored her she'd go away.

Yeah, right.

Every muscle in my body tensed. I held my breath waiting for her to ask why I was slumped over my desk instead of oo-la-la-ing along Le Seine with Le Dick.

Well, let her ask. She couldn't pry it out of me. There was no way in hell I'd—

"Did you hear?" she whispered. As she waited for me to take the bait, she glanced over her bony little shoulder then scooted her chair closer and leaned in. Her gaze searched my face.

What? Was this some sort of new gossip-gathering tactic? Loosen me up with a prime tidbit? Get me talking so she could move in for the kill? Uh, uh, uh, I'm onto you, gossip girl.

I put on my *you're annoying me* face and stared at her. If I didn't bite at her lure, maybe she *would* go away.

"On Friday twenty-five people bit the big one."

I dropped my pen. "What?"

"The paper laid off twenty-five people in editorial. Friday, just before five o'clock Rivers called them all in and they got the ax."

Friday? I'd started my so-called vacation Friday at noon. "Who?" I asked, hating to play into Zoe's hand, but this was major. Twenty-five people? I had no idea. Ohmigod, that was half of the editorial department.

No wonder the newsroom seemed quieter than usual this morning. I mean reporting wasn't strictly a nine-to-five desk job and it wasn't unusual for half the office to be out at once. Good reporters probably spent three-quarters of their time out in the field digging up the news and were only at their desk long enough to pound out the story under deadline, but this morning the place had been like a morgue. God, and I thought it was just me. My mood projecting a gray yuck on everything I came into contact with.

As Zoe rattled off a list of the casualties, a chilling thought wrapped around my windpipe. What if I was supposed to be on that roster and Rivers forgot I was taking the afternoon off? What if he'd planned to finish me off today? Was he sitting on his self-righteous ass knowing good and well what he had in store for me? Just like he knew all day long Friday what he was going to do to those poor unsuspecting suckers on *The List.*

If I thought my life was shit before. Now it was . . . I'd be dumped *and* unemployed? Nooooo! This couldn't happen! It was fundamentally wrong. Too many life changes all at once were bad. Way bad. That's how people grew old overnight.

"So your job's okay?" I asked, then held my breath. I'd worked at the *Daily* longer than Zoe.

She nodded, and I could breathe again.

Wait! She was a general assignment reporter, jack-of-all-trades, flexible, moldable. I, on the other hand, was the food critic. Can you say *disposable?* Like a box of chocolates in a dieter's kitchen.

Oh, God. Oh, God.

"They had security here to escort them out." Zoe's dark brown eyes sparkled. "John McCroy, the sports guy, made a big scene. I thought he was going to punch Rivers. McCroy was cussing and going on about how his wife's pregnant and all. Rumor has it more people are going to get it in three months if the advertising staff can't start turning a profit."

I swallowed hard. "More?"

Zoe's head bobbed up and down. She loved to take an already depressing bit of news and wring every bit of emotional impact out of it, even at the risk of sensationalism. It wouldn't be the first time she'd stretched the truth for maximum impact. I firmly believed that somewhere on her list of things to do before she died was garnering a piece of gossip worthy of inciting mass hysteria. Killjoy that I was, I refused to let this be the issue that allowed her to cross that one off her list.

"So that's all the layoffs for now?"

Her head bobbed again.

As if she would know if my job was safe. Then again, with her knack for being the first to know, maybe it wasn't such a stretch.

"Of course *Natalie Clemmons* kept her job." Zoe's left eyebrow shot up and she pursed her thin lips. "You *know* why."

"She's a decent reporter." I swiveled my chair back to my desk and picked up my pen.

Enough. The last thing we needed was for Rivers to catch us goofing when he was primed for letting people go. On good days he was moody. I sure didn't want to get caught in the crossfire of his *black Monday after bloody Friday* hangover.

"She's sleeping with VanHussen."

I shot her a *go away* look. But she just sat there and pointed toward the ceiling, toward the office of Chris VanHussen, the heir-by-marriage to the *Orlando Daily*.

His resume read:

Forty years old.

Six-foot-two.

Zero handicap golfer.

Gorgeous trophy husband to Marjorie McPherson VanHussen, oldest daughter of *Daily* owner Douglas A. McPherson.

"Oh, please." I tossed my pen aside. "VanHussen's married with three kids. He's not sleeping with Natalie Clemmons."

"That's not what my sources say."

"Your *sources?* Give me a break, the Magic Eight Ball is not a source. Do you really think Chris VanHussen would be stupid enough to sleep with an employee?"

She shot me a *that's-a-no-brainer* look. "VanHussen doesn't give a damn about the *Daily*."

Actually, she had a point, given the paper's financial nose-dive since he'd taken the helm. Problem was he was never at the helm. He spent more time out on the green—or somewhere—than he did in the office. Preoccupied with his balls—you can take that however you want.

VanHussen was a lot of things, but he wasn't a newspaper man like his father-in-law, who started the *Daily* to give the *Orlando Sentinel* a run for its money.

McPherson always said any town the size of Orlando needed more than one daily paper to keep the news and views unbiased. For that alone, I admired the man, despite his blind eye to the nepotism that was sending the *Daily* straight to hell.

"Wood! Logan!" I jumped at the sound of Rivers's booming voice. "Care to join us in the editorial meeting?" Zoe zipped back around to her side of the gray wall. I stood up fast and saw Rivers waiting in the middle of the newsroom, his arms bent at the elbow, his palms toward the ceiling as if he were shrugging.

Oops.

Apparently I wasn't the only one who'd had a rough weekend. Believe me, Rivers's misery was no consolation. I grabbed my notebook and raced toward the conference room.

Well, if I'd fallen through the layoff cracks, I'd find out in a few minutes.

My job was safe. Or maybe I should say I was still employed at the *Daily*. As for my job, it had kind of gone through a meat grinder during the editorial meeting.

It scarcely resembled the position I was hired to do. Rivers had informed those of us who were "*lucky* enough" to remain standing, we had the dubious honor of picking up the slack.

In addition to food coverage, I'd handle the arts because it seems they'd actually read my resume and remembered I had a minor in art. Didn't they read the fine print? My emphasis was art history.

So how did I get so lucky to get the ballet beat?

Ballet as in tutus and point shoes. That was the extent of my knowledge on the subject. With that they expected me to write a feature story on the Central Florida International Ballet and review their production of *Giselle*, which opened Valentine's Day evening.

Oh, goody.

I drew a series of spirals around the edge of my notes. They might as well have assigned me sports or international trade for all I knew about ballet.

For God's sake, I was a food writer, not a dance critic. A food writer who just happened to know the difference between a Renoir and a Rembrandt. But I knew nothing about Isadora Duncan. How in the hell was this supposed to work?

Baklava, I could handle. Ballet was harder to swallow, which seemed a fair exchange since ballerinas didn't eat anyway.

To me, watching a flock of women in tutus and men in tights prancing around onstage was about as stimulating as watching fish swim in a fishbowl.

I heard Zoe yacking on the telephone. For someone so little, her voice carried—no, more like reverberated—throughout the sparsely populated newsroom. I tried to tune her out by wondering what kind of a man got up every morning and put on tights to go to work.

Oh.

Never mind. Pretty obvious.

I tore off the page in my notepad that I'd scribbled on and folded it in half.

No, now wait. Mikhail Baryshnikov wasn't gay. He was hot, in that kind of artsy-sensitive, beta male sort of way. He'd certainly caught my attention in the movie *White Nights*. I doodled some more. Hmmmm, maybe watching buff men in tights wouldn't be so bad after all.

Okay, enough stalling. Time to get to work. I pushed aside my doodling and picked up my voice mail messages. Of the ten phone messages that collected on my phone while I was in the editorial meeting, five of them—count them f-i-v-e—were from Jimbo Giani, jackass extraordinaire. Tenacious jackass. I'd give him that much. But that was *all* he'd get from me.

He'd never bothered to come over and introduce himself Saturday night. So, according to the bet I made with Karen, I was off the hook as far as one Jimbo Giani was concerned.

Good. Five calls automatically scratched off the list. That made my day a little brighter.

I marked through Giani's name with the vengeance of a high priestess sticking a pin in a voodoo doll. Sorry, *Jimbo*, you can't always get what you want.

You can't always get what you want.

That stinking song was going to be stuck in my head all day.

Humming, I'd just pulled up the ballet's website on my computer to do a little research, when my phone rang. "Olivia Logan."

"So how in the world did you land the *bitch beat?*"

I glanced at the right wall of my cubicle, the one that separated my space from Zoe's. A flick of irritation zinged through me.

"Why are you calling me? You're right on the other side of the wall."

"You're in a mood today. So are you going to tell me why you're here and not in Paris?"

It was like hearing her in stereo, the way her voice carried through the empty newsroom. Through the phone and through the wall. No, I wasn't going to tell her.

"What's the bitch beat?" I asked, hoping she'd take the old bait and switch.

"VanHussen's wife, Marjorie, major bitch. She just got appointed to the Central Florida International Ballet's board of directors and is rabid for press coverage. That's why it's the *bitch beat.* She wants free advertising. Do I ever feel sorry for you. Rumor has it she's a piece of work."

"Zoe, *you're* a piece of work. We're both going to be out of work if VanHussen hears you calling his dearly beloved a bitch."

"So why'd you and Rich break up?"

"Because he's a dick."

Ahhhhhhhhh! I can't believe I'd just spilled it. She just wouldn't quit. "I've got to go."

I'd just slammed down the phone and it buzzed again.

Oh, for God's sake, Zoe, give it a rest. I grabbed the receiver.

"What?"

"Jeez, Liv, nice phone manners." In the ensuing silence, I heard Donna smacking gum on the other end of the line. "There's a gentleman here in the lobby with a delivery. Says he needs you to sign for it."

"Can't you just sign my name?"

"Nope. Tried that already," she said in her nasal whine. "Didn't work."

Oh, for God's sake. Why didn't they lay off her? Worthless. "Fine."

As I made my way from the newsroom into the lobby, I racked my brain and tried to imagine what could be so bloody important. An angry restaurant owner? No, I wrote my reviews under the pseudonym "Starvin' Marvin." Donna might be lame, but she knew better than to out me.

Some sort of a top-secret lead? Right, I should be so lucky. The mayor's girlfriend was waiting in the lobby prepared to spill her guts about the affair everyone in Orlando who had eyes knew about. Might be fun, if we handled stories like that. Even if we did, why would she ask for me?

Richard? My heart kicked into overdrive. Had he sent something? Was he here, waiting—

No! Forget him. The Richard I knew was dead. No, even worse, someone had given him a lobotomy which transformed him into Evil Dick and programmed him to marry The French Tart.

Think of anything else, but not The Dick. *You can't always get what you want.*

When I turned the corner into the lobby, I quickly realized some days started out bad and progressively went down the shitter. This was one of those days. Proof of that was the sight of Jimbo Giani, dressed in black jeans and a leather bomber jacket, standing in the middle of the lobby clutching a bouquet of a gazillion red, yellow, pink and white long-stemmed roses.

Oh, shit.

Maybe if I kept my head down I could keep right on walking out the door. But he'd already seen me.

Fury nearly choked me. I had to put an end to this once and for all. This pushy, brazen mule was used to getting what he wanted. Clueless. Avoiding his phone calls wasn't going to resolve the issue. I had to be frank.

I plastered on a smile and counted to ten as I approached him. He watched me, his eyes bright and expectant.

"Mr. Giani. I appreciate your interest, but when I accept a dinner invitation, it's because the man who delivers it has the manners to ask me out in person. He doesn't send a note via the bartender because he's too busy draping himself all over two blondes young enough to be his daughters."

Giani smiled like he was trying to understand a joke and he didn't quite get it.

"Excuse me? I'm looking for Liv Logan."

He glanced around the lobby.

"I'm Liv, live and in person."

He blinked and cocked his head to the side. His brow furrowed. Then he glanced around the room. I followed his gaze to Donna who was blatantly listening, of course. She looked back and forth between Giani and me, then pretended to busy herself. But I knew she was still listening, probably salivating at being able to scoop Zoe on a juicy morsel of gossip.

"Let's go in here." I led Giani to the conference room and shut the door. "Look, Mr. Giani. I appreciate your interest, but I'm not . . . interested."

He cleared his throat and stared at the flowers for a moment. I should have felt like a first class schmuck over the way I'd just acted. I mean the flowers were beautiful.

I gripped the back of the chair I stood behind.

Maybe Karen was right. Maybe someone like Jimbo Giani, a man who'd treat me right, was just the medicine I needed. A couple of dates didn't equal a serious relationship.

He clutched the flowers and shifted from foot to foot. "Well, jeez. I'm glad to hear that because I think I've made a big mistake. I was looking for a blonde. Tall, slim, long straight blonde hair. Knockout. She was sitting at the bar at Hue Saturday night with a friend."

What?

My mouth fell open. *Karen.* He'd meant the note for Karen, not me. For the life of me I couldn't figure out why, if I hadn't wanted to date the guy in the first place, his words felt like a swift round-robin kick to the gut.

I mean . . . Oh, God! I was totally invisible. He hadn't even seen me sitting right next to Karen. But I was there. I was *there!*

I turned away from him, walked to the conference room door, then held it open for him.

"Well." My smile felt like it was set in thin plaster. "Good luck finding your tall, blonde knockout. I'm sure she's a lucky woman."

He furrowed his brow again and stole a glance at me as he started out the door. He'd just stepped out into the hall when he turned back to me and said, "How'd you know my name?"

My insides squirmed. "Oh, well, you know, we've done stories on you here at the paper."

He frowned. "Right."

Again, he stared at the flowers. "Here." He thrust them into my arms. "Have these."

As I stood cradling the roses like a Miss America reject, he disappeared down the hall.

What the hell was I going to do with four dozen roses? Take them to Karen and tell her about the mistake? She'd be thrilled she'd outshone me after all. Or at least she'd better be thrilled after the way she pressured me to go out with him.

I walked past the reception desk on my way to find something to put the roses in.

"Everything okay?" Donna asked.

"Peachy," I muttered.

She eyed the flowers.

Oh, the conclusions her mind must have been jumping to. Well, let her jump. I hoped she didn't hurt herself.

In the break room, I found an empty plastic pitcher, ran some water in it and shoved in the roses.

Good enough.

I set them in the middle of the table and started back to my desk. It felt good to leave them there. Maybe someone would steal them.

I got back to my cubicle, dialed Karen's work number and asked her to meet me for lunch.

"Oh, hey, I'd love to, but I'm shorthanded today. Veronica called in sick. If you want to come to the shop we could order in."

About two years ago Karen had taken a wild chance and opened You're Putting Me On Again, a vintage clothing boutique in the heart of downtown. She'd invested her life savings and gone against the grain of everyone who told her she was crazy to give up her steady job doing hair to throw every cent she had into a pipe dream. Two years later she was too busy to track down the naysayers and flaunt her success.

I gathered the flowers from the break room and set out on foot to Karen's shop. Before I was even a block down the sidewalk, no fewer than six complete strangers asked, "For me?"

I smiled at each one, even though I didn't feel like it. I wanted to roll my eyes and say, "Oh, you're so original."

But the person who really took the cake was the guy dressed in the business suit who asked, "How much for the roses?"

I didn't smile at him. I had three words for him: I'm. Over. This.

"Yeah, right." It was all getting a little bit old.

He was walking alongside of me.

Get out of here, weirdo. Did I look like a walking flower vendor?

"No, really." He pulled out his wallet. "How much?"

I stopped in front of a health food restaurant and squinted at him. Behind him, I could see my reflection in the glass. Ohmigod, if I did look like a flower seller, I'd have to say the next option was a float in the Tournament of Roses Parade.

"Here." I divided the roses in half and thrust them at him. "On the house." That was one way to lighten my load.

The guy looked stunned. "Thanks, are you sure I can't pay you?"

I shook my head and left the man holding his wallet and half my burden.

I turned down East Church Street, walked past the bank building plaza and Pax Comedy Club to a little storefront with an ornate window display draped with yards of ivory and rose antique silks and laces. An old-fashioned dressmaker's dummy sported strands of pearls in various lengths and a picture hat with flowing pink ribbons and dried flowers. A hand-painted sign that read You're Putting Me On Again hung above the entry, suspended by ornate wrought iron hooks that had been painted white.

As I pulled open the door, a bell chimed. Karen looked up from the wrinkled dress she was steaming behind the counter. "Hey, Brenda Starr. Oh, my God, look at you. Did you rob a florist?"

My arms were still so full I could barely squeeze past the clothing racks. "These are for you." I dumped the roses on the display case that Karen used as a wrap stand.

"You shouldn't have," she said, staring first at the flowers then at me like I'd just gifted her with an alien.

"I didn't. Compliments of Jimbo Giani."

"Oh! He called?"

"Five times. When I didn't return his calls he paid me a visit." I reached out and plucked a petal off a pink rose, pinched it and sniffed it. No scent. Must be one of those cultivated hothouse varieties with the fragrance bred out of them.

Karen picked up the whole bunch and buried her face in the middle of the bouquet. "Look at all these roses. The guy's in love with you. When are you going out?"

"We're *never* going out, because the guy's not in love with *me*."

Karen gently laid down the roses. Her brow wrinkled into her pre-lecture frown.

"Save it," I said. "He's not interested in me." Ouch. I'd intended to preempt Karen's harangue, but my words turned on me and cut like a sharp knife.

Despite having no desire to date Jimbo the Jackass, admitting the truth of his misdirected attraction hurt.

Dumped by The Dick.

Invisible to The Jackass.

This was starting to become a pattern.

"Oh, come on. How can you say Jimbo's not interested in you? Look at this." She gestured to the flowers. "The guy brought you all these roses. There's got to be—"

"Two dozen. There used to be four dozen but I gave half of them away to a guy on the street." I straightened a display of brooches. "Each flower intended for *you*. Not me. The bartender gave Giani's note to me by mistake."

There. I'd said it. Time to move on.

Disbelief flashed in Karen's eyes, but was instantly replaced by pale blue pity. And if anything pissed me off, it was her feeling sorry for me. And what got me, I mean *really* got me where it hurt, was Giani obviously hadn't even seen *me* sitting there. I was invisible. Even if Juan had dolled me up and made me presentable, the Liv Logan Jimbo Giani came face to face with today wasn't the one he saw in the bar. That was assuming he'd even seen me at all.

I grabbed a handful of antique buttons from a silver filigree box on the counter and watched them slide through my fingers, like unshed tears held back so long they'd petrified into permanent angst.

I'd happily worn the cloak of anonymity most of my life, but lately it was starting to pinch and bind. I closed the glass lid on the little box and glanced up at Karen. "You're going to call him, right?"

She shrugged.

I dug in my purse and extracted Giani's card. "Go for it. It would do you some good to let a man take you out and spoil you."

There, how did Karen like her own words used back on her?

"Oh, Liv, I can't go out with him under these circumstances."

Okay, she could cancel the pity Liv party. I didn't need her to smooth balm on my bruised ego. It hurt like hell without touching it. So it was best just to leave it alone.

I winked at her, smiled and shoved the card toward her. "Oh, yes, you can." Karen hesitated for a moment, but accepted the card and managed a weak smile.

Standing right there in the middle of the boutique, I made a vow: I would damn well never be invisible again.

While I was delivering Karen's flowers, Marjorie VanHussen called and left me a voice mail. It seemed a little birdie had told her about my *Giselle* assignment. I was cordially invited to meet her at two o'clock, one week from today at the performing arts center where the ballet practiced.

"I'll *introduce* you," she said. No, more like demanded. Do not pass go, do not collect any information without first being introduced. I imagined her biting off the clipped words with perfect white teeth.

One word came to mind: bitch.

Judging from her tone of voice and the unspoken message between her words, I'd best not even think about saying no to Marjorie McPherson VanHussen.

Oh, yeah. Lucky me. I was on the bitch beat.

I'd do the happy dance, but I was too overcome with joy. I tapped my pencil on the desk.

God, why? What had I done that was so heinous to warrant this . . . this crap that was suddenly raining down on me? I looked at the ceiling. Whatever it was, I'm sorry. Didn't mean it. Really. You can stop now.

I wasn't a real religious person. I was spiritual, but whatever I did, couldn't absolution apply so I could start having good days again?

My phone rang and I grabbed the receiver. "Liv Logan."

Silence.

"Hello?" I said.

Nothing.

I waited a couple more beats and hung up.

An eerie feeling crept over me. I'd been getting a lot of hang-ups on my work phone. At first I didn't think anything of it, but now that Richard was gone, it was starting to give me the creeps. If he was calling and hanging up, he was a bigger dick than I'd thought.

Jerk.

Go call The French Tart.

I got up and looked to see if Zoe was in, but her desk was empty and her computer screen was black. She was obviously out for the rest of the afternoon. That sounded like a good idea.

I made a deal with myself. Women like Marjorie thrived on running the show. Since it couldn't hurt to make an ally of the publisher's wife during these uncertain times at the paper, I'd change my attitude and go with the Marjorie flow. In return, I would reward myself with Starbucks mocha grande and a cinnamon scone. Now that was almost a fair trade.

One week later, on the short drive over to the Central Florida Centre for the Performing Arts, I was surfing a wave of irritation, inspired by a week's worth of phone calls from *Mah-jorie* about what kind of story she expected me to write about the ballet.

Dammit. How dare she?

Her most recent call came just as I'd grabbed my purse

and notebook to head out to keep our appointment. The mere sound of her voice started me chafing from the micromanagement noose.

Why had I answered the phone? You'd think I'd have developed some sort of Marjorie radar by now. But I was waiting on a call from someone else and got, "Before you come over here, Olivia, I just want to make sure we're on the same page."

Look, bitch, if you say that to me one more time, I'll . . . I'll. . . . Okay, reality and good judgment dictated I wouldn't do anything rash. But after a solid diet of the boss's wife from hell, I deserved a whole lot more than the comfort of a Starbucks scone and mocha.

As much as I loved the treat, it didn't cut it right now. I'd have to think of a really, really good way to reward myself. Hmmm, the Chico's catalogue had come in the mail over the weekend. Maybe I'd treat myself to that pretty blue outfit.

Instantly, my mood brightened. I parked the car and made a new resolution. Yes, with that kind of incentive, I could deal with Mrs. VanHussen. I had Chico's. She had no influence in my life. Well, that was true if you didn't count the whole husband/boss situation, but I wouldn't think of that right now. I'd graciously accept her help and write the story my own way.

I was the reporter.

The three-story building was an old renovated power plant. All high arched windows and cream stucco walls. Light. As I entered the building, an attractive woman with jet-black hair and piercing blue eyes waved at me from an office behind the reception desk.

So this was Marjorie VanHussen?

Mid-thirties. Oooo, bad nose job. The nostrils were too high and the end was bobbed off a hair too short. Someone ought to tell her if she paid for that botched job she got ripped off.

She wasn't quite what I expected. But, then, what had I expected? I mean really. It stood to reason a man like Chris VanHussen would be married to a beautiful woman.

Other than her nose, Marjorie was perfect from her shiny black hair, to her black and white Chanel suit, down to her polished and painfully pointy-toed patent leather pumps.

"Olivia." More of a statement than a question, but yes, there was that *I-am-so-superior* tone.

I nodded and accepted her perfectly manicured hand. "Marjorie." Not Marge or Margie. Mah-jorie. "Thank you for offering to introduce me."

Oh, puke. I bit the insides of my jaws. I'd look soooo good in that new Chico's outfit. I was sooooo earning it.

She smiled with an air of gracious self-assurance.

"Thank *you* for taking the time to do this story. The Central Florida International Ballet deserves more press."

Oh, is that so, Mah-jorie. It was only the ten thousandth time she'd said it. What did one more hurt?

The name suited her. It personified the Junior Leaguer, the ballet board member, the type who came from money, married well and sent her children to expensive private schools.

"Come inside," she said, gently putting her left hand on my back to guide me. "The ballet's *exquisite*. You're in for a real treat. Are you familiar with the story *Giselle?*"

No, that's why I'm here. And I'm sure you'll tell me all about it.

Before I could answer, Marjorie turned to greet a group of five women who were on their way out.

I watched her as she warmly interacted with the women, whom she introduced as members of a service organization who were considering donating their time to help sew costumes. In turn, Marjorie called each one by name, made nice comments and astute observations.

Smooth.

Actually, if I tossed aside my Marjorie bias, she seemed quite warm.

Well, of course she did. She needed these women. She knew what she was doing.

What was it like to be Marjorie VanHussen? The woman who always knew the right thing to say, the appropriate thing to do. *Always* appropriate. Did she know about the Natalie Clemmons rumors?

For Natalie's sake, I hoped not.

Women like Marjorie VanHussen had ways of dealing with the competition. Delicate, but deceptively effective means. Like cleaning up a dead mouse dragged in by the cat without getting her hands dirty, without even really having to look at the mess.

If the Natalie rumors proved true, one day Ms. Clemmons would just disappear from Chris VanHussen's life. There one day, gone the next.

Poof.

The Olivias and Natalies of the world were expendable. Men never left the Marjories.

Before, during and after the affair, no one would ever see anything but a happy couple, a perfect family. People would look at the VanHussens and sigh, *oh, aren't they lucky*.

I watched the sun stream in through one of the huge windows. It bounced off the stucco wall, illuminating a *Swan Lake* poster of a man and a ballerina locked in an embrace. He was looking at her longingly, her head was turned away.

People used to think Rich and I were lucky.

Don't think about The Dick.

Don't! Don't! Don't! Don't!

Concentrate on your job. Think ballet.

I walked over to the reception desk and picked up a brochure about the company's season.

Think *I love my life.* Think *I am not invisible.* Think . . . You can't always get what you want.

"I'm so sorry for the interruption," cooed Marjorie, back at my side. "We're desperate for volunteers these days, but that's not the focus of your story. I had envisioned more of an interpersonal feature story focusing on the lives and relationships of our talented dancers."

The wave of irritation rose again. Wait just a minute, Mah-jorie.

You're starting to annoy me. You might be able to waltz in and tell your plastic surgeon how to do his job—and you see what that got you. But I'm a member of the press. I don't take orders from my interviewees. Who do you think you are? The daughter of man who owns the paper? The one who sleeps with the man who holds the fate of my job in his hands?

Well, except when he's holding Natalie Clemmons.

Hmmmm, where did Chris and Natalie do it? Did they grab a little afternoon delight in his office? Or did Chris make up excuses to steal away for secret rendezvous? I'll bet the whole golf thing was really just a cover, a convenient excuse to be incommunicado. Did he tell Natalie the intimate details of his horrendous layoff plans while he screwed her or did he spill them as he basked in the afterglow? Ew. My gut clenched.

"A story like that could work," I said, hating myself even before the last gelatin-spined syllable escaped my lips.

Marjorie flashed me an *I'm-glad-we-understand-each-other*

smile. "Come on." She motioned for me to follow. "I guar-
antee before you leave, you'll be as smitten with this dance
company as I am."

Yeah, promises, promises.

Feeling like I'd just sold my soul to the devil, I accompa-
nied her down a long hall and into a room labeled Studio
Two. Inside, jaunty classical music blared while a group of
emaciated women and—wow—impressively buff men in
tights rehearsed turns, leaps and moves that defied human
limitations.

Okay, so the whole men in tights thing was a little
funky. But, my God, what bodies. Okay, maybe this
wasn't so bad.

Marjorie and I silently made our way to some chairs along
a mirrored wall on the far side of the rectangular room. As we
sat down, I noticed one of the taller men in the company and
a tiny, strikingly beautiful ballerina in a frothy white tutu
seemed to be arguing quietly on the sidelines as most of the
corps danced.

He reached out to her, but she shoved his hand aside,
turned gracefully and stomped off flat-footed in her point
shoes to the other side of the room. I thought of the *Swan
Lake* poster in the lobby.

When he turned to watch her pace in the opposite corner, I
noticed he had the most incredibly flawless—no, absolutely,
positively the most exquisite—Adonis-like butt I'd ever seen.
It was accentuated to perfection by flesh-colored tights and a
little tunic-like jacket that stopped just at his hips. He turned
back to the front. I swallowed hard. Never mind the buns.
The guy was hung like a bull.

Holy cow.

His thigh muscles rippled as he transferred his weight
from one leg to the other. As he crossed his arms, I noticed his

broad shoulders and sculpted arms defied reason.

A work of art.

Every lean inch of him.

My appreciation returned to his tights, and I shifted in my seat.

Okay, so it had been six long months since I'd had sex—far, far too long. Regardless, a woman would have to be dead to miss the pure beauty of this living, breathing Rodin sculpture.

See, I knew quite a bit about art. At least I was astute enough to recognize a walking work of art when I saw one.

In fact, with the classical music playing in the background, I'd suddenly gained an even deeper appreciation for all things artistic. A reverence I'd never experienced in my college art classes.

My gaze traced the line of gold brocade adorning the front of his tunic. By the time my senses registered that his face, while pleasant—mmmm, nice smile—didn't quite match the superb magnitude of that bod, I realized he was watching me, watching him. And his smile invited me to look until I'd had my fill. So maybe this was proof that God had answered my absolution prayer.

"*That's* Alexei Ivanov," Marjorie purred. "He's Russian."

As if that explained everything I needed to know.

Alexei's gaze shifted to Marjorie. She straightened and I thought I recognized a nuance, nearly imperceptible to the untrained eye, transfer between them. Then Alexei turned away and prepared to dance.

Oh.

So maybe Chris had his reasons for screwing around with Natalie. Maybe that's what Ballerina Girl was all pissed off about. Maybe sweet Marjorie's ballet *charity work* went beyond the boardroom.

Yeah, more like bedroom.

Watching Alexei's steel buns as he performed athletic leaps and lifts, I could clearly see what tempted Marjorie. With moves like that, Buns would be hell on wheels in bed.

Oh, Lord.

When the music stopped, Marjorie stood and applauded and the man directing the dancers called a fifteen-minute break. As Marjorie scurried to his side, her high-heeled pumps clicking on the hardwood floor, I noticed the ballerina Alexei had fought with took flight for the door. Alexei followed.

Uh-huh.

"Konstantin, may I please have a moment with you?" Marjorie asked, syrupy sweet and more southern than she'd sounded earlier. "I'd like to introduce Olivia Logan." She motioned for me to join them. "Olivia's a reporter with the *Orlando Daily* and she'd like to write a feature story on the company."

I pulled myself to my feet and joined her.

"Olivia, this is Konstantin Alexandrova, the Central Florida International Ballet's artistic director."

We shook hands. For a slight man, he had a firm and commanding handshake.

"Pleased to meet you," he said, his voice heavily colored by a Russian accent. He smiled warmly. "We're happy to help you and you are most welcome to watch us as we rehearse, but may I ask a favor?"

I nodded. "Of course."

"We must concentrate as we prepare for our performance. Could interviews wait until we have worked through the troubled spots? Then we will be at your disposal. How about if you start one week from today? We will be in the theatre. You watch us in action."

"Absolutely, Konstantin," Marjorie chimed in before I could reply. "Olivia can find other things to do. She'll be back in a week."

Marge was definitely getting on my nerves. I gritted my teeth and managed a smile.

"Absolutely," I echoed.

I should know better than to say *never*. Because when I do, I always end up eating my words. And they're *never* soft and sweet. So let me backpedal a little bit here.

When I said I was sick and tired of being invisible, I must have been in a mood. And if, per chance, I wasn't in a mood then, I am now.

Shedding my cloak of anonymity left me just a tad exposed. Actually, it made me feel downright naked, and I wasn't sure if I was ready to let it all hang out.

With the ballet's rehearsal schedule, I thought I'd get a reprieve from Marjorie breathing down my neck, trying to direct my journalistic endeavors.

No luck. Not when I was on the *bitch beat.*

Offering to school me on the subtleties of ballet and the story of Giselle and dropping not-so-subtle hints about the expected glowing review of next weekend's *Giselle* performance, she not only made me wish I could disappear, she made me realize I just might be capable of committing murder. But I could easily plead insanity. Basically I was a nonviolent person, but if I didn't murder her, she was going to drive me to such madness that I would kill myself.

Hmmm, kind of like the lead character, Giselle, in the ballet. Well, actually, she collapsed and died over a man who controlled her heartstrings, not because of a control freak who drove her insane because she held the purse strings.

In the ballet, Giselle is so overcome with grief when she

finds out the love of her life is not the man she thought he was, she goes mad.

Hul-lo, girlfriend.

I was relating to ballet better than I ever thought I would. The story was a bit too close for comfort and could have made me very sad, if not for the brilliant distraction of Mr. Buns of Steel dancing the lead male role.

Ah . . . poetry in motion. But wait, I digress.

I started to tell you how I'd rediscovered the virtues of invisibility.

Sure, it had a little to do with evading overbearing Marjorie and her harangue over her brigade of men in tights, but more to do with happening upon a certain guy from a certain party, saying good-bye to a pretty redhead in the middle of the hallway early on a Sunday morning.

Chapter Five

One of the perks of being invisible is people don't see you. Well, duh. I know that's obvious, but think about it. Unnoticed, you can get away with things like crawling out of bed, throwing on a tattered terry bathrobe, and fetching the newspaper without witness.

It's not pretty, but fresh out of a long-term relationship with a man who detested high-maintenance women, this no-hassle lifestyle had become a habit.

Wait a minute. Could The French Tart be anything less than high-maintenance? I hoped she was karma coming 'round to bite him in the ass.

Forget The Dick, I was into comfort these days. So picture the scene when I opened the door and ran headlong into Hunter, who was casually leaning on the jamb of the apartment across the hall apparently saying good-bye to a tall, thin, beautiful woman. Both turned and looked at me.

Shit!

One hand frozen on the doorknob, I fumbled to pull my robe closed. And why? To hide my red plaid flannel jammies? As if the dingy robe with its torn pocket hanging down like a conspiratorial winking eye would make me look sexy.

Shit! Shit!

I gaped at him.

He straightened.

I wanted to disappear, but I didn't have anything like a byline to fade into. Frankly, a doormat would have worked fine if Juan believed in such *bourgeois* conformities.

The woman standing next to Hunter was stunning,

dressed in tight black jeans, a soft-looking moss-green sweater, a color I loved but couldn't wear because it made me look ill. Her long hair hung in spirals, mussed just enough to look sensual.

As I looked back and forth between Hunter and the stunning redhead, I felt smaller than a flake of dandruff and ten thousand times as ugly.

Oh, God! I had to get out of there.

I turned to leave.

"Olivia?"

Busted.

I was tempted to act like I hadn't heard him, slink back inside and shut the door, but instead I turned back.

He squinted like he couldn't quite decide if it was really me. And—

I sucked in a sudden breath. Ohmigod, he'd remembered my name.

"Good morning," I murmured, my voice still froggy with sleep. I swiped my free hand through my tangled hair. Of course it was standing on end. My frizzies were probably making obscene gestures.

What the hell was *he* doing here?

And who the hell was *she?* The Loft Slut, live and in person. Uggh, why'd she have to be so pretty?

Judging from the open apartment door, one of them lived across the hall. But something in the comfortable way Hunter leaned against the doorjamb gave me the sneaking hunch he was my neighbor.

Why did he keep turning up?

For that matter, why did my knees go weak when he smiled?

Okay, this called for a major reality check.

He was standing in the hall with a *woman* at five o'clock on a Sunday morning. I have three words for you: Saturday night sex.

Shouldn't that cancel out the woo-woo-this-guy-is-your-destiny pathos my heart was singing about? Yeah, unless I was a total masochist.

I glanced down at my sock-clad feet, which I'd shoved into fuzzy slippers, then glanced back at Hunter.

Ohmigod, I must look so ridiculous, and he was gorgeous in his black sweatshirt, sleeves pushed up to his elbows. A trace of a beard shadowing his angular face.

I definitely had to get out of there.

But then he smiled and pointed at my door. "Are you staying with—"

"Just moved in."

Instantly Hunter looked wide awake.

"With *Juan?*"

The look faded to one of puzzlement, like the equation's parts didn't quite equal the sum. An awkward silence stretched on. And on.

"You live here, too?" I finally asked.

"Yeah, I just got back," he said. "I've been out of town."

The woman watched him as he talked, a black jacket draped over her forearm and black leather backpack purse slung over her shoulder.

Her gaze flickered my way and she smiled. Uggh, no-body's teeth were *that* perfect.

My hand fluttered to my cheek. I felt what must have been pillow creases etched into the side of my face, which made me remember I hadn't even as much as wiped the sleep from my eyes.

Okay, time to go.

Hunter touched the woman's arm.

"Oh, sorry, Des, this is Olivia . . . ?"

"Logan," I said. Hmmmmm, if she was his girlfriend, how was he was going to explain me to her? I crossed my arms. Let's see him talk his way out of this one.

He smiled again. Okay, with that smile he could probably talk his way out of anything.

"Olivia Logan. We just met about a week ago." He said, looking at me, "Liv, this is Destiny Forbes."

Liv. Oh, he called me Liv. It made me feel all warm and—*Destiny?* Pa-lease.

"Hi," I said.

Figures she'd have a name like *Destiny*. I bit the insides of my jaws and hoped I hadn't made a face thinking about her name.

"Hello." Her voice was low and rich, like a perfectly tuned cello, played by a virtuoso. She'd been played all right. And so had I.

So *destiny* was involved after all. Only in a way I'd never fathomed. A gorgeous woman was *not* part of *this* daydream. Unless *I* was cast in that role. My bathrobe, my not-so-sexy bed-head and my morning breath weren't part of this dream either.

Shit! Shit! Shit!

"How was Paris?" Hunter asked.

Paris? I groaned inwardly.

"Paris?" Destiny said. "I love Paris." She looked at me expectantly, in that confident way that comes naturally to tall, thin, beautiful women with names like Destiny.

"Paris . . . was . . . is . . . fabulous."

Well, everyone *says* so. It wasn't exactly a lie. She shifted from one long leg to the other and leaned back against the wall as if she'd resigned herself to being there for a while. The pose accentuated her perky breasts. She looked at Hunter with sleepy eyes and an intimate smile that spoke volumes, but his gaze flicked back to me.

Well, baby, this is what a real woman looks like in the morning. I don't run into the bathroom and plaster on the makeup before I face my man.

I took a bolder look at Destiny and my heart sank when I realized she wasn't wearing any makeup.

I don't know what got into me, but before I could stop myself, I blurted, "I'm engaged."

Then I cringed. What a liar!

Hunter's gaze darkened or maybe he seemed a little surprised. I wish I could have stretched the truth to say he looked disappointed, but the days of deluding myself were over. Why would he be disappointed when he had a woman like Destiny?

I picked up the fat Sunday paper and hugged it to me. Its plastic bag crinkled. "I'd better go." I gestured toward the door with my thumb. "Good to see you again, Hunter. I'm sure I'll see you around. Since we're neighbors. And all."

He nodded. "Hey, congratulations on your engagement."

"Nice to meet you," Destiny said.

I ducked back inside and leaned against the door.

Ohmigod! I hate this robe. I hate these slippers. I want to burn them. I kicked one off and it went flying across the room. Then I stood in the middle of the dark foyer and replayed every excruciating detail of the horrific Hunter scene in my head.

Destiny. Ugh. Even her name sounded manufactured— like her bobbed nose, her permed and dyed auburn hair. She obviously had implants. Nobody that skinny had boobs that perky. I drew in a deep breath and tried to pull myself up and out of the green, slimy place my emotions had dragged me.

Concentrate on the high points of the conversation.

Forget the embarrassment. It's all in the attitude. I'm secure with myself. This is who I am.

High points.

What else?

There had to be more high points to the conversation. I just had to think a minute.

Ahh! The engagement bit. That was brilliant. Especially since I always thought of the perfect comeback three hours after the fact. At least once in my life I'd saved face when it counted. Yep, in the span of a heartbeat I'd managed to blurt a beautiful, bold-faced lie.

Ohhhhhh, why did I do that?

Why did I care?

I didn't need to impress Hunter. What? Like I wanted to get involved with anyone right now, especially someone who lived across the hall? That was too close for comfort.

Oh, for God's sake.

I tightened my bathrobe and sighed.

Why *did* I keep running into him?

Just forget it. I was too busy to ponder such a useless bit of coincidence. I had much better things to do. Like see if he was kissing her.

I dropped the newspaper and pressed my face against the door and watched them through the peephole.

They stood there, much as they had when I'd opened the door. Only the scene was distorted out of proportion by the peephole's fish-eye lens. Hunter still leaned on the doorjamb. Destiny's posture was still perfect. Jacket over one arm. A good three feet of space separated them.

Yeah, I know spying was pretty sad. But I had to look, because just two weeks ago, Hunter had plied me with wine and made me contemplate the unthinkable: He'd made me consider cheating on The Dick. I'd never cheated.

Never ever even considered it.

And in the hours Hunter and I talked, my subconscious had indulged in every erotic fantasy it could concoct. Even if my conscious mind denied it at the time, it was owning up to it now.

Boy, I could pick 'em. Another womanizer.

Shit.

Destiny laughed, reached out and touched his arm.

Flirt.

My heart pounded.

She stepped closer and wrapped her arms around Hunter's neck—

"What are you looking at?"

I let out a startled gasp and tried to turn around, jump away from the door and grab the paper all at once. An awkward move that had me banging my head against the door somewhere in the middle of the motion.

"Ow."

Juan stood in the hall, shirtless, rubbing his hand over his face.

" 'Livia? What are you doing?"

"I was just getting the paper."

He shrugged. "You want some coffee?"

I nodded. "What are you doing up so early?"

"Ron and I are driving up to St. Augustine this morning." His voice trailed off as he walked into the kitchen. At least he didn't look out the peephole himself.

I took a deep breath, pressed my face to the door, and stole one more look out into the hall.

They were gone. Wait! Where did they go? Back inside to satisfy their heated passion? Did she leave? I'd never know because I didn't get to see.

I snorted as I turned away from the door and bumped

smack into Juan, who stood behind me again. This time mere inches.

"*What* are you looking at?"

"Nothing," I said nonchalantly.

This time he looked out the peephole himself.

Fine, let him look. There was nothing to see.

I walked into the kitchen and put the paper on the table.

How well did Juan know Hunter? Maybe I could plumb Juan for details.

I filled a kettle with water and set it on the stove.

Not that Juan was the type of person Hunter would hang out with. Hunter exuded 100 percent, grade-A, hot-blooded heterosexual male vibes. Just the kind of hot-blooded heterosexual male who might ask Juan why he had an engaged woman living with him and when I was getting married.

Ahhhhhhh! Oh, dear God, what had I done? I'd better talk to Juan and tell him what I'd done. He'd cover for me until I could fix things.

"Do you have time for breakfast?" My voice cracked. I cleared my throat. "I have to write an article for the food section about easy and elegant at-home Sunday brunches. I need to test the recipes."

Stupid! Stupid! Stupid!

I poured coffee beans in the mill and pressed the grind button. The smell of freshly ground beans was somewhat of a comfort.

But still, how could I have been such an idiot telling Hunter I was getting married? Maybe this was the reason I was supposed to wait three hours to formulate a good comeback. The three-hour jobbies usually didn't get me in trouble.

This is why I didn't lie.

But actually, I did lie. I was a big, fat liar and I was going to look like a big, fat idiot if I didn't fix this quick.

"Juan?"

I picked up a hand towel. If Hunter asked Juan about my being engaged, and Juan told him I'd moved in because The Dick dumped me, I'd . . . I'd. . . .

Juan rounded the corner. "Did you offer to cook for me?"

I dumped the ground coffee in the French press, then poured in boiling water.

"You bet."

The aroma filled the whole kitchen and I watched Juan inhale deeply as I started collecting the items I'd purchased yesterday for the menu. "How does this sound—wine country steak and hot eggs. Polenta. Bellinis?"

"Sounds wonderful," he said.

Just tell him.

"What's a Bellini?"

"Champagne and peach puree."

Confide in him about Hunter. First, ply him with a couple of Bellinis and then over breakfast say, "You know our neighbor across the hall . . . ?"

He'd nod.

We'd talk about how Hunter was a nice *asset* to the neighborhood. And I'd slowly bridge to the a-funny-thing-happened-when-I-was-picking-up-the-paper story.

This could work. Juan said we'd have good *girl talk*.

I popped the cork on the champagne. In fact, this might be fun.

I picked up a couple of peaches and held them under the cool running water.

"May I invite Ron?"

No! *Not* fun.

Maybe Juan hadn't noticed, but it was plain as the patronizing smirk on Ron's face that the guy didn't like me. This week I'd seen him a total of five times and each time he'd acted as if he smelled something rotten.

Someday I was going to tell him the foul stench stinking up the place was his bad attitude.

If I let myself, I might take Ron's cold shoulder personally, but I wouldn't give him that satisfaction.

No way. It was his problem.

I dried the peaches with a green hand towel, then ran a finger over the velvety skin.

Maybe Ron had something against women in general. Hmm, come to think of it, I'd never seen him act particularly cordial to Karen either.

"Sure." Invite away. He won't come.

"Great! I'm sure he'll sacrifice an early start for a fine breakfast like this."

I stirred the coffee, then depressed the plunger, sending the grounds down to the bottom of the carafe. There was nothing like good, rich French roast made in a French press.

Despite all that Frenchness.

The Dick and The French Tart did not own all things French. They would not steal these pleasures from me. In fact, I would love all things French to spite them.

It was just a shame they had to taint Paris before I had a chance to visit. I'd always wanted to go there. And I would.

Someday.

Just not right now.

I took two china cups from the cupboard and poured the deep, rich, steaming liquid. A splash of half-and-half in my cup and mmmmmmmm . . . heaven.

Nearly dancing with glee, Juan took his cup and went to call Ron, leaving me alone to peel the peaches for the Bellinis and sort out the mess I'd made.

I peeled a peach and set the delicate, fleshy fruit on the

cutting board. Droplets of sticky juice slid down my hand to my wrist.

A vision of Hunter licking the ambrosia from my fingers, from my lips—I could almost taste the essence of Hunter and peach, and a tingling started in my stomach. Until I remembered Destiny putting her arms around him in the hall earlier. It was probably a good thing that I didn't get to watch the good-bye grand finale.

This way, I could create my own ending—just like in the kitchen mysteries I wanted to write.

Maybe she'd just hugged him, then left and he'd gone back inside without a steamy kiss.

Maybe she'd died in his arms from malnutrition.

Maybe they'd both gone back inside.

Back to bed.

Which is exactly where I should have gone.

Not with Hunter.

Well, of course not. He was in bed with Destiny.

I should just go back to my big, lonely bed, all by my lonely self, and pull the covers over my head. . . .

Naaaa, I'd rather eat.

What a mess I'd created. I tossed the peeled, pitted peaches into the food processor, pressed the on button and watched the fruit explode into tiny bits.

Okay, this was the plan: I'd just casually mention to Hunter that the engagement was off. He'd never know I'd never been to Paris.

I pressed the off button, scooped out peach puree into two crystal champagne flutes, poured some bubbly into the glasses, then sampled a taste. The bubbles tickled my nose.

I took another sip.

The heavenly concoction usually put me in a good mood,

but this morning it made me think of weddings and my engagement lie.

Had they served French champagne at The Dick/French Tart wedding?

An ache stirred deep down in the dark hollow where my heart used to be. I downed the rest of the Bellini and forced myself to think of something else.

Like how I didn't know for certain that Destiny was Hunter's girlfriend. But what was the alternative? That she was just a lucky strike he'd picked up last night?

I poured another Bellini, sipped it and set the glass aside so I could lay the steak out on a piece of waxed paper and grab the meat tenderizing hammer.

Had he given her the same seductive eyes he'd given me?

Bam.

I flattened the steak with a hard blow of the tenderizer.

Had he softened her up with wine like he had me?

Bam. Bam.

Was that his smooth operator MO?

Bam. Bam. Bam.

Pretty good one.

Bam. Bam. Bam.

If I hadn't been ready to fly off to Paris to meet The Dick, it probably would have worked on me, too.

But no.

Bam. Bam.

I was loyal to the ugly end.

Bam. Bam. Bam.

And The Dick had already gotten married.

Bam. Bam. Bam. Bam.

I was such an idiot.

Bam. Bam. Bam. Bam. Bam.

Well.

Bam.

That.

Bam.

Was.

Bam.

Then.

Bam.

This was now.

Bam. Bam.

I was a new woman.

Bam. Bam. Bam.

And I certainly wouldn't fall for another

Bam.

two-timing—

Bam. Bam.

Womanizer.

Bam. Bam. Bam.

Even if he was hot.

Bam.

Especially because he was hot.

The tenderizer slipped from my hand and landed on the counter. I stared at the flattened steak.

The best thing I could do was forget Hunter and channel my energies into work. God knew I needed as much strength as I could gather to deal with Marjorie.

Juan rounded the corner again. His eyes were wide. "Are you cooking or remodeling?"

"Sorry, I probably woke up the neighbors." No, no, the neighbors were already awake. They'd been *up all night,* obviously.

"Ron's on his way," Juan said.

Huh?

"Oh. Great."

I definitely should have gone back to bed.

Was that terrible? Did it make me a horrible person who handed out empty invitations?

I sliced the end off an onion and peeled off the paper-thin skin. The pungency made my eyes water.

It wasn't an empty invitation. It wasn't an invitation at all. Juan was the one who invited Ron.

I glanced up from the onions I'd been chopping and saw him brooding—honestly brooding—like a big, pouting boy, staring at the floor, bottom lip thrust out, hands shoved in the pockets of his copper-colored corduroys.

"What's the matter?" I asked with an increasing suspicion it wouldn't be a good time to broach the fake engagement cover-up.

"Nothing," Juan snapped.

Okay. I set aside the onion and laid into a green pepper.

Juan sighed.

"Everything. Ron's got his panties all in a wad because I had the audacity to suggest a change of plans at the last minute."

"You don't have to change your plans. I don't want to mess up your day."

I scraped the onion and peppers into a skillet, added a little olive oil and a smidgen of butter, and turned on the burner.

Believe me. It's fine if you take your boyfriend and his wadded panties straight to St. Augustine. It was challenging enough to be around Ron on a good day, but the thought of sharing a meal with him in a mood gave me indigestion.

"No. No. No. We'll be happy to dine with you. St. Augustine will still be there no matter what time we arrive. What can I do to help?"

That was a loaded question.

The butter and oil sizzled as the vegetables cooked.

Dump the curmudgeon.

Ohmigod, how I wanted to say that. But given that Juan and I had been roommates for sixteen days, my better judgment said it was best to save that bit of sage advice for another time. Say maybe two or three years down the road.

If Ron was still around.

My money said he wouldn't be.

I smiled at Juan and handed him a champagne flute.

"First, you can drink a Bellini. Then you can start chopping these carrots and start on the garlic."

Pinkie extended, Juan held the glass to his nose and sniffed it, then sipped.

He closed his eyes and noisily smacked his lips.

"Ahhh, goddess nectar," he said. "Medicine for my weary soul."

While he sipped his drink I went and changed clothes. When I returned, I refilled both of our glasses. Pheww, I was starting to feel a little tipsy. But, hey, we needed all the fortification we could get before Ron arrived.

I added the carrots and garlic and stirred while Juan told the abridged version of *The Ron and Juan Story*.

One bottle of champagne later, we heard a key in the lock.

Ron had a key?

Oh, for God's sake. The realization ripped through me. I may be the new roommate, but it pissed me off.

He pissed me off. But that was another *wan of corms*.

Wan of worms.

Whatever.

Waddif I wanted to walk around in my underwear? Or naked? I could dance naked in my *home if* I wanna. Betcha The French Tart pranced around naked all the time. That's how she stole my boyfriend. Destiny probably pranced naked, too.

Men stealers.

Really *pizzez* me off.

I added a cup of boullion to the vegetables and turned the burner to simmer.

Juan looked a little *pizzed* himself.

Ha! We were both *pizzed*.

Nope. Hee-hee-hee. We were both drunk, we were.

Hee-hee.

I tipped back the last of the champagne-soaked peach, smacked my lips like Juan had to get the full effect of the goddess nectar. Hey, if Destiny and The French Tart could prance naked, I could be a goddess.

God-dess.

Yes, that would be me.

Anif ol' Ronnie ol' boy had a problem *wif* that, he could *juss* go—

"Since the prevailing attitude is *the more the merrier*," Ron announced, a *schnotty* edge to his *schnotty* tone, "I've invited a guest."

Ugggg. He's so *schnotty*. Why doss he *alwase* have to be so schnotty? Well, Schnotty Boy, if you think you can take that schnotty tone in my *kisschen*—

Uh-oh.

"Heeeey, Hunter," I stammered. "Long time no see."

Chapter Six

I can honestly say it was the first time I'd been smacked by a hangover without the pleasure of enjoying the buzz.

As I stood staring at Hunter, I felt ill. And completely sober. And very stupid. All I could think of was I barely had enough food for three. Why didn't I think of that excuse earlier when Juan first brought up the lame idea of inviting Ron, who obviously had some ulterior motive for dragging Hunter to the party.

What the hell was that about? Ohmigod, if anyone might spill the beans about how The Dick dumped me, it would be Ron.

Don't panic. Just steer the conversation away from weddings and engagements and Dicks.

Ron and Juan had retreated to the living room and were talking in low voices. But even if the words didn't carry, the bad vibes of the strained tone did.

Hunter stood just inside the kitchen door watching me cook. I searched for something to say. Something that didn't have to do with Destiny or my hideous appearance in the hall this morning. Ron would definitely get off on that. He'd have great fun at my expense. I could foresee this great fun becoming his new favorite pastime. What a classless moron.

Mo-Ron.

Ha! How fitting.

Hunter walked over and leaned his hip on the counter right next to me. *Right next to me.* He was so close I could smell him. Mmmmmm . . . God, I loved the way he smelled. Clean like soap and spice and another pure masculine scent I couldn't quite put my finger on—hair gel? Aftershave? What-ever it was, it made me want to lean in and see if he tasted as good as he smelled.

I stole a glance at him.

He smiled, and I felt all weak and loopy. Maybe I wasn't quite as sober as I thought. I wished he'd say something. I was afraid to speak in case I slurred my words. Great, finding me drunk on a Sunday morning after the bathrobe ensemble. Let's see how much more unattractive I could make myself. Speaking of—

"Would you like a Bellini?" I enunciated the words.

Before he could answer, I found myself inside the walk-in pantry. The door swung shut behind me.

I stood stupidly staring at the hearts of palm and Kalamata olives, table water crackers and spices on the shelves in the pantry. Okay, so I knew we didn't keep the champagne in the pantry, but maybe I'd find my senses in here. Or at least come up with a plausible way out of the Paris/engagement lie.

Forget the Bellinis, steak and hot eggs; I just knew Ron would find a way to serve up my personal life as the main course.

My head spun and this time I knew it wasn't entirely due to the effects of the champagne. I leaned against the wall and tried to take a deep breath, but couldn't quite fill my lungs.

Think.

Oh, did you think I said I was getting married? No, silly, you must have misunderstood. My boyfriend is the one who got married. To someone else.

"Is this a bad time?" I heard Hunter's voice on the other side of the louvered pantry door.

Was he talking to me or Juan?

I could see his silhouette, the pure sexy bulk of him, and I knew I had to face him sometime, unless I decided not to come out. I had plenty of food in here. Bottled water for a month. By that time, maybe they'd forget about me.

Or maybe if I closed my eyes and was really quiet, I'd disappear. Become invisible. If only the pantry didn't spin when I did that.

I opened my eyes and—Oh, shit! Hunter was standing there looking at me. I hadn't heard him open the door.

"Are you okay?" I couldn't quite tell if he was concerned for me or if he thought I might be a little crazy.

No, I'm not okay. I'm a miserable liar and you—"Exactly what color are your eyes, anyway?"

Did I say that out loud?

Please tell me I didn't say that out loud.

I couldn't believe I said that—out loud. While Hunter stood there in the dim pantry, his eyes looked almost black.

He shrugged. "Blue?" He pulled the chain that turned on the light.

I blinked against the sudden brightness. Ahhhh, yes, they were blue. Dark blue.

"Like midnight blue," I murmured. "Almost indigo."

He smiled.

Ohmigod, he probably thought I was so weird.

"I've never really thought about it."

My head had stopped spinning and my face felt all warm and tingly. Actually, the pantry was kind of cozy. Hunter standing there. Just a few inches between us.

"Can I ask you something?" he said.

Just a few inches and one big, fat lie. Okay, here it comes. Better to just tell him the truth. I was suddenly sober, like I'd been pulled over by a cop.

"Why are you hiding in the pantry?" he asked.

I blinked. Huh?

This time I shrugged and sighed as my shoulders fell.

"I'm not hiding."

Maybe I should tell him that since I'd seen him, The Dick had called and told me he'd gotten married. Well, it had happened since I'd seen him, if you didn't count seeing him this morning. It was a "Paris is nice" kind of twisting of the truth.

"Maybe I should come back later," he said. "Ron asked me to come in because he wanted some advice about surround sound stereos. But I didn't know you were cooking. I don't want to interrupt your breakfast."

"Nonsense." Ron, who was now in the kitchen, put his hand on Hunter's shoulder.

Horror glinted in his eyes. In one smooth move, he turned and was inside the pantry standing next to me, both of us facing Ron.

"What's going on?" I heard Juan ask.

Oh, if you only knew.

Ron scowled at me, and shoved back a blond wisp that had fallen in his eye.

Oh, like that was supposed to intimidate me? You're not Hunter's type, Ronnie boy. And Juan is way too good for you. You don't deserve him.

I shifted from one leg to another, taking a stance like a cocky gunfighter preparing for a shoot-out. My arm brushed against Hunter's and I jumped.

Good thing I didn't have a gun because I would've hurt someone. I'd like to think it would've been Ron, but I probably would have shot myself.

The warmth of Hunter's bare arm against my own reassured me. Like having someone on my side.

Juan stepped up next to Ron. "Is the party in here?"

First, Ron looked straight-faced at Juan, then sneered at

me before his gaze pointedly swept over Hunter.

From head to toe.

Ewwwww! My skin crawled. I couldn't even imagine how Hunter felt.

And poor Juan. I glanced at him, staring at Ron. Lips pressed into a tight line, Juan had obviously gotten the full gist of his boyfriend's lewd nonverbal innuendoes.

Hunter stood rock still. Next to me. His arm still barely touching mine. I loved a strong man.

"Well, Julia Child, are you going to spend the morning in the pantry with our *very* attractive neighbor, or are you going to get this show on the road and cook?" Ron said. "It's plain to see there's not room in there for three. And I'm sure there will be even less room with all that butter and cream you're trying to force feed us. That's got to be enough fat grams for a week."

His assessing gaze sliding to my hips, Ron raised his eyebrows, looked back at Hunter and laughed.

Wait just a minute, you stinking son of a—

Ron clapped his hands twice. "Chop, chop. Juan and I have places to go."

Ooooh. Ooooh!

That jerk.

That—That bastard.

Why did Juan put up with him?

Misogynist pig.

Juan shook his head and looked at me apologetically. "Sometimes he's positively caustic. I apologize on his behalf."

"I'm only joking," Ron said.

He crossed his arms and a plastic smile spread across his face. "Someone doesn't have a sense of humor," he singsonged.

Hunter took a step forward, towering over Ron, and he seemed to shrink.

"You've got a pretty twisted sense of humor. You might want to tone it down a little."

Hunter was defending me? What little air I'd managed to pull into my lungs whooshed out. I stood there blank, amazed and a little touched that Hunter would go to bat for me. That was very kind.

Hunter's gaze shot back to me. "Don't let him bully you," he said, his eyes the deep dark blue of a stormy sky.

He walked out of the pantry. Ron had to step back fast to get out of his way. "I have to go," Hunter said. "Liv, hopefully another time."

Another time? Like, him and me?

Okay.

But then I remembered he thought I was engaged and realized he was probably just being polite. I turned off the pantry light, stepped out and closed the door just in time to see Hunter turn to Ron. "Don't ever let me catch you bullying her."

Certain realities are cold, hard and ugly, no matter how you view them. Even people in total denial, can't merely wish away these truisms—no matter what kind of bull the affirmation gurus feed them. The truth will eventually rear its ugly head and bite.

Hard.

It's taken me thirty-two years, but finally I've learned some axioms are self-evident: Eat more calories than you expend, you get fat; drink too much champagne early on a Sunday morning, you spend the rest of the day nursing a headache; fall for a philandering man and your heart gets minced into little itty-bitty pieces.

Can you see a cause-and-effect pattern forming here?

As I stood in the bathroom, trying to clear the Monday morning haze from my brain, each and every bit of truth to which my eyes had been opened yesterday was taunting me.

After Hunter left, Ron and Juan took their lovers' spat to St. Augustine, leaving me alone to eat every bite of the Sunday brunch myself.

Well, I couldn't let it go to waste, could I. And to tell the truth, after being thoroughly humiliated, eating a whole skillet of steak and hot eggs felt like a hug from a good friend. The kind of soothing comfort I'd yet to find in a man.

Then I'd spent the rest of the day holed up in my room sleeping off the champagne buzz, thoroughly disgusted with my lack of self-control.

I slipped out of my robe and studied my body in the mirror. Yep, there it was. Yesterday's brunch, right on top of all the other emotional, recreational and work-related feasts I'd eaten my way through.

I turned to the side, aghast at the flaccid belly and orange peel bum waving at me from the mirror.

Ohmigod, when did this happen? More importantly, why hadn't I seen it before Ron so gleefully brought it to everyone's attention?

Could be that I didn't own a scale. All the magazines said toss the scale, go by how your clothes fit.

And my clothes, well, I'd never been one to embrace a snug fit. Loose and flowing was more my style.

Okay, okay, so since Rich moved to Paris, my loose and flowing wardrobe had started shrinking. I thought it happened in the wash. No, really. I'm serious.

I've never been petite. I think I was born bigger than petite. I was about a size twelve when Rich left, and he never complained.

Now I was a . . . a tight size twelve. Look, the average American woman is a twelve, or so they say.

Whoever *they* are.

I took a hard, assessing look and tried to find something to love about my body.

If the average size is a twelve, I was above average. So there. Who wants to be average? But why did it have to be my size and not my bank account that was above the norm?

I picked up my hairbrush and raked it through my snarled, curly brown hair.

Give me a break, I wasn't the fashion editor. I was the *food* reporter. I slammed down the brush.

Dammit, *this*—I grabbed a handful of excess hip—*this* was a hazard of the job.

I let go of myself. My skin was all red and blotchy where I'd mishandled it.

Why hadn't Karen told me I was getting fat?

What kind of friend was she?

Why hadn't I seen it?

Was I suffering from the opposite of anorexia nervosa? Was there such a disease? Rather than seeing a fat person superimposed over a skeleton, a person saw a healthy woman in place of the hefty girl staring back?

Whatever.

Thanks to Mo-Ron, my eyes had been opened.

Seeing myself clearly for the first time in God knows when, I knew I needed to do something about it, but what?

Join a gym?

Go on a diet?

Giving up the food I loved was like saying good-bye to a beloved friend. The mere thought made me want to run down to Starbucks and drown my pain in a grande mocha and a cinnamon scone with extra butter.

It probably stemmed from the same perverse character flaw that attracted me to Hunter despite the fact he was involved with another woman.

I stuck my toothbrush under the faucet, then smeared a dab of toothpaste on the wet bristles.

This whole food thing was messed up. Why didn't we crave the foods that were good for us? The food we were naturally drawn to such as butter, crème brûlée, chocolate mousse and blue cheese dressing should *not* make us fat. That was just wrong.

Why weren't carrot sticks as satisfying as a bag of potato chips? They're both crunchy, but one leaves you *largely* unsatisfied, like you should go scratch an *eat-five-fruits-and-veggies-a-day* goal off your To Do list. The latter just left you *large*.

And who was the idiot who decided thin was in? During the Baroque period corpulence was a sign of status. A sign of well-fed prosperity. I was born at the wrong time.

I set down my toothbrush and put my hands on my hips and tried to look at my large breasts with love. I would have been a babe in the seventeenth century. Probably one of Rubens's favorite models. Ha! Me, a supermodel.

I felt the makings of an article for the paper coming together. *We're not fat. We're Rubenesque. We are undiscovered works of art.*

I tried to make myself believe it, but I couldn't drown out the voice in my head that kept screaming, "Good God, you *are* fat."

I turned off the tap and placed my toothbrush back in the holder. Then I yanked back the burnt orange shower curtain, turned on the water and waited for it to steam before I stepped under the hot stream.

Away from the mirror the mocking voice changed its

tune. "So you're unhappy. What are you going to do about it?"

True, I'd never had patience for people who sat around and whined about their troubles and did nothing about it.

My eyes had been opened. I was delusion-free. Well, maybe except for the blind faith that someday they'd invent a hair product that really would keep wavy hair from frizzing in the Florida humidity. Hey, a girl's got to have something to hang her hopes on.

This epiphany might be the first step toward loving myself. I ducked under the showerhead and whispered my affirmations:

"I am worth more than my appearance."

"I enjoy healthy foods that nourish my body."

"I am not attracted to Hunter. He has a skinny girlfriend, and the last thing I need is to get involved with another cheating womanizer."

Huh? Where did that come from? It was true, but I certainly didn't need to make Hunter a part of my morning ritual. Frankly, philandering men left a bad taste in my mouth. Kind of like a sip of grapefruit juice after brushing my teeth.

As I lathered with my lavender and rosemary soap, I repeated the affirmations, leaving out the one about Hunter. Water trickled into my mouth and nose, and I waited for the magic words to fill up the aching hollow in my heart and the cracks in my self-esteem.

Like putty for a broken soul. Only this wasn't sticking. Like an epoxy seal that had broken before it had a chance to set.

I finished washing my hair, shut off the water and stood for a moment in the tub, letting the steam envelope me.

But how about the way Hunter stood up to Ron on my behalf? It was the first time a man had defended me.

Against my good sense, warmth started to fill up the cracks and crevices the affirmations had missed.

He didn't have to defend me.

And how about the way Ron shut up?

Ha! The look on his face?

It was almost worth the humiliation.

Well, no, actually, it wasn't.

Snuffed by the hand of reality, the flame sputtered. As I stepped out of the shower and grabbed a towel, I caught another glimpse of myself in the fogged mirror. I studied the distorted image.

Voluptuous?

Womanly curves?

Again, I grabbed a handful of excess flesh.

Nope, nothing more than thirty pounds of excess flab.

Voluptuous and womanly were just sugar-coated synonyms for middle-age spread.

And I wasn't even middle-aged.

Oh, God.

Ron was right.

No wonder Rich left.

I hugged the towel to me. Suddenly, I was twelve years old. I wanted my mother. I wanted her to hold me and tell me I was beautiful like she used to. To tell me I could do anything I set my mind to. That Ron, and Rich, and my father who'd bailed out on us didn't matter.

But my mother wasn't here. Like everyone I'd ever cared about she was . . . gone.

Well, damn my father and Ron and Hunter and Rich and his skinny French Tart, too.

I'm sure she was thin. Have you ever seen a fat French woman? Someone told me overweight French women locked themselves in the house because they were too ashamed to set foot in public.

Maybe it was a blessing in disguise I didn't get to go to Paris. The Fat Police would have probably been waiting for me at customs.

"Chubby American woman, you are under arrest for attempting to smuggle your unsightly blubber into our country. You should be ashamed. Bad fat girl. No croissants for you."

Fat equaled shame.

Made you insignificant.

Less of a human being.

It meant you didn't feel or think or hurt.

But it did hurt.

I hurt.

I wrapped my arms around myself and watched the fog on the mirror dissipate.

I'd never had a bad self-image. I squeezed my eyes shut. I wasn't going to develop one now.

Once I read, "A woman never loses anything if she has herself."

Like it or not, I was all I had left.

Today was the first day of the rest of my life on the bitch beat with Marjorie and the Corps de Anorexics. It really did feel like a life sentence. Like the school year seems to last forever for a kid. Only this was like being dammed to eternal hell without tasting the forbidden fruit.

Marjorie could direct and push all she wanted, but in the end, the words belonged to me. I could smile and nod, but it didn't mean she owned my soul. Or my story.

I went to my closet to choose an outfit. I'd pushed my *shrunken* clothing to the far end. The three or four staples, mostly Chico's Travelers, hung within reach.

My gaze selected the black ensemble. Ah, black to match my mood. Not because it was slimming.

I pulled the silky pants off the hanger and fingered the elastic waistband.

Once upon a time, I wouldn't have been caught dead in pants with elastic anywhere on the garment. But Chico's had managed to stylize the impossible, liberating the over-thirty woman by camouflaging the expanding waistline.

I contemplated whether I should hail or curse Chico's.

It was their fault I hadn't realized I was getting fat. There should be a caution tag inside Chico's pants, like the warning label they slap on a pack of cigarettes.

WARNING: *Elastic waistbands can be hazardous to your girth. Don't be fooled by fashionable appearances. Forgiving fabric has been known to lure unsuspecting women into a false sense of security, allowing ample room to grow a gargantuan spare tire and cultivate an ass the size of a tractor trailer. Wear with caution.*

I finished dressing, applied a little makeup, and set off for the kitchen for a *light* breakfast.

"I can do this."

My stomach growled a protest.

At least I'd managed to stay the Starbucks craving. I was stronger than I gave myself credit for and was getting stronger every minute.

I popped a piece of bread in the toaster, then picked up the phone and dialed Karen's number.

"Hello?" croaked a sleepy voice.

"Hey, it's me. Do you remember your sixteenth birthday party when your grandmother gave you that pair of brown polyester stretch pants and we all nearly went into convulsions trying to keep from laughing?"

"Ummmmmm."

"Didn't we swear we'd never let each other make the fashion faux pas of wearing something so hideous? When did we forget that oath?"

"Hmmmmmm?"

"When did elastic waistbands become fashionable?"

"I don't wear . . . elastic waistbands." Karen sounded more asleep than awake.

"What? Oh. Never mind. I thought you were my friend."

"I am your friend." She sounded a little more alert. "What's wrong?"

"My butt."

"There's nothing wrong with your butt."

"No, except that I should be wearing a wide-load sign."

Karen yawned into the receiver. "Did I miss something here? I'm not following you. I could have sworn you were just talking about those revolting brown poly stretch pants Grammy gave me for my sixteenth birthday."

"Why didn't you tell me I was getting fat?" I wailed.

"Because you're not. You're big-boned."

"Oh! Why don't you just come over here and slap me in the face. Big-boned? That's what people say about their fat friends to keep from hurting their feelings. Do you describe me as having a good personality, too? Come on, the cat's out of the bag, thanks to Ron. I tried to call you yesterday to tell—"

"Hold on a sec—"

I heard a muffled voice in the background.

"Is someone there?" I asked.

"Wait a minute—" Karen said.

More muffled voices, like Karen had put her hand over the receiver. Then I could have sworn I heard her giggle.

No way.

Karen did not giggle. She hated women who giggled. Only

living *Barbie dolls* and topless dancers named Bambi giggled.

"Is someone with you?" I asked.

"Yeah, can I call you back? And I'll see you Wednesday. We're still going to Monica's then, right?"

Wait, Karen *never* let guys spend the night. She had her way with them, then booted them out before the sun came up. It was part of her "attach yourself to no one" creed.

"Who's there?" I asked.

"No, you can't talk to her," Karen said.

"What?" I asked. "*Her?* Her who?"

What in the hell was going on? Karen was liberated, but not—

"Hello?" A man's voice came over the line. "Jimbo Giani here."

Oh, shit!

"Karen will talk to you later."

Chapter Seven

After my eight o'clock editorial meeting at the office, I headed to the Bob Carr Performing Arts Centre where the ballet was in dress rehearsal for their weekend run of *Giselle*.

I'd driven this route hundreds of times, the shops and businesses and fast food joints all looked the same. The sun had set and risen like everything was normal, but the world was upside-down and nobody seemed to realize it but me.

I should have been making plans to move to Paris, instead I'd moved in with a gay hairdresser. And then there was Hunter—forget Hunter.

I wished Karen could forget a certain jackass who kept turning up like an overzealous Jehovah's Witness, finally landing in my best friend's bed.

I couldn't believe Karen let Giani spend the night.

At least with the Witness I could preempt the annoyance by not answering my door. They eventually went away. I had a sinking feeling even if Giani had a door slammed in his face he wouldn't go away.

What if Karen didn't want him to go away? That was ridiculous. Karen could have any man she wanted. Why would she choose an oily, old man who was a—a jackass?

This was not like Karen. We must have a long, long talk.

But for now I had a more immediate situation demanding my full attention.

I pulled my car into the performing arts center parking lot and saw Marjorie, dressed in a hot pink pantsuit, waving at me from the stage door.

Yes, the world was truly upside-down when I had to take

editorial direction from the boss's wife.

I steered my car into a parking place, grabbed my purse and notebook, and steeled myself for the day from hell.

If misery loves company, I'd found a soul mate in Giselle.

In the ballet's first act, Giselle is happily living a carefree life until she falls in love with Loys, a deceitful man who leads her to believe he'd marry her when he really has a hidden agenda.

Upon discovering his lies, Giselle dies of a broken heart and spends the entire second act roaming the earth, a mournful, distraught spirit.

Okay, so I could feel for her in Act One, but we parted ways in Act Two. There was no way in hell The Dick or Hunter or any man was going to relegate me to the underworld. I was stronger than that. I didn't need either of them.

I milled around backstage trying to gather information for my ballet feature, while the company warmed up with the artistic director, Konstantin.

Marjorie introduced me to a handful of people she grabbed as they ran here and there.

The first was Cathy, the wardrobe mistress, as she whizzed by with a rolling rack of costumes.

In the stage wings, two middle-aged women dressed in tights, leotards and leg warmers compared notes on clipboards. They didn't look up as we approached, but do you think that stopped Marjorie?

"Olivia, this is Roberta Renninger, our ballet mistress," Marjorie said.

"Hello." Roberta nodded politely and returned her attention to her conversation with the other woman.

Marjorie gestured to the other woman. "Anna is Konstantin's assistant."

What? No *mistress* in Anna's title? Obviously not, seeing how Anna didn't even warrant a last name.

Ballet mistress? Wardrobe mistress? It sounded a little kinky to me. Like they should wear masks and stiletto knee-boots and carry whips to keep everyone in line.

Marjorie would be Mistress of Making Everyone Miserable. I'll bet she'd get into the whole dominance-submission act. As long as her Junior League cronies didn't catch wind.

Marjorie smoothed her hair, her eyes narrowed, and her gaze flicked back and forth between the two women.

"Olivia is a reporter from the *Daily*." An imperious tone edged her words. "She's going to follow *us* this week, write a story about the ballet, and review *Giselle*. Konstantin wants everyone to make Olivia feel at home. I'm sure you'll help her with everything she needs. Yes?"

Anna didn't look up from her papers, but Roberta's humorless gaze snapped from the clipboard to Marjorie. For a second I thought I'd witness a Mistress Smackdown. Then Roberta looked at me and even managed a half-smile.

"Certainly," she said. "But right now you'll have to excuse us. We have a rehearsal in five minutes and we have some issues to iron out."

"*Certainly.*" There was no mistaking the mocking note in Marjorie's tone. But Roberta and Anna didn't even glance at Marjorie as they walked away.

I just couldn't look at her either. I didn't want to see the expression on her face. Maybe it was to let her save face, maybe it was because she was irritating me with all this *us* and *we* talk. Like Marjorie had an official role with the company beyond buying herself the title Resident Pain in the Ass and making eyes at Mr. Buns of Steel. Speaking of whom, I hadn't seen him yet.

I turned my attention upward to the men in the catwalks

adjusting lights and cables. When I looked back down, I nearly got run over by a man racing past with cases of bottled water, double-stacked. I sidestepped out of his way and narrowly missed bumping into a stagehand carrying a large rolled-up banner.

Everyone seemed to be on a mission, to have a purpose, except for Marjorie and me. We were clearly in the way, like a couple of fat thumbs on a hand of long, slender fingers.

"Why don't we go into the theatre and watch the rehearsal?" Marjorie said, a bit subdued. "It looks like they're about to start."

Yes, please.

She ushered me to the third row of the empty hall. I sank down into my seat, into the shroud of lovely darkness as the orchestra played the overture and the dancers leapt onstage.

This was more like it. Here, I felt smaller. The dancers seemed bigger. Larger than life.

But wait. Where was Buns? I scanned the dancers onstage, but I didn't see him and his glorious backside.

"Is this the whole company?" I whispered.

"No, the first run-through is with the understudies," Marjorie said. "The principal dancers have a later call."

Suddenly, Marjorie started waving at someone over on the side of the theatre. I had to squint into the darkness after watching the brightly lit stage. But as my eyes adjusted, a perfect form materialized in the shadows. Like an apparition, there was Buns in the flesh. The Prince of Tights.

Marjorie was making such a commotion trying to get his attention I just knew Konstantin was going to stop the rehearsal and throw us both out. I glanced back at him in his seat five rows behind us watching the action onstage. But finally Buns saw Marjorie and came over and sat in the empty seat next to her.

"Alexei, darling," Marjorie said, taking his arm. "This is Olivia Logan, a reporter with the *Daily*."

Alexei, *darling?* Oh, give me a break.

He leaned across Marjorie and offered his left hand. Marjorie still had firm possession of his right arm.

"Alexei Ivanov." His voice was colored by a rich Russian accent and he looked me right in the eyes. "Very pleased to meet you, Ms. Logan."

Oh, no, no. *The pleasure is all mine, Mr. Darling Buns.* "Nice to meet you."

He had a Tom Cruise–like smile. Kind of looked like him, in fact, only taller and with longer, slightly curly blond hair.

Wow, with that smile and those buns, I had a feeling Alexei darling had a knack for mesmerizing every woman he spoke to into a speechless puddle of goo.

Those who weren't immune to the charms of players, that is. Ha! You may be one gorgeous specimen, but I've been there, done that, and I ain't going back no more.

Alexei was still smiling and leaning across Marjorie, and I realized I still had hold of his hand. I let go and scrunched down in my seat and wished the darkness would swallow me whole.

Marjorie held firm to his arm. When he settled back into his chair, she leaned over and whispered something in his ear.

He laughed.

I didn't want to know.

For God's sake, had she forgotten I worked for her *husband?*

An electronic rendition of *Ode to Joy* shrilled in the darkness. Marjorie jumped to grab her purse.

She fished out her cell phone.

"Hello?" she said in a hushed voice. "Hold for a moment, please."

She smiled at Alexei and me.

"Excuse me for a moment. Normally, I would turn this off but I've been waiting for a call. Your phone's off, isn't it, Olivia?"

So the rules applied to everyone but her. She probably thought she was perfectly entitled to be married to Chris and fool around with Buns. Another bitch with *entitlement syndrome.*

"My phone's in the car," I said.

"Good, good." She stood and turned to Alexei. "Don't go away."

Marjorie had barely cleared the door when Alexei moved into her seat, right next to me.

Okay, this was awkward.

He leaned forward and rested his arms on the seat back in front of us. I crossed my arms and kept my gaze glued to the stage. To keep myself from fidgeting, I pulled my notebook and pen from my purse, and pretended to write notes about the performance.

"You like the ballet?" he asked.

"I'm learning to appreciate it."

"Americans look at ballet different than we do in Russia. In Russia it is a privilege for boys to study the dance. Here, people think they are, how you say, gay?"

I glanced back at Konstantin, to see if our conversation was annoying him. Wasn't it rude to talk during a performance? Even if it was only a rehearsal. As intense as everyone seemed, who knew what Konstantin might do.

But Konstantin seemed wrapped up in the performance, directing, taking notes and drinking in every move onstage.

"I would like to talk to you more about it," Alexei said. "I think it is very important that American boys understand you can love the dance and still be a man. For instance, in Russia, male dancers are heroes."

I looked at him, really looked at him.

He was serious.

"I'll be here all week," I said. "I'd love to talk to you about it."

"Yes, would be good story," Alexei said. "In my country, I am hero of many. You should write about that. Good publicity for the ballet, here, where people not think so much of the dance."

He flashed that smile. Probably his way of sealing the deal.

I saw Marjorie sliding down the aisle and I busied myself pretending to take notes.

When she reached us she loomed for a moment, eyeing us as if looking for clues that we'd committed some flagrant carnal sin.

"You're in my seat," she said to Alexei, her lips pressed into a thin smile. As if there weren't nearly 2,000 other empty chairs in the theatre.

Alexei grinned at me again and stood. "I must go dance."

"He's definitely wanting publicity for the dance company," Karen said Wednesday night as she steered her T-Bird into the far left lane of Interstate Four.

"He's pretty self-obsessed," I said. "He called himself a hero."

Karen laughed. "Haven't you ever wondered what it would be like to have sex with a guy so physically perfect? In *every* area from what you've said."

Maybe after a thousand Pilates classes and a year-long fast. " I'd be too obsessed with my jiggling fat."

In my former ignorant state of chubby bliss, I may have

wandered blindly into delusions of a hot affair with Mr. Buns of Steel, but not now.

"Don't you think *you're* being a little self-obsessed?"

No. This was completely different.

"Mine is self-preservation. Not self-obsession. I've never had anyone run out of the room after I've taken my clothes off, and I don't want to start now."

Maybe I should join a gym.

Wasn't in the budget. But I did need to start exercising. "Besides, dating rule number one is never date a guy whose butt is perkier than yours. Rule number two is never date a guy who gets paid to put his hands on a woman's crotch."

"What?" Karen shrieked.

"Well, he doesn't exactly put them on her crotch, but close enough. When he lifts Lara, his dance partner, he slides his hand up her leg in this way."

I tried to demonstrate in the air, but it lost something in the translation. "No, really, it is so sensual. It takes my breath away."

I stared out the window for a minute and wished I were Lara, that Alexei was touching me the same way he touched her, that his big strong hands were all over my body as we danced a bedroom *pas de deux*.

Dance for two. Ha! See, I was learning. Maybe there was hope for my future as a dance critic. What about hope for *pas de deux*ing with Alexei?

Not with Lara Minsky in the picture.

I didn't ménage à trois.

Minsky.

Even her name sounded tiny.

Minsky.

Minuscule.

Miniature.

Eensy-weensy-Minsky, the Russian princess.

"Do you really think he's sleeping with Marjorie?" Karen said as she rolled down her window. I'd told her how Mahjorie was all over Buns.

"I don't know. That's hard to say. Sometimes I'd almost swear to it. Other times it seems like he looks right through her. She's a real piece of work. She's trying to tell me how to write my story—already informed me the review *would* be positive. I don't know why she just doesn't write it herself."

"Sounds like she's used to everyone jumping when she's calling the shots."

Except for Alexei. Maybe they weren't sleeping together.

Maybe they were. Bet she didn't give up that easily. Maybe they were just being discreet.

"If she is having an affair, shouldn't I be the one in the power position here?" I mused. "I'm the one who has the goods on her. Shouldn't she be worried about me telling on her?"

Karen slanted quick glances at me as she drove. "Let's see, *she's* the one with the money, her husband is *your* boss, and he works for *her* father. If you have a southbound train planning to purposely derail at top speed, how long does it take it to crash and burn? You do the math."

We rode in silence for a few miles.

Hmmmmm, in a way, Alexi and I were up the same creek. We had to put up with Marjorie because she was in control.

"Ask Monica what you should do," Karen said.

Monica was Karen's psychic. She lived in Cassadaga, a spiritualist community a short drive northeast of Orlando. Last week, Karen made this appointment for us.

"My treat," she'd said. "I want you to know all the wonderful things you have ahead of you. If anyone can tell you, it's Monica. She's *always* right."

I'd never been to a psychic. I didn't know if I really believed if anyone could see the future or if it was all a bunch of
hooey. Or maybe I wasn't quite sure if I really wanted to know
what my future held. I just needed to retreat and heal.

"What do you call a boy ballerina anyway?" Karen asked.
"A ballerino?"

"Makes sense," I said. "Ballerin*a* is the feminine form of
the word. Ballerin*o* must be the masculine."

"Sorry," she said. "It all seems feminine to me. I can't
imagine anything masculine about a guy who wears tights. I
always thought all *ballerinos* were homos."

She propped her arm on the open window. The cool evening breeze blew her long blonde hair every which way.

"Baryshnikov's not gay," I said. "And Alexei kind of reminds me of him. You'd just have to see him. He's just so . . .
so Russian."

Karen slanted another glance at me.

"Oh, God, you *do* like him?"

"No, let's just say I've discovered a whole new appreciation for ballet. He's—" I waved away the thought. "Naaaa,
never mind."

She shot me a quick glance.

"Say it. Tell me."

I adjusted the shoulder strap of my seat belt and tried to
translate my thoughts into words.

"This is kind of lame, but he's just so regal, so elegant.
He's like a storybook prince come to life."

Karen laughed. "Yep, that's lame."

"I know." I scraped my fingernail across the grain of my
corduroys. "He's a good distraction. It's just fun. Like a
crush. Someone I'll never have. It feels safe and exciting at
the same time."

"Oh." Karen sighed. The glow of the dashboard illuminated her face and she looked as if she were seriously contemplating the situation. "Okay, crushes are good. But, Liv, the tights and those little slippers have to go."

I laughed and buttoned the last few buttons of my coat. The night air was a little chilly.

"Come see *Giselle* with me Friday night," I said. "I have to write a review and I have no idea what the hell I'm supposed to say. It's not exactly like a restaurant review."

"It is if you sample the goods," she said, an evil glimmer in her eyes.

The thought of sampling Alexei's goods both exhilarated and terrified me.

"No. Remember, safe distance. Besides, the paper doesn't publish stories like *that*. Will you come with me?"

Karen nodded. "Then I can see Buns of Steel in action. See if he's good enough for you."

"I just met the guy. I just think he's hot."

"Sure, that's what they all say."

"Speaking of meeting men, what gives with you and Giani?"

Karen stared straight ahead.

"Oh, I got so engrossed in hearing about Buns, I can't believe I almost forgot to tell you," Karen said. "Guess who I saw last night?"

I frowned.

"Don't change the subject."

"No, listen. This is really wild." Karen continued on as if she hadn't heard me. "I saw your friend Hunter."

I groaned. I hadn't seen him since the pantry humiliation, and as far as I was concerned, I didn't want to see him again until I'd dropped a good thirty pounds and one fake fiancé.

I knew it was ridiculous. I was losing weight for me, not

because Ron shamed me into it. Certainly not to impress Hunter, who already had a skinny woman camping out in his apartment.

"I saw him at the Blue Note," Karen said. "His band, Altered Ego, is playing there."

"Hmmmph." I shrugged.

"I thought you liked him?"

"I don't know," I said. I stared out the side window at silhouettes of trees and a fenced-off pasture that blurred by my window. The moon was just starting to rise. "I think he has a girlfriend."

"Judging from the way the women at the Blue Note were acting, I'd say he might have a few."

My gaze snapped to Karen. Don't ask my why, but suddenly I felt sorry for Destiny. There were few things worse than being the last to know.

It had happened to me. I watched it possibly happening to Lara, though it was right in front of her face. Now Destiny, too. Maybe we should form a society for scorned women. No, sounded too lesbian. Even if men were cheating dogs, I couldn't live without them. That's just the way I was wired. Was there not one man in this world who could be faithful to one woman? If so, he was the man for me.

"What was Hunter doing?" I asked, not really sure if I wanted to know.

"Well, it wasn't so much what he was doing. The women in the audience were all but throwing their panties at him while he sang. One woman flashed everyone and the bouncers threw her out. Then Jimbo wanted to go and we—"

Karen stopped suddenly as if she realized she'd turned the conversation back in the direction I'd intended it to go in the first place. She added quickly, "You're right. Hunter's probably not the guy for you. Cute, though. Why couldn't you have a crush on him instead of the ballerino? I mean, what's the difference? From what you've said, it sounds like Alexei has a couple of girlfriends."

"Hunter lives across the hall from me. That's a little too close for comfort. I'm not interested in Hunter or Alexei."

Liar. Man, you're getting good at this. Spitting out fibs like watermelon seeds.

They're crushes.

I can have crushes without falling in love.

"I don't know, across the hall sounds pretty convenient to me." Karen winked at me.

"Quit changing the subject. What gives with you and Giani?"

A silly smile spread over Karen's face. She looked like a smitten nine-year-old.

"He's . . . He's fabulous."

"Please tell me you're kidding?"

Karen closed the window and turned on the heat.

"I'm not kidding." Her voice sounded thin and a little edgy. "I really like him, Liv."

She *really liked* him? A vague Twilight Zone feeling rushed over me because Karen dated many, but *really liked* few.

"Liv, I've never been with anyone like him."

"You let him spend the night. You never let men stay all night. You haven't even known him that long. How many times had you been out before you slept with him?"

"Does breakfast the morning after count as a date?"

"No, because he'd already spent the night. Please tell me you didn't sleep with him on the first date."

Karen merged off the interstate and followed the off-ramp to a dark, tree-lined road.

"Why? What difference does it make if you sleep with him on the first date or the third date? You know you're going to do it. Why play games if you click with someone?"

With the heat on full blast, the car was getting a little stuffy. I unbuttoned my coat.

"You don't even know him. What about all those women he was with that night we saw him at Hue? What if he's sleeping with them, too?"

"He's not," she said. "Or at least not anymore. Have you ever met someone who you just clicked with the minute you laid eyes on him?"

My thoughts jumped to the night I met Hunter, how we'd talked about everything and nothing. But I blinked away the pipe dream and shrugged.

"It's strange," she said. "I feel like I've known him all my life."

I turned down the car's thermostat. I couldn't believe Karen was so blind. Didn't she see Giani for what he really was—a salesman?

"I'm sure his millions don't hurt."

I meant it as a joke, but Karen rolled her eyes.

Hmmmm, there was a chemistry between Hunter and me that first night. Hypothetically speaking, would I feel different about him if I knew he was a millionaire who could take care of me for the rest of my life, rather than being a starving artist who had to dance to the tune of the piper with the cash?

In all fairness, I didn't know whose tune Hunter danced to.

Destiny's tune.

My mind supplied the good-bye scene in the hall I didn't get to view through the peephole. Destiny slipping her arms around Hunter, then a long, deep, hot kiss. The kind that curls your toes and makes the world disappear. Hands groping. His hands on my cheeks, in my hair, sliding down my back, down to cup my bottom and pull me hard against his—Whoa, wait, that was *me* he was kissing, not Destiny.

Ohmigod, that was good.

I glanced at Karen, who was staring out the windshield, probably lost in Jimboland.

Nope. I'd much rather be a poor man's wife than jockey for position in the stable of a rich playboy.

"What kind of a car does lover boy drive?" I asked. "Probably something expensive and flashy, right?"

She shot me a what's-wrong-with-you look. "Why are you being so judgmental?"

"You're changing the subject again. *What* kind of a car?"

Karen drummed her fingers on the steering wheel.

I knew I was being a bitch, but I couldn't help it. It was like an itch I had to scratch.

"A Ferrari," she said.

Oh, ohhhh, how typical. I almost laughed out loud. The writing was all over the wall, in bright neon letters. This guy was such a player. Karen, yes, Karen, queen no-one-walks-away-from-me-because-I-walk-away-first (and that's a direct quote), was setting herself up for a big fall.

"I'll bet it's bright red, right?"

She fidgeted a little, pulling the collar on her sweater away from her throat. Then looked at me real serious. "Yeah, so?"

I snorted.

"That is *such* a penis extender."

Karen didn't laugh. Uh-oh, maybe I'd crossed the line. Even I had to admit that was a little harsh.

Then a smug smile spread across her face.

"Believe me, he *doesn't* need a penis extender."

"Oh."

Karen reached over and gave my arm a little shove.

"Yeah, *oh*," she said. "So shut up about it already."

Deep breath. Back off, Liv.

"All I'm saying is he's not your typical type."

"Maybe that's why things are different with him. I'm tired of my *typical type*. I'm tired of the dating rat race. I think I'm ready to settle down and make a life with someone."

Surely I hadn't heard her right.

Maybe I was having hunger hallucinations since I'd barely eaten today. This was one worse than the Twilight Zone. This bordered on alien abduction—because someone or something had obviously replaced my friend Karen with this . . . this Jimbo Giani–loving alien. She looked like Karen. She sounded like Karen. But the words coming out of her mouth were decidedly unKaren-like.

"After one date with a man, you're talking 'til death do us part? He must have been really good in bed."

Karen pulled into a driveway, which I assumed was Monica's, and put the car in park. She sat staring out the driver's side window for a while before she spoke.

"Liv, you've been my best friend since the fourth grade. Just be happy for me. I really think I've found the real thing."

She pulled the collar of her navy pea coat up around her neck.

The real thing. Ohmigod. Coming from Karen, that was heavy. I wanted to be happy for her. Really. But if I dug deep down, I had to admit I was a little disappointed that my free-spirited friend had found someone just as I was free. That was selfish. Pathetic, actually, and I knew I'd better get over it real fast.

I tried my best to smile. "Let's go ask Monica."

We got out of the car, tension still hanging between us, and picked our way through a maze of plants and bushes to the small, white bungalow's lit front porch. In the dark yard I could barely pick out a couple of gazing balls, a birdbath and statuary.

As we stepped onto the porch, the cold night air tickled the five sets of wind chimes hanging from the eaves, striking a discordant chorus. Just above the doorbell hung a sign that said *Madame Monica, psychic. By appointment only.*

Karen rang the buzzer.

In my mind's eye, I saw Madame Monica, a middle-aged, frizzy-headed woman swathed in flowing robes and a purple turban with a big gaudy pin in the middle of it like a third eye.

So you can imagine how surprised I was when a young, petite blonde sporting jeans, a pink turtleneck and a very red nose answered the door.

"Hey, Monica," Karen said and stepped forward to give her a hug.

Monica stepped back and sneezed into a blue tissue.

"Sorry, hon, I've got a terrible *code.* I don't want to give it to you." Her voice sounded one step away from laryngitis. "I almost called you to reschedule, but I thought ehhh, what the heck."

She shoved the tissue into her front pocket.

Okay, maybe I'm not so good at forming accurate mental pictures. But mental pictures and first impressions were two totally different things.

I'd seen Giani. I'd talked to Giani. I knew Giani's phony jackass game. And he didn't merit the adoration of my best friend. Most important, I didn't want Karen to get hurt.

But who was I to say? I'd let Madame Monica deliver that sage advice since Karen seemed to hang on her every word.

"You must be Olivia." Monica took my hand. And all I could think about was how she'd just sneezed into a tissue which she'd been holding in that same hand.

Ew.

"Oh," Monica said. "Oh!"

She squeezed my hand then let go and gaped at me with wide blue eyes.

"What? What?" Good God, what did she see?

"Lucky girl," Monica said to Karen. Then she turned back to me. "Olivia, did you know you've recently met your soul mate?"

Soul mate? Ohmigod. Karen and I looked at each other. I nearly choked. Karen's face brightened.

"Please, come in," Monica said. "Come in."

We stepped inside a small living room that smelled of sage and sandalwood and—Sniff. Sniff. Was that garlic?

"Normally we'd have some tea and chat for a while, but if you don't mind, we'll get right down to business. I felt some strong messages coming through for Olivia and I don't want to lose them. Do you mind if I work on her first, Karen?"

"Go ahead." Karen nudged me. "Soul mate, huh? I'll forgive the tights and slippers if you'll be nice to Giani."

"Who says it's Alexei?"

Karen's right eyebrow shot up. I was relieved her mood had lightened and she was acting more like herself. I was afraid it would have been a long, quiet ride home. I'd never seen her get so defensive over a guy, and from what I could discern about Giani, he violated most of the rules Karen had carved in stone about the men she got involved with.

We followed Monica down the hall to what looked like a spare bedroom. In the middle of the room was a round table covered with a white cloth. Draped over the top was a smaller purple cloth with a white pillar candle in the middle. In the corner I spied an incense burner emitting a fine trail of smoke. The space had a calm, peaceful feel about it. Ahhhhhh, relaxing.

"Have a seat," Monica said. Karen and I sat down as Monica walked over to a shelf along one of the walls and chose a tarot deck. I looked around the room at the various crystals, books and candles displayed on shelves and tables.

Soul mate?

I knew this reading was a good idea.

But Alexei? Hmmmm . . . I just couldn't see it.

Hunter? I gulped.

"Are you taking anything for that cold?" Karen asked.

Monica sat down at the table and lit the candle. "Vitamin C, echinacea and loads of garlic. But I had to break down and take a decongestant tonight. I hate to do that, but I couldn't breathe. May I hold your ring, Olivia?"

I must have had a strange look on my face because she explained, "I like to hold an object that belongs to the person I'm doing the reading for. It helps me see things clearer."

Okay. Made sense.

I slid off the pearl ring that used to belong to my mother and held it out.

Aaaaa-cheeewwww! Monica sneezed again, this time into her sleeve.

"Ugggh, I'm sorry." She pulled out her tissue, wiped her red nose, then reached for my ring.

Ewwwwwww. Yuck. I hesitated for a split second, until the word "soul mate" echoed in my head and convinced me to relinquish the piece of jewelry.

Monica sat with her eyes closed and held the ring for a good two minutes before she looked at me and spoke.

"I see several men in your life."

Karen whistled a catcall. "You go, girl."

I rolled my eyes.

"And one is definitely your soul mate," Monica continued. "But you need to be careful, you're very vulnerable right now. You've been through a lot lately. Right?"

I nodded. "I've met three men recently—"

"Three?" Karen asked. "Hunter, Alexei . . ." She ticked the names off on her fingers. "Who's the third?"

"Juan," I said.

Karen blew a raspberry. "He's not a man."

"He is, too." I turned to Monica. "A soul mate doesn't always have to be romantic, right?"

Monica sniffed. "True. But I'm getting a vibe yours is."

A chill started at the top of my head and tingled its way down to the tips of my toes. Then currents of electric anticipation coursed through me. This was the stuff I always hoped to read in my horoscope or find in my fortune cookie. Oh, please be right. Please don't have the currents crossed with some other Olivia Logan out there in the universe.

"So, there are two men in particular," I said. "I've met both of them recently. Can you tell me which one is my soul mate?"

Aaaaa-cheeewwww! Monica sneezed again and groaned.

"Mon, you're really sick," Karen said. "We could do this another time if you'd rather."

I nodded, but inside I was pleading, "Please give me a name first."

Monica shook her head. "I'm fine. Besides, I'm getting some really good messages for you, Olivia."

Inwardly, I breathed a sigh of relief.

"Can you tell me a name?"

Monica squeezed her eyes shut again. Karen and I exchanged anxious glances. After a good minute, Monica shook her head and rubbed her temples. "Uggggh, this cold makes everything so fuzzy. Wait . . . I see the letter 'O'. Does that mean anything?"

The letter "O"?

"Olivia starts with 'O'," I said, trying not to sound desperate. "Are you sure you don't mean 'A or I or H'?" I asked.

Monica sniffed. "No, definitely 'O'." She squeezed her eyes shut. "I think. Ugggghh." She placed my ring on the table and rubbed her eyes. "I'm so congested."

So "O" was a definite maybe. I hoped the whole soul mate message wasn't just one big sinus headache.

"Maybe she means 'O' as in 'Oh! Oh! Oh yes! YES!' " said Karen.

"No, that would be your reading, not mine," I said.

Karen kicked me under the table. I kicked her back.

"I'm getting a hazy message," said Monica. "I can't quite make it out. I want to consult the cards."

She asked me to cut the cards and dealt ten in the shape of a cross.

The first card she turned over was the "love" card. My stomach dropped to my knees.

Next was the "sorrow" card.

My heart dropped three stories.

Dammit. Figures. Love, followed by sorrow. The story of my life.

I was doomed. As if I needed a psychic to tell me my love life was filled with sorrow.

She must have sensed my panic because she immediately started to explain, "The first card tells about the situation. The second card tells what's affecting the situation. So love in your life right now is colored by sorrow. You've had some disappointments, haven't you?"

I stared at the card without answering her. I didn't want to supply too much information. I wanted to see how good she was.

"Now this card"—she flipped over a third card, the lovers—"is your destiny card. Yes, see, this is what makes me think your soul mate is more than a friend."

One by one she flipped over the cards and told me what she saw.

"Hmmm, interesting," she said. "I do see two men in your life. One will bring you great joy, the other has the potential to bring you great sorrow."

Well, that was a no-brainer. Come on, Mon, if you really want to impress me, tell me specifics—like a name.

As if she read my mind, she tapped a card and said, "I see the one who brings you sorrow surrounded by many women."

Great.

That could be either Hunter or Alexei. Thanks for the warning. Maybe I should steer clear of both. If Richard, the international computer geek, had a French mistress, what would happen with these two? Hunter's vocation by nature inspired women to flash their breasts and toss their panties. Alexei's required him to put his hands all over women's bodies. Both situations were too much of a temptation for any red-blooded man to resist.

When Monica picked up the last two cards, she looked a little panicked. She replaced them facedown, then opened her mouth as if she wanted to say something, but didn't.

"What?" I asked. "Tell me. I can take it."

She looked straight into my eyes, her forehead wrinkled into a sad frown as if she didn't quite know what to say. Instead she took my hand.

"It's not over yet," she said. Then squeezed her eyes shut and shook her head as if trying to blot out a terrible image.

My heart pounded. I knew it. Something terrible. Something horrendous was going to happen. That was my life. That was the hand I'd been dealt—literally.

I reached out and turned over the last two cards—the death card and the emperor.

She was really starting to freak me out.

I pointed to the death card. "What does that mean? Am I going to die?"

My heart pounded. Would I be trampled by a stampeding herd of rabid rock and roll groupies or was Marjorie going to hunt me down and kill me when Alexei and I announced to the world we were soul mates and destined to be together?

Figures my soul mate candidates would come from heaven's scratch and dent store. They're perfectly fine men except for these nearly microscopic flaws: one's the object of desire of every twenty-something slut in Orlando, the other's the boy-toy of a deranged, high-profile socialite, who, in one swipe, could take everything away from me—my job, my soul mate, my life.

"No, the death card means change." Monica's gaze flicked away from mine. "Ummm, usually."

Oh, great. "In this situation does it mean death, or does it mean change?"

I swallowed hard and realized I didn't want to know.

"Olivia." Monica grabbed my hand again and looked at me with pleading eyes. "I'm not myself today. I'm sick. I should have rescheduled your reading. It's just that the messages were pouring through so strongly—Aaaaa-cheeewwww!"

She sneezed into her arm again, then got up and pulled a fresh tissue from the box. She blew her nose, then rubbed it and tried to smile. "You're a strong woman. You'll be fine."

I'd be fine. The world could end and I'd be fine. Olivia Logan, the last woman on Earth, is doing just fine.

Monica slumped down in the chair. "I really feel much worse than I realized. Karen, can we reschedule your reading—I'll do it on the house." She turned to me. "I'm not going to charge you, either. In fact, disregard most of what I said. It may or may not have been accurate." She slumped over and put her head in her hands. "I'm just so foggy from this cold and all these decongestants."

Karen hopped up and went over to Monica and started massaging her shoulders. "You poor baby. Go right to bed and get some rest. Do you want me to make you a cup of tea before we go?"

Aaaaa-cheeewwww!

"No," Monica blew her nose again, "thanks. I just need to go to bed."

As she walked us to the door, I thought about the death and sorrow cards and shuddered. Could I at least keep the soul mate as a parting gift? Rather than asking, I walked silently out into the cold, dark night.

Chapter Eight

I got home from Monica's around nine-thirty. Before I put my key in the lock I felt the thump of heavy bass and—

What was *that?*

Barry Manilow's "Copacabana"? I pressed my ear to the door and felt the pseudo Latin *thump, thump, thump* down to my solar plexus.

Juan was home.

Finally. I hadn't seen him in three days. Since he left for St. Augustine with the Mo-Ron after the pantry incident.

I didn't expect him to check in with me. Really. It's just that . . . Okay, so I didn't know what I expected.

We'd been roommates for a little over two weeks and were still getting to know each other's rhythms and patterns. All I knew was I could certainly live without this annoying Barry Manilow rhythm shaking the walls.

I slid my key in the lock.

Seriously, Juan had gone AWOL for three days. I was starting to get a little worried, especially since the last person I saw him with was that psycho of a boyfriend of his. And they weren't exactly swooning over each other.

I paused before I opened the door and pondered if I should voice my concern, but quickly decided against it.

No one wanted to live with a nag.

I *wasn't* a nag.

Juan was a big boy and didn't need a hall pass every time he decided to take leave. Besides, I suppose if I'd really wanted to know where he'd gone I could have called La Galleria. Surely he would have let the salon know where he was going.

Wouldn't he?

I pushed open the door and walked into a dark apartment. Barry bellowed on and on about the hottest spot north of Havana.

I flipped on the hall light and about three seconds later someone silenced Barry, mid cha-cha.

I froze, afraid to take another step. Scary visions of Ron and Juan in a compromising conga line danced through my head.

I'm liberated, but there are some things I just don't need to see. Like Juan and Ron dancing naked.

Ahhh!

I flipped off the hall light, as if the action could black out the image.

If I sneaked through the kitchen and didn't look to my left, I might be able to make it to my bedroom unscathed. Jeez, I'd never be able to listen to "Copacabana" the same way again.

Just as I was making my break from the kitchen to my bedroom, Juan said, " 'Livia, is that you?"

I froze and stared straight ahead. "Yes."

Do not look in the living room.

Do not look in the living room.

"Why are you walking in the dark?"

My gaze darted to the dark room, but all I could see were silhouettes of furniture and shadows cast by the streetlights coming in through the sheers. I closed my eyes. Tight.

"Are you alone?" My voice squeaked on the last word.

"Yes," he muttered. "I am *utterly* alone."

Huh? I opened my eyes and strained to see into the living room. I thought I heard him sniff. Did he have a cold, too?

I felt my way along the kitchen wall, flipped on the light and saw Juan sitting on the edge of the living room couch hugging a pillow. His eyes were red and puffy. He'd either been crying or hadn't slept in the three days he'd been gone. I had a sneaking suspicion I knew the cause.

"Why are you sitting in the dark?" I walked over and sat next to him.

He moaned and buried his face in the pillow.

I reached out and rubbed his back. "What's wrong?"

My heart thudded as I remembered the death card Monica had turned over tonight. Please, no. I really disliked Ron, but I'd never wish him—

"I broke up with Ron Sunday," Juan said into the pillow.

Oh, yes. Yes!

Instant relief flooded through me.

I almost felt ashamed for the near joy blossoming inside me. I knit my brow and puckered my lips, but it took everything I had not to smile.

Yea!

You should feel bad for Juan. He's distraught.

Ding dong, the Mo-Ron's dead!

Juan was obviously hurting, and it wasn't funny.

Maybe the card meant *change.*

That had to be it.

Change was *good.*

The mean Mo-Ron, the wicked Ron. Ding dong, the wicked Mo-Ron's dead!

I studied my hands so Juan wouldn't read the delight in my eyes. Ohhhhhhh. How could I be so happy about something that made my friend so sad?

This would build bad karma.

Yea.

Stop it. I didn't need any more bad karma.

148

"What happened?" I asked.

Yea.

Shut up.

"I couldn't take it anymore."

I nodded. At least he had the strength to end a dead-end relationship rather than looking the other way long enough until he could convince himself all the broken dreams were exactly what he wanted.

All he deserved.

"Are you okay?"

He nodded. Shrugged. Shook his head and sighed.

"I'm not right now, but I keep telling myself I will be. I'm better off."

Yes, you are, you smart boy.

I rubbed his back again. I didn't want to say too much. Just in case he and Ron somehow got back together in the middle of the night.

"Sunday? That was three days ago. Where have you been?" I feigned a stern look at him, then smiled. "I was really worried about you."

He brightened a little.

"You were worried? About me? I went where any good Spanish boy would go in the throes of a crisis. Home to *Mami*."

A pang of envy plucked at my heartstrings. I hadn't been able to run home to mom in years.

"But next time I go away," he said, "I'll let you know where I'm going. So you won't worry."

I smiled at him. " 'Copacabana'? It's not exactly a sentimental breakup song."

Juan's face clouded, and I wished I hadn't asked.

"It was our song."

"Okay, sorry I asked." I had to say something to keep him

from slipping back down into the black hole I'd just pulled him out of. "I should have known."

My stomach growled and I realized I hadn't eaten since lunch. Not on purpose. I'd been so busy I hadn't had a chance to grab lunch. I worked late and had to meet Karen to go up to Monica's.

I knew I really shouldn't eat so late, but I looked at Juan feeling so down and knew a good black bean quesadilla was just the medicine he needed.

"Are you hungry?" I asked.

"I'm always hungry."

"How about if I whip up a quick feast and we can eat and watch a tape of the American Ballet dancing *Giselle*? I need to watch it as a basis of comparison for the review I have to write of the Central Florida International Ballet."

"*Giselle*?" His accent made the word sound like *G-sell*. That *Juanism,* that little twist his accent put on words, warmed me up inside and made me feel like everything was going to be okay. We may have known each other for less than a month, but already we'd become a family. So it wasn't a typical Beaver Cleaver family, probably more along the lines of the Osbornes. But he was my family and, hey, I'd take it.

"How do black bean quesadillas with mango salsa sound?"

"Like heaven."

"Good, you can help me. You peel, I'll chop."

As we walked into the kitchen, Juan picked up a red, white and blue Priority Mail envelope. "This came for you."

I took it and glanced down at the package. Barely visible beneath the rerouting slip reflecting the change of address from Rich's house to Juan's condo I'd filed with the post office, was my handwriting.

"Oh, no." The words escaped my lips before I had a chance to stifle them.

"What's wrong?" Juan asked.

I sighed. "Nothing. Nothing at all." I contemplated whether I should open the package now or just toss it and spare myself the pain of yet another rejection.

Tempting as it was, the eternal optimist in me, that annoying little voice that refused to let me stay in bed and pull the covers over my head or crawl into my cave clad in my comfy, threadbare, gray sweatpants—which was looking more and more tempting as each day passed—piped up and urged, "What if it's an acceptance?"

The post office had a change of address, but the editor to whom I'd sent the first three chapters of my "kitchen mystery"—a story featuring a chef heroine who's drawn into a world of intrigue when a former lover turns up dead in her kitchen—had Richard's old number. The number from which I'd disconnected the answering machine.

What if someone actually wanted to see more of my work, and I missed the boat because I threw away the acceptance letter out of fear?

I felt Juan's gaze on me as I ripped open the envelope and yanked out the paper inside.

Dear Author,

Uh-oh.

Thank you for your submission. Unfortunately it does not meet our need at this time . . .

Blah, blah, blah, blah.

Standard, smudged "Dear Author" rejection form. It looked like a copy of a copied copy that had obviously been Xeroxed a few too many times. The wording wasn't even aligned straight on the page. I shoved it back in the envelope.

I ran my thumb over the black ink of my writing. When I

mailed the package off, so full of hope and determination, I had no idea how my life would change.

I walked over to the sink, opened the cabinet door and pitched the lot into the garbage, manuscript and all.

Maybe Monica's death card meant the death of a dream.

One by one, my dreams were dying slow, painful deaths.

I squeezed my eyes shut for a few seconds, determined not to let the welling moisture escape. I didn't want to explain to Juan. This was his night to feel sorry for himself. He didn't need to share the hankie.

Focus on the good, Olivia. That's what my mom used to tell me.

I got to keep my job.

Soul mates.

Alexei's buns.

Soul mates.

Hunter's blue eyes.

Soul mates.

Monica saying disregard everything I told you.

No! Think positive thoughts.

The soul mate parting gift.

But who?

Thursday morning I was armed with a new attitude. It's amazing what a good night's rest will cure. Or how even a few hours' restless sleep can lend a whole new perspective to a dark mood.

Who needed to publish a book?

I didn't need the grief.

Not that I was tossing my pen. You might say that for the time being, I was giving my rejection-weary soul a much-needed respite.

Besides, I didn't have time to fuss with future submissions. Right now, I had a full-length newspaper feature to write and exactly two days to figure out how in the hell I was going to pull off this ballet review.

I'd watched the tape of *Giselle* twice last night, once with Juan's commentary, and again after the food was gone and the novelty of the ballerino's *bulging assets* had worn off. Tired and melancholy, Juan had passed on the second screening and gone to bed. I took notes on the show. It made me feel like I was accomplishing something, but I didn't know exactly what to do with notes, and truthfully, I didn't know if I was any closer to figuring out ballet.

Oh, well.

Company rehearsal call time at the Bob Carr was ten o'clock. I'd landed in the office at eight to research ballet reviews done by other reporters at other papers.

The write-ups I pulled mentioned the mood of the ballet, the choreography, the power and grace in the dancing, the chemistry between the dancers, the set, the lighting. Oh, look, one mentioned costumes.

But no mention of how the men filled out their tights.

Okay, so I still had a lot to learn in a very short time. Marjorie was clamoring for a good review, but before I faced that music, I had to finish the company feature, scheduled to run on the front page of the Friday "Weekend Living" section.

I'd spent the first three days observing and interviewing the various cogs that turned the wheels of the Central Florida International Ballet. The photographer had shot Monday's rehearsal.

All I had left to do was interview the principal dancers, Alexei and Lara.

Should be a piece of cake, right?

Wrong. Dancers don't eat cake.

And Lara, our little Russian prima ballerina, didn't speak

English, or so I'd learned after knocking on her dressing room door.

During the week's rehearsals, Konstantin, Lara and Alexei always spoke Russian to each other, but I figured it was just habit or a way to remember the old country. The three of them had worked together for years. They'd come to Florida together. They had that Russian bond going on.

Alexei and Konstantin spoke English fluently, so I just assumed Lara did, too.

Alexei came around the corner and stopped to observe our game of charade communications.

My face flamed.

I hated myself, but my heart started thudding. How ridiculous. How sophomoric. I'd been doing just fine until Monica starting going on about soul mates. Now, all of a sudden I was struck dumb in his presence. Overnight, he'd transformed from Buns of Steel, man in tights, to someone who might matter.

No longer just a crush, he didn't feel safe anymore.

I'd lost my bearings. I didn't want to care about him. I didn't want to leave myself wide open again.

Stepping into the middle of Alexei, Lara and Marjorie's love triangle wasn't exactly my idea of the perfect start to a union of soul mates. If I got involved, would it transform the triangle into a love square? Would Alexei keep adding women until they ran out of geometric shapes and had to invent a new one? They'd probably name it after him.

The Alexeigram.

Monica said I'd just met my soul mate. That narrowed it down to two men, if you didn't count Juan. Why, why, why were both of my soul mate candidates egregious Lotharios?

I couldn't look Alexei in the eye.

He touched my arm. "What are you trying to tell her? I'll

interpret for you." He said something to Lara in Russian.

She shot him an icy stare and walked away without re-plying.

Ooooooh.

I watched him as he watched Lara walk away and I could have sworn I saw a flicker of pain in his eyes, which confirmed that there was no soul mate connection between us.

Besides, if a man's going to be with me, he's going to be with *me*. Exclusively. I didn't even want to be number one if there was a number two. I didn't share with ballerinas or French Tarts.

Meeting a soul mate should feel better than this.

Like gazes meeting across a crowded room then—

Bam!

Boom!

Fireworks and harp music.

I thought of Hunter that first night at Hue.

But the potential for pyrotechnics fizzled at the thought of Hunter and Destiny in the hall that Sunday morning.

Nope, I'd know it when I met my soul mate. It'd be all warm and fuzzy and moon dust in your hair and golden stars up in your eyes of blue—Oh, wait. That was from the song "Close to You."

I hated that song.

Well, actually, I secretly liked it because it was one of the few songs I could sing where my voice sounded halfway de-cent. But basically, it was an annoying song and it stuck in my head like gum on the sole of my shoe.

Laaaaaaaaa la-la-la-laaaaaaa close to you. . . .

Alexei Ivanov didn't feel like a love song or my soul mate.

Once you got past the awe that this man had a body that made a Rodin sculpture look inadequate, the soul mate po-tential plummeted to an all-time low.

Besides, the situation was way too complicated and seemed to be getting stranger by the minute.

The Diva was pissed.

She'd obviously been *dissed* by Alexei, for some unknown reason. And Marjorie had been strutting around looking smug, like a mean cat that planned to eat a little bird for lunch.

And me? Right about now, I'd mortgage my soul for drive-thru liposuction.

Marjorie rounded the corner in her cashmere suit and pearls. I'd bet fifty bucks she'd been lurking the whole time listening to everything.

"I guess I could ask Konstantin to interpret, if you absolutely *must* have her input," she said, acting all annoyed.

See, what did I tell you? She'd heard every word.

Marjorie clucked her tongue, then reached out and plucked a piece of lint off Alexei's leotard. Her hand lingered on his chest and smoothed a crease or wrinkle I couldn't detect.

"On second thought, Konstantin's very busy," she said. "Too busy to deal with this *nonsense.*"

I raised an eyebrow. Interview nonsense or prima donna nonsense?

"You want a good story?" I gave her the old stare-down treatment. "I'll let you make the call."

She crossed her arms and studied me with her steely blue gaze. Her three carat diamond winked at me as if it were saying, "Take heed, minion, better watch your step."

She blew out a breath through her nostrils. "Fine. I'll ask him, but don't count on it."

As she walked away, it suddenly dawned on me that Marjorie had met her match in Lara. Lara was an exotic mix of fragile strength. The prima ballerina had diva power, something Marjorie couldn't pay a plastic surgeon to install.

Something I couldn't even pretend to compete with.

Monica was wrong.

Way wrong.

No soul mate for me. At least not here. And if I knew what was good for me, I'd put such crazy notions right out of my head.

Damn those decongestants. It should be against some spiritual law to get a girl's hopes up by talking about soul mates.

Flagrant foul!

Alexei shrugged. "Lara is not so happy with me."

I teetered on the edge of temptation, wanting to ask him *why,* to hear him admit he knew darn good and well *why* Lara was not so happy with him. But I couldn't get the words past the lump in my throat.

I took a deep breath. "Do you have time to talk to me this morning?" I said. "I need to ask you a few questions for my article."

Now he was smiling. Ah, you like that publicity, don't you, Buns?

"We must rehearse in a few minutes," he said. "Can you stay? My Oma is coming to watch. You could interview her, too. She is eighty years old and still rides the bus."

"Oma? Isn't that German for Grandma?"

"Yes, my mother was German, my father Russian. They were both dancers. They meet when they traveled with the same company."

Ahhhh, two kindred spirits.

Now that was romantic.

Laaaaaaaaa la-la-la-laaaaaa close to you. . . .

His accent was killing me. Since when did I become a sucker for foreign men? Let me rephrase that—men with very broad shoulders and buns of steel and Russian accents that dripped over my soul like honey on a piece of hot buttered bread.

My heart pounded. I looked up and met his gaze and realized those same eyes that seemed to be only for Lara were now watching me intently. My stomach performed a series of perfect *grand jetés*. Oh, God. Okay.

"My deadline is four o'clock. When will she be here?"

"She'll be here in an hour. For your four o'clock . . . how you say, deadline?"

I nodded.

"You write for me, 'Alexei Ivanov likes Orlando very much and wants to open people's hearts to the dance.' "

I gulped.

People's hearts? Could you be more specific? Which hearts did you have in mind? Say, mine for instance. Then it would be singular—person's heart. Olivia's heart. But we have the rest of our lives to perfect your English.

Oh, and that smile was killing me. Mmmmmmmmm. Was he doing that on purpose? Probably. To butter me up to make me stay and interview Oma.

"All right, I'll stay and meet your Oma."

I heard Marjorie's heels clacking on the wooden floor. "Konstantin's much too busy," she said in a satisfied I-told-you-so voice. "Lara will just have to miss out on the publicity."

The publicity.

Oh. That's right.

Alexei wanted publicity from me.

That's all.

Actually, it felt better that way, somehow safe again.

In that new reality check, I tried to convince myself he wouldn't stoop so low as to have an affair with Marjorie. Would he? Please say no.

Lara was so small and beautiful, and when Alexei looked at her his eyes were tender and passionate. When he looked at Marjorie it was the *close the deal* smile.

"I must prepare to rehearse," Alexei said. He nodded at me.

Marjorie and I watched him walk away. For once the two of us were in perfect unspoken agreement as we stared at the finest ass in possibly all of . . . the world?

"When will the feature be finished?" she asked, without removing her gaze from Alexei.

"My deadline's four o'clock."

"Did Alexei give you everything you need?"

Oh, don't I wish. How about you? Have you gotten anything?

I nodded. "I'm going to stay and observe for another hour or so, then I'll head back to the office to finish the story."

Alexei disappeared and Marjorie turned to me. Did she realize she was so obvious?

"Remember, positive, positive, positive."

Of course the story would be positive. Unless I could figure out a way to work in a bit about the overbearing bitch of a board member who desperately wanted to get in the tights of a certain company member.

Two waifs in skimpy leotards floated past us. Marjorie eyed them, assessing them head to toe. She frowned.

"Did you ever dance?" The words slipped out of my mouth before good sense prevailed.

Marjorie looked a little surprised and, for the first time since I'd met her, she seemed to soften. With a faraway look in her eye, she said, "A long, long time ago."

"Why did you stop?"

She blinked. Her eyes refocused on me, cold and hard. "I

want to see the article before it goes to press."

Now I understood.

Even with all her Daddy's millions, she was no happier than the rest of us. She got away with treating people like shit because people let her get away with it.

She may have had the good fortune to be born into money, to attend some Ivy League college and have all the advantages money could buy. But when it came right down to it all the money in the world couldn't make her happy. It couldn't buy a good marriage. It couldn't buy love or fulfill unrequited dreams.

And it couldn't buy a person's soul.

"You'll have to talk to my editor, Nolan Rivers, if you want to see the story before it runs." I glanced at my watch. "I'll do well to get it to him by deadline."

Marjorie opened her mouth to say something, but the music to *Giselle* began.

Like children under the spell of the Pied Piper, Marjorie and I turned in unison and walked to the wings to watch.

The stage was set for the beginning of the second act—a surreal graveyard nestled amidst majestic weeping willow trees. A lake reflecting a huge, glowing moon was painted on the backdrop. Upstage sat a tomb bearing an ominous cross draped in ivy.

The dancers were scattered about, and Alexei and Lara burst onto the scene on a crescendo of brass and percussion.

As Alexei started to lift Lara, he slid his hand up her leg. I got goose bumps all over again.

Did I mention how much I was beginning to *love* ballet?

I wondered how Marjorie felt, wanting so badly to be cast in the role of prima ballerina, to have his hand on her leg, but having to play the lonely bitch instead.

And for someone who'd been so pissed off, Lara looked

pretty darned content in Alexei's arms.

Downright happy.

Like . . . like she was in love.

They were rehearsing the part where Giselle had died and Albrecht, the role Alexei danced, realized how much he still loved her.

Isn't it just like a guy to realize what he lost after it's too late?

I stood rapt, hidden in the cloak of the black curtains that created the wings of the stage.

Alexei, or I should say, Albrecht, ran after Giselle, arms outstretched, begging forgiveness for deceiving her.

Yeah, dream on, loser.

But what did Lara, I mean Giselle, do? She forgave him, because she loved him.

She *loved* him.

Giselle loved Albrecht.

Alexei loved Lara.

Giselle danced with Albrecht to protect him from the queen of the Wilis who was bent on killing him.

He was damn lucky, too. I wouldn't want to mess with the Wilis bunch. They were a troupe of scary women who were really pissed off because they'd died of broken hearts after the men who'd once loved them and promised to marry them abandoned them.

I could certainly understand their bad attitudes. Sounded perfectly justified to me. Since my father kicked my mother to the curb, she might have been a good Wilis candidate.

The rest of the ballerinas in the company danced the Wilis roles. Whirling, swaying and sweeping their arms in a circle around Giselle and Albrecht.

Mournful and distraught, the *corps de ballet*'s dance really looked like angry spirits bent on revenge. They circled the Wilis queen.

Hmmmm. I have a question. How did the Wilis queen get to be queen? It's not a title passed down through the bloodline.

Oh, I know! Maybe whoever gets dumped worst gets to wear the crown? You know, like those clubs where whoever has the worst week gets the prize.

If so, look out, queenie. I could've given her a run for her crown.

My heart hurt *way* worse than her heart.

Yea! I'm The Queen.

It's good to be The Queen.

And since I am The Queen, I get to kill The Dick.

Can I kill The French Tart, too?

But The Queen has elected to have someone else do her dirty work because she doesn't like violence.

Yea! I always knew I was royal.

The Wilis closed in, while Giselle threw her body in front of Albrecht to protect him.

Then again, I don't know if I'd want to be queen of such an angry court.

Olivia, Queen of the Scorned and Eternally Dammed.

I don't think so.

Hmmm, after the way my father left us, maybe the title could've been handed down through the bloodline.

Naaaa, I couldn't see my mother doing the angry spirit afterlife.

So much for that theory.

True, she never quite recovered from my father leaving and breaking her heart, but she wasn't angry and bitter. On the contrary, she always emanated love.

Was I still bitter about him leaving?

How could I be bitter when I hadn't talked to him since I

was seven? My mom and I had a wonderful life. If anything, maybe I was mad at the Universe for taking my mom away before her time.

Don't go there.

Don't go there.

Don't go there.

It won't do any good.

Think positive.

I am not bitter.

I didn't even know what happened to my father.

The thought created a little fissure in the tiny scar in a forgotten place in my heart, a fissure which threatened to tear wide open.

I sighed and closed my eyes to escape the agitated Wilis. The fissure was so similar to the large gaping hole Rich created when he called me nearly three weeks ago.

Time healed my *father wound* to an ugly scar I could almost forget if I didn't look at it, didn't touch it.

The *Rich wound,* on the other hand, was still too fresh, too new. Even a simple thought like whether I should forgive him ripped the lesion wide open, and made it feel just like the day he said good-bye.

Don't do this.

Think positive.

I love my life.

I am beautiful just the way I am.

I am strong and healthy.

I am not a Wilis.

I opened my eyes and saw the Wilis dance in a circle, closing in on Giselle and Albrecht. As long as he kept one hand on the cross over her grave, he was safe.

Naaaaaa, I couldn't see my mother joining the scorned specters society.

I didn't want to be a Wilis either.

Not even if I got to be the queen.

The queen can have back her crown.

I am a free spirit.

As Alexei and Lara danced, they looked into each other's eyes, their bodies pressed together between leaps and lifts. I wondered whether Lara's looks of love were genuine or an act?

Together.

Apart.

Together.

Apart.

The rhythm of their passionate lives.

Ultimately, Alexei always pulled her back to him, a gesture so strong, but so gentle and elegant, I could almost understand why Lara softened.

If I were critiquing this dance right now, I'd have to say Lara Minsky and Alexei Ivanov were . . . perfectly matched.

A prince and his princess dancing in their own private storybook kingdom. They created fireworks in a never-never land that even Marjorie and all her daddy's money couldn't buy.

A place I'd certainly never known.

Chapter Nine

Just before the Wilis dance ended, a sturdy white-headed woman wearing a brown plaid housedress and black lace-up shoes shuffled past Marjorie and me. The older woman, who looked to be in her eighties, knocked into me as she made her way through the wing to the edge of the stage.

When she stopped, her large frame blocked my view.

Marjorie snorted and craned her neck to see the final moves of the dance.

This had to be Alexei's Oma.

How sweet.

She'd taken the bus all the way across town to watch her grandson's rehearsal. That was worth a mention in the story.

She must be so proud.

As the dance ended, I tried to see around her to watch Alexei's reaction to his Oma.

He grabbed Lara's hand and together the two of them approached to greet her.

"Five-minute break, everyone," Konstantin called.

The rest of the company members scattered. Konstantin walked over toward us.

Oma said something to Alexei in German and enfolded him in her meaty arms. Then she stepped back and held his face between her hands as she gazed up at him and continued muttering in German.

She hadn't even as much as looked at Lara, who stood at Alexei's side, her beautiful face expressionless even as Alexei turned to me and said, "Oma, this is Olivia Logan, she is a newspaper writer."

A little unsteady on her feet, Oma took a few seconds to turn her body in my direction and focus her gaze on me.

"Olivia, this is Berta Weil, my Oma. W-e-i-l, so you spell right in the article."

Oma took firm hold of both of my hands and squeezed.

"Oh, she's a *big* girl," she said, the words emphasized by her thick German accent.

A sudden loud ringing in my ears muted anything else she might have said. My cheeks burned and I was sure I was turning about twenty shades of scarlet.

Would you please give me a break, people?

Why was everyone suddenly so compelled to point out my size? I'm working on it, okay?

"Nice to meet you, Ms. Weil," I managed to say, pronouncing the *w* like a *v,* just like Alexei had done so her name sounded like veal, which was food, and then I felt stupid because everyone knows *big girls* are always thinking about food.

"Alexei, why you not marry a girl like this?" Oma took hold of my arm and jerked me toward him.

Oh!

Oh, shit.

Don't say that.

Well, wait, the marriage part was good, but why'd you have to make the *big girl* comment?

I glanced at Lara who was still standing there with a blank face because she didn't speak English and had no idea her future Oma-in-law was trying to marry off her Alexei.

"Vhat your name?" Oma asked.

I cleared my throat. "Olivia Logan."

Oma eyed me like she was assessing a fatted calf.

"She is not so scrawny like a bity-bity ballerina." She made an angry gesture toward Lara and I wondered what the tiny dancer had done to piss off Oma.

"This girl sturdy. Give you many babies."

Babies?

Making babies with Alexei?

Mmmmmmm. Go, Oma. I think you're onto something here. In fact, I think I might love you, Oma.

We might have become good friends, if not for the fact that thanks to her big girl and making babies comments, all gazes were now on me, Marjorie, Lara, Konstantin.

No! Stop! Don't look at me. I'm the invisible one and, to tell you the truth, I like it that way. Because when I was invisible, no one said anything about my size and nobody broke my heart.

Alexei's gaze was burning my body, looking at me as if he were seeing me—I mean really seeing me as a *woman*—for the very first time.

I looked away.

I didn't want to know the results of the assessment. I just wanted to die right then, right there. Just shrivel up and blow away with hopes that nobody would try and find me.

Of all the times I prayed that a man like Alexei Ivanov would notice me, this was not how I wanted my prayers answered.

The left corner of my mouth began to twitch, and I dug down deep and pulled out a kind, be-nice-to-the-crazy-old-woman expression and asked, "So, how many great-grandchildren do you have?"

After the day I'd had, I deserved an extra grande mocha and a cinnamon scone with gobs of butter. From mortifying Oma pointing out my sturdy, childbearing worthiness to two hours of full-length feature deadline hell, I needed a treat. The only thing standing between me and my reward was the unusually long afternoon line at Starbucks.

Maybe the whole city suffered from bad-day blues and had turned up for a much-deserved pick-me-up.

By the time I'd freed myself from the publicity-hungry clenches of Alexei and his matchmaking Oma—during which I'd received the abridged version of the *Life and Times of Alexei Ivanov, Volume One*—I barely had time to write and submit the story before my deadline came crashing down around me.

By the way, for the record, I did not tell Rivers that Marjorie wanted to proof my story before it ran.

If she wanted to see it so badly, she could ask Rivers herself.

As I stood in line, breathing in the heavenly aroma of coffee and eyeing the assortment in the goody case, I saw one lonely little cinnamon scone sitting there waiting for me.

Ahhhh, lightly browned with a hint of cinnamon sprinkled on top.

It had my name on it.

I really should make scones myself. I hadn't made them in eons.

"Olivia, hi."

A deep, southern-tinged voice behind me shook me from my analysis of the perfect cinnamon scone.

I turned around, knowing good and well who stood there.

Hunter in faded jeans and a button-down chambray shirt. The espresso machine wheezed and gurgled.

"Hi," I said and felt my cheeks warm. Go away. I can't order extra butter and a fully loaded mocha with you standing here.

"So how's life treating you?" he asked.

Did he notice me eyeing the treats?

No one else in line after him. So he couldn't have been standing there very long.

"Great." My gaze darted to the scone—Good, still there. Safe and sound—then counted one, two, three people in line ahead of me. "I've been busy. They just had a big reorganization at the paper and my duties have been kind of rearranged." Maybe Hunter just popped in to say hi. Maybe he'll have to run before they take my order. A couple fell in line behind him. "But I'm taking it all in stride. You know, lucky to still have my job."

Hunter nodded as I spoke, and I realized I was talking very fast. I took a breath and consciously slowed down.

"My friend, Karen, said she saw your band at the Blue Note."

He was standing so close to me, his arm brushed mine. The contact made me inhale.

He smelled good. Mmmmm. I loved the way he smelled.

I breathed in again, this time longer and slower and wondered if he was aware of our body contact. Because it didn't seem to faze him.

But, mmmmm. It was the same way he smelled when he stood so close to me in the pantry almost a week ago.

Uggggh, speaking of which, after what Ron said, I definitely couldn't order the scone and mocha in front of Hunter.

Okay, if he's still here when it's time to place my order, I'll sneak back down and get my scone later.

No, with my luck I'd probably run into him and then I'd really look like a pig.

You know us *big girls,* we just can't get enough.

I took a step back to reclaim my personal space, all the while telling myself if I didn't stand so close to Hunter, I wouldn't have to bend my neck back to look up at him.

"You're tall. How tall are you?"

I could always tell him the scone was for Juan.

"Six-four."

His arm brushed mine again. But I'm not 100 percent certain it wasn't me who stepped closer this time, disregarding his personal space.

"That's tall."

He smiled, which made his eyes crinkle at the corners. Okay, this guy was full of sexy little surprises just waiting to be discovered.

If Destiny was his girlfriend, how did she feel about his habit of invading others' personal space?

"When did your friend come in?" he asked.

What? Oh, Karen. "Last week sometime."

"I wish I would have known, I would've gotten her in without a cover."

Giani was probably just the type of cheapskate who'd love a freebie. Probably how he afforded his Ferrari. "You'll have to come out with her sometime and hear us play," he said.

"Yeah, I'd like that."

If I accepted the freebie, did that make me a cheapskate, too? No. It didn't apply to those of us on a budget.

B.F. (before Ferrari), it's frugal.

A.F., it's cheap.

And it's cheap if a guy uses a freebie or a coupon within the first month of the first date.

Dating rule number three: No cheapskates. Even if they do drive red Ferraris.

On the other hand, guys who offer to share their resources—i.e., Hunter offering to get my friends and me in to hear his band without a cover charge—earned extra points.

That was so sweet of him, so nice. Maybe that's what it was about him. He was just a nice, decent, cool kind of guy whose attentions were misconstrued when he really didn't mean any harm or womanizing.

Rich never used to flirt, and I liked that about him. Not that I was calling Hunter a flirt. He was just a little more outgoing than Rich.

Once I moved in with Rich, we never really went out. We'd go out to dinner or see movies and there was this one couple we used to do things with. But they moved and we didn't really have any other couple friends.

Why didn't Karen have a boyfriend then?

Why did she have to wait until I was single to decide to settle down? On second thought, if she would've chosen someone like Giani, I wouldn't have wanted to double-date.

Rich and I having no mutual friends certainly cut down on the who-keeps-the-friends custody battle. Made the split nice and tidy. Well, so would the fact that he was on the other side of the Atlantic and—"Huh?"

I'd just realized Hunter asked me a question, and I had no idea what he'd said. I stared at him blankly.

"You're up." Hunter gestured to the guy behind the counter who looked mildly annoyed at my temporary mental sojourn. Or maybe he looked that way because his lower lip piercing hurt. How *did* they fit a piercing gun down there? Better yet, why would someone want a piercing there?

I stole one last glance at the scone in the case. "Decaf. Small."

I will definitely start making my own scones. That way I can enjoy them whenever—

"Mocha grande and a cinnamon scone, heated, please," Hunter said.

Ohmigod. How weird was that? My stomach did a little drop, and I breathed in to catch it before it fell.

So Hunter and I shared a mutual weakness.

Who'd a thunk?

I knew I liked him.

He had good taste.

I ignored the hopeless spiral of warmth that unfurled in my stomach.

He was a good guy and, if worse came to worst, he'd make a great friend. A great, gorgeous friend.

Who knows? Maybe by the time I was ready to trust again, he and Destiny would have gone their separate ways.

I took another step back, before I entertained any stupid notions of falling for him before he and the big D broke up.

Destiny was a very lucky lady.

Yep, very, very lucky.

Look at the bright side. Hunter just saved me a gazillion calories. For some reason, that thought didn't satisfy my craving.

Maybe the second best thing to eating a cinnamon scone was eating one vicariously through Hunter.

That could help with the craving.

What I wouldn't give to *be* that cinnamon scone right now.

No! Stop that.

I am not pathetic.

I enjoy healthy foods that nourish my body.

I am in control of my hunger, it does not control me.

I am not soul mate obsessed.

No, wait, keep it positive.

My soul mate will find me when the time is right.

There! That's better.

"Six-forty-seven," said Mr. Weird Piercing.

Ugh! What's wrong with me? I forgot to say separate

checks. "We're not together." And what a shame.

I pulled out my wallet, but Hunter said, "Put it away." He handed Weird Piercing a ten. "This is on me since you've been working so hard."

Oh.

Wow.

"Thanks," I muttered. "Next time I'll treat." Happily, because if I treated, that concluded there would be a next time.

Weird Piercing handed Hunter the change and his scone in a little bag, and we stepped down to the end of the coffee bar.

It was just a cup of coffee. A small cup of decaffeinated coffee, but it meant more to me than a mocha and a scone or a man bringing me four dozen roses he'd actually meant for me.

"So when's your band playing again?"

I hoped he didn't think I was trying to score free cover on top of free coffee.

"Tomorrow night. Want to come?"

Darn it. I hate ballet.

"Wish I could, but I have to work."

Our order was up and we grabbed our cups and wove around people doctoring their coffee with cream and sugar, and the tables and chairs gone askew during the afternoon rush as we edged toward the door.

"At the paper?" he asked.

"It's opening night of the ballet *Giselle*. I have to write a review."

Darn it. Darn it.

"You're into dance."

He sipped his coffee and broke off a piece of scone.

"I'm not. It's part of the rearranged duties I mentioned earlier."

He broke off another piece of scone and held out the bag. "Did you ever try these things? God, they're good."

"I know. They're fabulous." But I waved off his offer, knowing I wouldn't be able to stop with just one taste. I glanced up at him, then my gaze slid to his mouth. Nope, one taste would never be enough for me.

He held open the door, and I walked out.

"Are you heading home?" he asked.

"I am."

"Walk you up?"

"Sure, if you're heading in that direction."

He nodded. "I have to work tonight."

"At Disney or is the band playing?"

We started walking.

"Disney."

"How long have you played the banjo?"

He rolled his eyes and smiled that little half-smile that was one of the first attributes that drew me to him.

The half-smile and those intense eyes.

"Forever," he said. "It pays the bills."

I tried to picture Hunter playing his banjo in one of those corny Disney costumes and couldn't make the jump. It just didn't translate, like painting a pair of pants on Michelangelo's *David*.

"I hope Altered Ego will start paying the bills soon."

"Does it look promising?"

He shrugged.

"I should know something in the next month. We've been talking to a label about a deal. But in the meantime, it's Frontier Land for me."

I watched him as we walked—those intense blue eyes, his Roman nose, strong jawline. I'll bet he could be stubborn. But he was also kind.

A spiral of warmth unfurled in my stomach and rendered me breathless. I couldn't think of anything to say, and I racked my brain to remember all the things we'd talked about so effortlessly that night at the party four floors up.

"So—" we both said at the same time. Then we laughed.

"You go first," he said.

Suddenly, I felt stupid because I really didn't have anything deep and meaningful to say, just nervous chatter to fill the silence.

"What's your last name?" I asked. "I don't know what made me think about it"—other than the fact that you're hot and always hanging out on my mind's back porch—"but I realized I don't know your last name."

He smiled. "Monahan."

Nice. "Irish."

He nodded.

I paused so he could say what he'd started to say, but we walked along in silence—again. Okay, this was a little awkward. Why couldn't I just be content to walk with him in comfortable silence? Maybe because it wasn't comfortable. If it was comfortable I wouldn't feel the need to fill in the gaps. But what if he hates chatter? What if he thinks I'm boring or we don't click because of the long stretches—

"Destiny seems nice."

"She's great. She got a callback on her Disney audition." *There, that's better, he was just looking for a jump start.* "That's why she was here over the weekend. If she gets the job she's going to move down."

What? She doesn't live here? Hunter's been over there in that apartment all alone all this whole time? Like I would have put on the big moves if I'd known. But it was a fun thought.

"Down from where?"

175

We turned down the lobby corridor. I had to quicken my pace to keep up with his long stride.

"New York. She's been up there modeling, but she's tired of the scene. Wants to try something different."

Okay, I hated her. She was beautiful. And talented. And she had Hunter.

Bored with the Manhattan modeling scene. Oh, yawn, yawn.

Spare me.

Hunter opened the glass door. I entered, walked to the elevator and punched the up button.

"I'll bet you'll be glad when she's living in the same city with you. Those long-distance relationships are tough." He'd just better hope she hadn't already hooked up with some Calvin Klein underwear model. Personally, I hoped she already had, but if she'd slept with Underwear Boy and Hunter didn't know about it and slept with her—which he'd obviously done over the weekend—and Underwear Boy had AIDS or some other terrible disease—it would be really tragic.

I realized Hunter's brows were knit, and he looked baffled and very, very cute. The elevator doors wooshed open. We stepped inside.

"You do know she's my cousin, right?"

Chapter Ten

Ohmigod.

Cousin? As in related? As in *I-can't-sleep-with-her-because-it-would-be-disgusting-and-probably-illegal* type of cousin?

Oh, yea.

Ohmigod. Ohmigod. Ohmigod.

"Oh." Deep breath. "I thought she was your girlfriend." *Cousin? She's his cousin. Oh, thank you, God.* Stay calm. "You know . . . I thought . . . I mean, she's just so pretty."

Breathe, dammit.

Oh, I love her. She's beautiful. She's talented. And she's Hunter's *cousin.*

Monica was right about my soul mate.

And if Hunter and I got married she'd be my cousin, too. I'd always wanted a beautiful, talented cousin. Oh, yea! Hunter and I will have beautiful, talented children. They'll get his musical ability and my knack for the written word, and I'll cook for my family.

The elevator door dinged and opened on our floor.

"You didn't introduce her as your cousin."

"I didn't? I don't remember."

What?

He doesn't remember?

He hasn't been kicking himself for the past five days for *not* introducing her as his cousin?

Didn't it occur to him that I might think she was his girl-friend? Didn't it matter?

Oh, no, we're not getting married. Destiny's not going to be my cousin.

177

Wait! He thinks I'm engaged. So it wouldn't have mattered at the time if she was cousin or girlfriend.

Yea, wedding was back on.

"I'll catch you later, Liv," Hunter said as we arrived at our doors.

"Bye. Thanks again for the coffee."

Was this our first date? Someday I'd tell our grandchildren how he bought me coffee and ordered a cinnamon scone—

I heard his door squeak open and I said, "I really want to hear your band play sometime. Let me know when you're playing again, okay?"

Over his shoulder, he smiled his half-smile. Not exactly Alexei's Tom Cruise smile, but Hunter's was sexier. By far. I nearly melted.

"The Blue Note. Friday nights. Sets at nine and eleven."

I tried to act nonchalant, but I was screaming inside.

"Maybe I'll surprise you and show up sometime."

My heart was beating so loud it reminded me of the other night when I came home to Juan blasting "Copacabana"— the part about them falling in love.

"Hope so. You should get out and live a little, Liv."

The way he looked right then, all smoldering and seductive and just downright edible—but then again, I suppose he could have been playing his banjo and singing "Yankee Doodle," and he still would have looked smoldering and seductive and downright edible—he inspired me to do something really embarrassing like blush, which I'm sure I was doing; or grin stupidly, which I was probably doing; or run over and kiss him, which I was highly tempted to do.

Before I embarrassed myself, I turned around and put my key in the lock and thought about how I'd eat every single one of those womanizer accusations.

Mmmmm, sweet. Who needed scones?

Cousin. Ohmigod.

I wanted to do the victory dance, alternately woofing and waving my fist in the air, then walking side to side like an Egyptian.

No, that would be embarrassing.

Very undignified.

"Liv?"

Huh? Ohhhh, I loved the way he said my name. Sounded like poetry. I turned back to him. He was facing me.

"When are you getting married?"

If you can imagine the noise of a phonograph needle scratching across "Copacabana," that's the sound that blasted in my head.

I'd told him I was engaged. This was it. The moment of truth. I had to tell him now or . . . or nothing. I had no choice. Say it. Just tell him, dammit. I crossed my arms in front of me. "I'm not."

His right brow shot up and he leaned back against the doorjamb the same way he'd stood four days ago when I saw him in the hall with Destiny. "Oh." He nodded. " 'Kay." And a grin markedly bigger than his usual sexy half-smile spread across his face.

Bam!

Boom!

For the first time in my life I could've sworn I saw fireworks and heard harp music. And it would've been really cool except now that I knew Destiny was his cousin and he knew I was a free woman, maybe the *bam* and *boom* were the sound of my nice, safe, protective barriers exploding. All the barricades I'd placed between myself and my feelings had fallen away. I was left standing here in front of Hunter, vulnerable, exposed. Just him and me. And my desire.

"Is that a good thing?" he asked.

I don't know, Hunter. Is it a good thing? Or am I an idiot to hope so, setting myself up? Richard all over again? But Hunter was talking about the end of my fake engagement, not my feelings for him, for us.

"It's not a bad thing," I finally managed to murmur.

"Good." He nodded again. "Good. Well, I've got to go . . ."—he motioned to his door— ". . . to work."

As I let myself inside the apartment, I'd already started free-falling from yea-she's-his-cousin to ohmigod-where-does-this-leave-us.

In the hallway, I pressed my back to the wall to steady myself.

I'd told him the truth. Well, at least half the truth. If the old saying, "The truth shall set you free" was, indeed, true, then why did I feel so bound and gagged by my emotions?

I cringed and slid down the wall to a crouching position.

At least he'd heard it from me, not Ron, not Juan, or some other secondhand source that might have dug me in deeper.

Even so, I still had some explaining to do. Like how I'd never, ever set foot in Paris. I cringed again. Thank God Hunter hadn't asked questions.

I hugged my knees.

What was going through his head right now? That just four days ago I was engaged, and now, it was easy come, easy go. Poof. Instantly single, and living to flirt.

I didn't flirt with him.

Did I?

Would that be good or bad if he was thinking I did? Well, I guess it would be good if he was thinking about me at all.

Ohmigod, what if he *wasn't* thinking about me, or if I'd been so damned transparent out there in the hall, babbling like an idiot about wanting to *come hear his band play* that he'd seen right through me and had lumped me in with the groupies?

Stop!

Stop!

Stop!

Think positive—the way he smiled at me. The way he makes me feel like I'm the only woman in the world. The way Destiny's his cousin, not his girlfriend. Yea!

A giddy rush spiraled through my stomach.

I took a long, slow, deep breath and decided I definitely needed a cinnamon scone. Like a junkie jonesing for a fix.

I got up and went into my bedroom, tossed my purse on the bed, then pulled my mother's red recipe notebook from the drawer of my bedside table. Of all my possessions, this collection of her handwritten recipes meant more to me than anything in the world.

I took the book and my coffee and settled myself in the big maroon chair by the window. Smoothing my hand over the notebook's red vinyl cover, I tried to quiet my mind. Tried not to think of the what if's and what's next with Hunter.

Somehow holding the recipe book made me feel calmer, like my mom was with me. If I closed my eyes, I could almost feel her arms around me, and hear her telling me everything would be fine.

Just fine. . . .

I turned to the first page. The paper had started to yellow. It had been ages since I'd turned to this book. I thumbed to her cinnamon scone recipe, then traced her neat script with my fingernail. She had such pretty handwriting.

My heart ached. A rich, deep, delicate ache in a different place than the part damaged by my father, by Rich. A spot deep in the core no one had ever touched. A place that whispered "take a chance, live a little."

The thought scared me to death. Take a chance? What if Hunter didn't want to take a chance with me? What if I had nothing left to give to chance? What if Richard took it all?

I closed the book and put my hand over my heart.

About a year after my mother died, I tried to make her scone recipe, but it didn't turn out. I tried once, failed and promptly put the book away.

Simple as that.

It just dawned on me that without intending to, I'd tucked away my dreams with it. The dream of our bakery. Of freedom and running our own business. Stuck it away in favor of a go-nowhere, no-risk life.

Why? What was wrong with me?

I could almost hear her saying, "Olivia, you've *got* to take chances."

Ha, *this* from my mother who always played it safe? I looked down and realized my hands were shaking.

Is that why I want to play it safe, Mom? Because, like you, I've come to terms with having no one to fall back on? One thing I've learned that you never taught me—at least not directly—is that each of us weathers the world alone. Like the changing seasons, everyone comes into your life and leaves eventually, one way or another.

"But, Olivia, you've got to take chances." The thought struck me like a kid anticipating a shot. The more I dwelled on it, the more panicked I got.

No. This was nonsense.

I picked up my cup of coffee and sipped it. It was cold now from sitting too long.

I held the cool liquid in my mouth.

Humph. Let anything sit too long and it turned cold. Tuck your dreams away and they'll grow old and stale and never come true.

I took another sip of cold coffee. If I were going to take chances, I should get my butt in gear and send my manuscript out to another publisher.

I drummed my fingers on the cover of the notebook.

I could do that. I *should* do that, if I really wanted change in my life. If I wanted to take a chance that might pay off.

Or I could make scones.

That felt better.

I got up and grabbed a piece of paper and a pen from my desk, flipped to the scone recipe and started jotting down the ingredients. Each one seemed strange, yet familiar as I remembered helping my mother gather each component, then standing next to her on a stool as we mixed batches together.

The phone rang. I didn't even look up. Probably Marjorie with a template of how she wanted me to write the review. I let the machine pick up the call and finished making my grocery list.

Should I make a batch of scones for Hunter?

No! Not now. That would seem too desperate, like I was trying too hard.

I was making these for *myself*. I tapped the pen on the desk. In celebration of the new me, the Olivia who went out into the world and claimed what she wanted. The Olivia who took a chance on life.

A little voice deep down inside me laughed—loudly. Uhhhh! Well, I had to start somewhere, and making my mother's scones after all these years seemed like a darned good square one.

That same voice suggested Hunter's bed would be a better place to start, and I laughed right back, knowing I should stick to the scones and leave the possibility of me landing in Hunter's bed up to the fates of the Universe.

I started to change clothes, but the blinking message light caught my eye. It was probably Marjorie, but what if it was someone fun?

Like who?

Hunter.

Get real.

Monica calling to tell me the soul mate part of the reading did, indeed, stick and she'd just had a vision of me talking to my soul mate in the hallway of my building?

Oh, grow up.

I grabbed the phone and retrieved the message.

"Hey, Liv, it's Karen. I'm really sorry, but I have to cancel for tomorrow. It's Valentine's Day. I completely forgot, but Jimbo didn't. I'll make it up to you. Promise."

She didn't.

Click, she hung up.

She did.

I couldn't believe she'd bagged out on our plans.

I hung up the receiver and stared at the phone for a second.

What about our girls' night?

What about Alexei's butt?

Don't make me do this by myself, Karen.

I picked up the phone again and dialed her number.

After the first ring, her answering machine picked up.

I hung up without leaving a message. She was probably in bed with Giani.

Dammit, Karen . . . thanks a lot, friend.

I knew how to handle this. I'd go down to the City Central Market and along with the scone ingredients, I'd buy a big box of Godiva and drown my irritation.

I drummed my fingers on the desk. Thinking of all kinds of mean and nasty things I'd like to say to Karen and—No, I didn't need Godiva, but I did need the scones.

My first inclination was to throw on my old gray sweatpants. I mean, we're talking comfort here. They were as much an old friend as Karen, only more faithful.

As I grabbed them out of the drawer, I spied a moth hole in one of the legs.

Would be just my luck if I threw them on to go to the store, I'd run into Hunter again.

My stomach did a strange twisty thing that sort of felt like going down a sudden hill on a roller coaster. You know, kind of fun, kind of scary at the same time. It momentarily neutralized the gnawing irritation brought on by my so-called friend, who thought she could trade me in for a jackass and make it up to me at whim.

I tossed the gray pants aside—sorry, old friend, maybe another time—and pulled out a newer black pair that I'd never worn because they weren't nearly as well broken in and hence not as comfortable as my gray pair, but they hadn't shrunk halfway up my leg, either.

What is this phenomenon with sweatpants that over time they shrink up and get shorter vertically, while simultaneously stretching horizontally? It's like the fabric shifts and grows in a different direction.

I pulled on the black sweats—Whoa.

What was this?

They weren't as tight as they used to be.

Wow, not even a week and I had room to move in these babies?

I did a deep knee bend—or a *plié* as they say in the ballet world.

Had I lost weight?

I *had* lost weight.

Ha!

For once in my life I wished I had a scale so I could know how much I'd dropped.

My automatic reaction was to call Karen.

Arrrrrrr.

Nope, I was mad at her right now.

Who could I celebrate with?

Juan was at work, and I couldn't run across the hall and tell Hunter that—

I'd just have to celebrate by making scones. It would be like celebrating with my mom.

I deserved them. I hadn't even really been dieting. A combination of cutting down and being too busy to cook, not to mention covering the ballet rather than restaurants.

I tugged at the waistband of the pants.

Wow, results in only a week.

I pulled off my navy twinset and donned a T-shirt.

Not a huge difference in the fit.

Wait, yes, as I pushed my shoulders back, I actually didn't feel like the shirt was ready to split at the seams.

If this were a button-down, it might not even gap.

Leave it to me to be one of the few women who celebrated a smaller bra size.

Feeling pretty darned proud of myself, I tied my walking shoes, armed myself with the recipe and took the steps instead of the elevator.

Karen was darn lucky I had this small victory to temporarily distract me from her bailing out. I'd chew on the sweet taste of weight loss for a while—at least until I'd extracted all the flavor—and give her the stink-eye later.

On my way down the steps I made a bargain with myself. Since I'd mentally put back the box of Godiva, I could have two scones if I took the long way to the market.

Long way as in head the opposite direction on Summerlin,

go west on Washington and cut over by Lake Eola, rather than simply turning the corner and walking a block to the market. The long way was probably about a mile.

Okay, I said I wanted to start an exercise program. This was my opportunity.

Here I was actually doing it.

Yea me.

Outside, the February afternoon air was crisp and fresh. I breathed in through my nose and exhaled fast and through my mouth.

Then I rounded the corner and saw the Valentine's Day display in the window of the soap shop near Starbucks. Funny, as many times as I'd walked by, I hadn't noticed it. I tried not to look as I strode past.

But the reality hit me that tomorrow, while all of the world would be celebrating love, I'd be at the ballet—alone. Hunter would be singing to all the groupies in Orlando. The thought settled over me like a wet blanket on a humid day.

February had just become my least favorite month.

A couple walked by holding hands, and I heard the woman say, "Oh, look, isn't the window beautiful?"

No, it's not. It stinks.

Who wanted to be single in February?

Single amidst all the happy couples.

I quickened my pace.

Hearts and flowers.

Broken hearts and wilted flowers.

Four dozen roses.

Roses meant for Karen, the no-good friend who'd dumped me for a jackass.

Four dozen ugly dead roses.

Stop!

Think positive.

Destiny was not Hunter's girlfriend.

Hunter was single.

Ohhh, and since Hunter asked me to come hear the band play tomorrow, it probably meant he didn't have a Valentine's Day date, either. But I didn't know that for sure. What if I did show up and he did have a date and he introduced me like he was introducing one of the guys?

I had to stop as a BMW with a cute guy behind the wheel and, of course, a woman in the passenger seat, turned into the 7-Eleven parking lot.

Tomorrow was Valentine's Day, and I'd spend the evening with Giselle and the Wilis, because my best friend was dating a jackass and Hunter would be too busy getting women's lingerie thrown at him.

I kicked a rock out of my path, turned the corner and started walking toward the lake.

At this rate, I'd be queen of the Wilis after all. I'd end up dying alone and bitter just like Giselle. As I stepped onto the sidewalk that ran alongside Lake Eola, I picked up my pace a little to a slow jog.

No, Giselle wasn't bitter, she forgave. Even after all the crap Albrecht put her through.

My pulse was hammering, but I pushed on.

Get a life, Giselle. Maybe if you'd had a sense of self before you turned body and soul over to Albrecht, you wouldn't have found yourself in this pickle.

I breathed in through my mouth and out through my nose.

Some women never learn. Look, Giselle, this forgiving and forgetting business was giving us all a bad name. It was plain to see it didn't get you anywhere. You saved Albrecht's life. He probably returned the favor by marrying someone else and was living a long, wonderful life with her. Probably married a thin French woman. And what did you get? You got an eternal life sentence hanging with the nasty sisters.

A couple in a swan boat laughed as they tried to pedal the boat backward.

At the very least, it seemed like Giselle should have had the chance to choose a happier ending. Not this oh-I'm-such-a-martyr grand finale.

I listened to the rhythm of my feet hitting the pavement.

She should have made him suffer.

She should have gone out and found her soul mate.

My *father fissure* tore a little more and the *Rich wound* throbbed. Soul mates were heavy, scary territory. I veered to the right to give another jogger room to pass and remembered my mom telling me to take a chance.

Maybe Giselle thought she'd found her soul mate and that was what landed her with the Wilis.

I mean, how much could a girl take?

What would happen if Rich came back proclaiming his love and begging forgiveness. Could I find it in my heart to take him back?

Wait, wait, wait.

A stitch in my side slowed me to a walking pace.

Erase that ridiculous thought. Whether I forgave him or not, Rich was married and wouldn't come crawling back to me.

Forgiveness was a moot point.

I stopped under the branches of a large oak tree and realized I'd walked past where I should have turned to go to the market. I cut north on Magnolia and walked over to Robinson Street.

It was five o'clock and people were just starting to get off work and spilling out into the streets from the downtown high-rises.

When I turned south on Orange Avenue, I spied the wig

shop, walked two doors past it and stopped in front of the space where my mom and I used to dream of opening our bakery.

How long had it been since I'd stood in front of this space?

There was a "For Lease" sign in the window. It was as if my mother was calling my bluff. *Here's the dream. Do it. Quit the newspaper and the Riverses and Marjories of the world, and be happy. Take a chance.*

How many times had we stood here with our noses pressed against the glass? Checking out the cavernous space, planning where the ovens, tables, chairs and cases would go.

I could see my reflection in the window and I shifted my focus to the busy people rushing past behind me, en route to the people they loved and places they had to go. I squinted my eyes as I reached out and touched the glass. Their images blurred and rippled like an Impressionist painting. For a moment, I thought I could see my mother standing beside me. But it was just the reflection of a woman in an advertisement painted on the side of one of the city buses that had stopped on its route.

I pulled my hand away and stepped back.

I'd have to walk up here again and remember to bring a pen and a piece of paper so I could write down the number.

A voice nagged that I could just call the Realtor. Maybe I would, but right now I had to get to City Market before it closed to get my supplies for the scones.

"What's an Oma?" Juan grabbed another scone from the plate on the kitchen table, sliced it and slathered on the butter.

"Oma is German for Grandma." I set my demitasse on the saucer and broke off a piece of warm scone. The rich, cinnamony confection melted in my mouth and reminded me of better times. Pretty good if I did say so myself. Almost as good as my mom's, but not quite. The spicy-sweet aroma made me think of how Hunter had offered to share his scone earlier and how knowing Destiny was his cousin put the chemistry coursing between us in an entirely different light.

"So the actress Uma Thurman," Juan said, "she's a German grandma?"

"Huh?"

"Uma. Uma Thurman. We should call her 'Grandma Thurman'?"

I laughed. "No, you dolt, it's *Uma* Thurman. U-m-a. Grandma is *O*-m-a."

Sometimes I couldn't quite tell when to take Juan seriously. But all kidding aside, he had a great sense of humor, and I loved him for it. Even though his breakup wounds were fresher than mine, he'd managed to rebound pretty fast—or at least he put on a happy face. I was probably better off spending time with him than listening to Karen go on all night about the virtues of Jimbo Giani.

Guilt tugged at my insides. What was wrong with me?

I should be happy for Karen. That's what friends do. They say, "Yea!" when you're happy and they tell you how lucky you are and what a great guy you're dating. They understand that you'd rather spend Valentine's Day with your new boyfriend than accompany a freshly dumped friend to the ballet.

I pinched off a bite of scone.

Okay, that was the way I *should* be. But I was far from it. So, yes, I was probably better off spending Valentine's Day with Juan.

Of course! Why didn't I think of that sooner?

"Do you have Valentine's Day plans tomorrow night?"

Juan looked up from his *Hair Today* magazine and grimaced. For a split second I saw a flicker of pain reflected in his dark brown eyes.

Before he had a chance to answer, I said, "Be my date to the ballet."

He glanced down at his magazine, turned a page.

This would be great. Juan was kind of like my Fairy God-mother—no pun intended—because not only would his art-istry transform me into a lady presentable for a night at the ballet, with him I'd have a wonderful time and probably only think about Hunter fifty times rather than a hundred.

I contemplated telling Juan about the latest developments with Hunter, but decided to wait and see if anything actually developed—like a first date.

In the meantime, Juan would appreciate Alexei's buns as much, maybe even more than Karen would. And he was much more deserving, that's for sure.

When he looked back up at me, he seemed more himself.

"I'd love to, but I'm supposed to go to Tampa tomorrow night to prepare for a hair show on Saturday."

My heart sank. I saw my coach turn into a pumpkin before I'd even had a chance to ride.

He closed his magazine.

"Although, if you promise not to keep me out too late"—Juan quirked a dark brow—"I suppose I could leave very early Saturday. Tampa's only an hour and a half away."

I jumped up and hugged him.

Maybe I didn't hate February as much as I thought.

Chapter Eleven

In the Monday morning editorial meeting two days after my ballet review ran, Rivers announced Natalie Clemmons would cover the next ballet.

"No offense to you, Logan," he said. "Great review. We just want to mix it up a bit. I think we'll have you focus on modern art—popular music, theatre, food. Clemmons will cover the ballet."

Humph, I didn't know if getting bumped from the *bitch beat* was a promotion or a demotion, but did he say music? Yea! I'd take banjos over ballet any day.

Guess Marjorie didn't like my style? Whatever. At least I didn't have to deal with her, and this gave me a valid excuse to go see Hunter's band and write a story on them. How convenient was that? My stomach flipped at the thought.

Zoe elbowed me and whispered, "Nat is so out of here."

I had to admit it did seem befitting that the boss's alleged mistress would get the pleasure of working with the missis. But why would Chris VanHussen agree to send his girlfriend into the ring with his wife?

Unless he didn't have a clue, which was probably the case. Maybe Marjorie had picked up the scent of marital improprieties and wanted to keep closer tabs on the lovely Ms. Clemmons.

Good riddance, Marjorie.

It's been nice knowing you, Natalie.

But there was more to that meeting than the latest reshuffling of assignments. Things felt funky. Rivers was acting strange, even more uptight than usual. He didn't mention more layoffs and nobody had the guts to ask, but something was definitely cooking at the *Orlando Daily*. I could smell it as strong as a Florida thunderstorm brewing in the dead heat of summer.

And speaking of powerful forces of nature, Hunter and I had some vibes of our own zinging back and forth, white-hot currents of lightning way off on the horizon that struck every time we ran into each other, which seemed to happen a lot after the cousin Destiny revelation.

We'd run into each other four times this week. Once in the hall, another time in the lobby as I was leaving and he was coming home from work at Disney. Then twice on the stairs. I'd traded in the elevator for the sixty steps between our floor and the ground. Not bad for a girl whose past exercise repertoire was limited to walking to the break room for coffee and walking back to her desk to pound out another story. The rewards of running into Hunter were worth the exertion.

"Lookin' good, Ms. Logan," Hunter said as we nearly bumped into each other on the landing.

Did I mention how much I was beginning to love exercise? Standing there, we'd talk and talk about everything and nothing, each in no hurry to say good-bye, but finally one of us would make the break. Ohmigod, the undertow of attraction was so strong it almost dragged me out to sea.

Then I'd go my way and he'd go his, and the reality that he hadn't asked me out would settle around me, keeping me firmly tethered to the here and now.

Maybe I was sending out funky vibes as a defense because, in the back of my mind, I knew I should keep him at arm's length. It *was* the safest way.

But then, something inside me shifted. Maybe it was caused by shock therapy from all this electricity zinging back and forth between Hunter and me. Maybe it was too much

194

oxygen to the brain from all this exercise, but I had a gutsy moment when Karen called me at work to apologize for bagging out on the Valentine's Day ballet.

"You can make it up by coming with me to hear Hunter's band next Friday night."

Silence filled her end of the line, but I waited, tapping out the seconds with my pen as I remembered the old negotiation trick about whoever spoke first when a deal was on the table put themselves in the weaker position.

"Okay," she finally said. "Did you talk to him? What's going on? Tell me."

Relief rushed through me, and I sat up straight in my chair. Yea! Now I wouldn't have to be mad at her. I had my best friend back.

In a hushed voice, I relayed the latest happenings—running into Hunter at Starbucks, learning all about *cousin* Destiny, telling him I wasn't getting married, his asking me to come hear Altered Ego and the very convenient excuse of writing a story about his band.

"Man, it's only been like three days since I talked to you and all this happens," she said. "Remind me never to stay away so long."

"Don't ditch me and you won't miss out."

Karen and I made plans to meet at the loft after work Friday. We'd grab a bite to eat and walk to the Blue Note.

"No excuses this time," I said. "Okay?"

She laughed. "No excuses. Promise."

"So is this a real story you're doing," Karen asked on Friday night as she spooned guacamole onto her quesadilla, "or just your cover for the night?"

We'd stopped at the little Mexican cantina on Wall Street to grab a bite to eat and catch up on a little girl talk before we headed down to the Blue Note. Or in my case, to down a couple of Margaritas and bolster my confidence, which was wearing thinner by the minute.

I stared at the line of people forming at the terra-cotta hostess stand and remembered Juan's words of wisdom as he worked to make me presentable. "Girl, we're going to give you a new attitude."

With a devilish look in his eye, he'd sashayed over to the stereo, chosen a CD from his towering collection and shoved it in the player. Patti LaBelle belted about her famous "New Attitude," about knowing where she was going and feeling good from head to toe.

Ugggh. Another woman with *attitude*. Tonight, I would don attitude like a hat and a pair of strappy sandals. If I could, I'd go out and buy a bitchin' ensemble and tell the world to look out.

If only. I'd better start with attitude first.

Juan danced around the living room and played the song over and over until I finally got up and danced with him as he sang, *"I've got a new attituuuude."*

He also had a second date with Tim, a guy he'd met at the hair show in Tampa last week. So Juan was in rare form and was bound and determined to help me cultivate a new 'tude of my own.

I should've told Hunter I was coming tonight. Forewarned him. Why? Would he have done anything differently if he knew I was coming? Like baked a cake?

I could do this. I took a deep breath. It was all in the attitude.

A server walked by with a sizzling skillet of fajitas. The aroma wafted its way over to our table. Uggh, I hoped I wouldn't smell like a Mexican cantina when we left.

I sipped my Margarita for fortification. The tangy-sweetness refreshed me. "Of course the story's legit. I'll have to produce an article or I'll look like an idiot. I'm writing it for the *Daily*'s 'Weekend Living' section. Maybe I'll do a whole series of profiles on up-and-coming local bands. You know, so I don't look biased." *Or* don't look like I'm trying to win Hunter with free publicity. I was waiting for Karen to jump on the anti-publicity band-wagon since I'd been so critical of Alexei's promotion grubbing, but so far she'd resisted. Good, because this was different. The tables were turned. And Hunter was not Alexei.

"Does Hunter know you're coming?"

I trailed my finger through the salt on the rim of my glass. "No, I wanted to surprise him."

Our server set a round of drinks on the table next to us and looked at us to see if we needed anything. I waved her on and pushed my soft taco, of which I'd taken two small bites, around on my plate with my fork.

"Good for you," Karen said. "I like your attitude." She studied me and nodded. "And your new do. In fact, I *like* the new Liv Logan. Though there wasn't a thing wrong with the old Olivia."

The new Liv Logan had attitude. Or at least she was trying to have one.

"In celebration of the new you." She raised her beer and clinked it against my glass.

"To the new me," I murmured. And to the old me quivering behind this Juan-painted façade. The me who would just as soon dash home and duck for cover. But I wouldn't dare.

Karen set down her beer, pulled a tiny neon-green gift bag from her large purse and handed it to me. "I have a present for the *new* you."

I wiped my hands with my napkin.

"What's this?"

"Open it. I have a sneaking suspicion they'll come in handy soon."

I peered into the bag. "Oh, my God!" I closed it fast and glanced around the crowded restaurant as a slow burn crept up my neck. "Condoms? *What* am I supposed to do with these?" I shut my eyes. "No! Never mind. Don't answer that."

Karen grinned and raised her beer to me again. "To the good times ahead."

Karen and I got to the Blue Note about nine-thirty. We fell in line behind a couple of blondes in miniskirts, belly-bearing blouses and ridiculously high heels. One of them had a belly button ring. They looked barely old enough to drive.

"Hey look, it's Mary-Kate and Ashley," I murmured to Karen. "Nope, can't be, I'm sure these girls aren't old enough to be the Olsen twins."

I heard them giggle and rolled my eyes at Karen. Must have fake IDs. There was no way anyone would believe these two were of legal drinking age.

The bouncer, a burly guy dressed in tight jeans and a denim jacket, eyed them from head to toe, smiled his approval and waved them through without asking for identification. Walking in after *the Olsen twins,* I felt like the babysitter. "I had no idea it was such a young crowd." The bouncer didn't ask for our IDs, but did manage to give us the slimy once-over.

I was suddenly very glad I'd let Juan tame my curls into spirals—something I never had the patience to do myself—and spend twenty-five minutes applying my makeup.

But these heels he'd insisted I wear—"Girlfriend, they

make your legs look ten miles long"—were another story. They weren't walking shoes, and I'm sure we'd walked at least a mile and a half by now. Why did everything that looked good have to be a torture device?

Inside the dimly lit dive, smoke hung in the air like a gauzy veil. The place reeked of stale cigarettes, alcohol and cheap perfume.

Dread lodged in my stomach like a heavy stone, and I felt the energy being sucked out of my body by some invisible power.

What was I thinking coming here? I hated places like this. Since my future felt so tenuous at the *Daily*, I should be at home right now working on my book.

Wait. I was *here* to write an article. This was work. Yeah, for a job that might not be there next week. I should be home putting together a resume—just in case. Dammit, I should be doing something constructive, not standing here in line with a box of condoms in my purse, waiting to see my hot neighbor, trying to convince myself I was here to write a story.

Who was using the lure of potential publicity to her advantage now?

But I had a new attitude.

As we walked down some steps toward a cashier collecting the $5.00 cover charge, I heard the band playing a heavy rock song, but I couldn't see them.

Was that Hunter singing? Every nerve ending in my body went on high alert. Wow, great voice.

Ha! This was kind of cool.

I stepped up to the cashier, a skinny woman with stringy, jet-black hair and eyeliner and tattoos to match, who sat behind a card table.

"Can I have a receipt, please?"

She looked at me like I'd asked her for a reserved table in the no-smoking section. "We don't give receipts."

It didn't seem like an appropriate time to whip out my press pass, so I simply slapped down a five and moved on.

Past the cashier, we turned left and fell into a sea of groupies in the room where the band played. Through the crowd, I saw Hunter front and center onstage, looking particularly fine in a plain black T-shirt and black jeans, belting a song into a microphone on a stand, lost in his own little hard-rockin' world.

I stopped in the flow of traffic to savor the vision. He *did* have a great voice. And wow, look at him all hot and sweaty— mmmmmm, that's what he'd look like after a long hot night of serious sex.

My breath caught and my heart beat to the pulse of the music, as I thought of Hunter and remembered the box of condoms tucked inside my purse.

I tried to share my thoughts with Karen, but the screaming guitar rift drowned out my words. Then a brunette in tight leather pants bumped into me as she walked backward talking to her friends. She'd been pointing at the stage when she slammed into me, and it coincided with one of those in-between notes in the song. I heard her say loud and clear, "He's sooooooo hot."

Uhhhhhhhhh!

She shot me a dirty look, and I noticed that she looked like she was about sixteen years old. Barely. Hey, chickie, watch where you're going. And watch who you're calling hot.

The Olsen Twins tottered by on their high heels, drinking beer in brown bottles. Did they steal those shoes from their mother's closet? Probably sneaked them out in a bag with their miniskirts and belly shirts and changed down the street in the Taco Bell bathroom.

Several women were dancing in front of the stage.

If I felt like the baby-sitter before, now I felt like the house-mother. Were these girls into banjos?

Bet they didn't even know Hunter played one. But I knew. I eyed the stage, the four other members of the band, and the various instruments and gear behind them.

No banjo. And that made it seem like we shared a secret.

Karen waved to me from a table in the corner and smug with my *secret,* I walked over, sat down and mentally prepared to gather information for yet another story I knew nothing about.

The problem with reporters was we knew a little about a lot of things, but we didn't know a lot about anything. That wasn't entirely true.

I watched Hunter sing a slower number, something about an elusive woman he wanted so badly it hurt. He closed his eyes and moved to the music.

I definitely knew what I *liked.*

I sat back, content I could watch Hunter without him knowing I was there. But about fifteen minutes through the first set, he did a double take in our direction and my cover was blown.

He waved and several heads turned to see who he was waving to, then he carried on singing just like before. It didn't seem to faze him that I was there. Well, maybe he smiled a little bit more—smiled at *me.*

When the song ended, the audience applauded and hooted and whistled. When the commotion died down, he thanked them, then said, "Hey, Liv, glad you could come out tonight."

Karen elbowed me and hooted and clapped. People turned and stared. Groupies glared. Heat rose in my cheeks. Stop looking at me. I hated all this attention, especially since it wasn't good attention. But I sat there smiling at him, trying to pretend like there weren't at least 100 hateful women giving me the evil eye. Thank God, in a flash, all gazes were back on Hunter as the band broke into another heavy number.

"Someone's glad to see *you*," Karen said over the music, but the waitress came over to take our drink order before I could respond. Just as well, because then we both ordered beer with a mug, thank you very much—it just wasn't a Cosmopolitan kind of place—and settled back into our corner and watched the last couple of numbers in the set.

When the live music stopped, my ears rang. Over the murmur of the crowd, Karen commented on how much she liked Altered Ego's style. I nodded and tried to focus on what she was saying rather than watching how Hunter had disappeared into the drove of people crowding the stage.

The waitress was just setting our beers on the table when Hunter cleared the masses and made his approach toward us.

"Here he comes." Karen kicked me under the table.

My pulse beat a steady cadence with each step he took toward us. I tried not to fidget, tried not to stare. I didn't want to look too anxious, but I didn't want to seem too aloof, either.

Just be cool.

I refused to behave like the groupies who swarmed the stage. I lived right across the hall from the guy. I knew he played the banjo at his day job. I'd seen him at five o'clock on a Sunday morning when he didn't expect to run into anyone in the hall—oh, wait, scratch that, it was me who looked hideous that morning. Hunter looked gorgeous, as always. I'd never seen him look bad—rewind and strike the five a.m. thought from the record.

"Put their drinks on my tab and bring me a Bass ale,

please." He pulled out the chair across from me and sat down. "Hey, stranger, you made it."

"Hey, yourself," I said.

He hugged me, and held me a little longer than just a friendly, hey-how-ya-doin' kind of hug. He usually stood close, but this was the first time we'd been *this* close. Nice. I breathed in deep. Mmmmmmmm. I thought for a split second he could hear my heart thumping, but then we broke the contact.

Be cool. I was just a friend turning out to support a friend's artistic endeavor. Oh, right, and to write a story for the paper.

"I was hoping you'd show," Hunter said.

Hoping? As in thinking 'bout me? Be still, my heart.

I smiled at him. "Thanks for the drinks. You remember Karen? You met at Hue that—ummm, first night at the party. God what was that? Like a month ago?"

He nodded. "I remember. Hi, Karen."

"Hey, Hunter." Her accent sounded particularly southern tonight. Most men found her irresistibly attractive, and I guess I'd just resigned myself to losing a little part of every man I'd ever set my sights on to Karen. It wasn't a competition or that she purposely tried to lure them away or that she even tried. It was just a fact of life. Guys always had a hard time *not* looking at Karen because she was so pretty.

"I love your band," she said. "Who writes your material?"

"I do," he said.

Ohmigod, there was something terribly sexy about a man who could set his thoughts to music. Like poetry, but one better. Could you imagine being the inspiration that moved a man so that he had to sit down and write a song about it?

I could live in that fantasy.

"Liv said you were here a few weeks ago." He smiled that

little half-smile. "Thanks for coming back and bringing her."

He leaned his forearms on the table and looked at me.

Me.

Not at Karen, at me.

Yea!

Hunter, baby, you could score big points for that. And he was already racking them up—that first night when we were doing the eye-contact-across-the-bar thing, his gaze didn't fall from my eyes to my boobs, and now his gaze chose me, not Karen.

"What'd you do to your hair?" he asked.

My hair?

He reached out and tugged a spiral.

"I let Juan have his way with me."

His smile transformed into a mischievous kind of grin that made him look boyish. He was usually so intense and I'd never seen him like this. It sent a funky-hot vibe careening through my veins—wow—which felt pretty darn cool. Again, my mind skipped to the condoms in my purse.

Right on cue, God bless her, Karen stood and smiled at us. "Excuse me for a minute, I'll be back."

"How was the ballet?" he asked.

"Great. And speaking of work, I have a surprise for you. I'm here to write a story about you and your band."

He looked a little taken aback, like he wasn't sure he heard me right.

I nodded. "Are you up for it?"

He blinked. "Yeah, that's great."

This was good. He was interested, but not overly. Sometimes in the face of publicity, people change, but Hunter seemed pretty unaffected.

The waitress brought his beer.

"Would you like another?" he asked me.

"No, thank you."

She handed him the bottle and walked away.

"What are your plans for tonight?" he asked. "If you're going to be here for the second set, I'll introduce you to the guys and we can figure out what you need."

What I *need?* Oh, what a loaded statement.

"Okay. But my deadline's not until next Thursday, so we have almost a week."

"Good, I'm glad we have time. Because it'll be next to impossible to get anything done in here."

We had *time.* For things we couldn't do *in here.* Okay. Right. Now I was trying to read meaning into plain and simple words.

"But I have to get back to work. If you're up for a late night, after I'm finished here, I'd love to take you out for coffee or dinner or breakfast, whatever you want." He shoved his hands in his pockets. "Just don't go away. Okay?"

Had he just asked me out? Ohmigod, he'd just asked me out. Finally. Oh, yea! Oh yes!

I nodded. "I'd love that."

He stood and reached out and touched one of my curls. Right then and there, I decided I'd be Juan's personal slave if he'd do my hair like this every day.

I watched Hunter walk through the crowd, stopping to talk to a few people along the way. I didn't care if they were men or women or the Olsen Twins. He was with me after the show.

Altered Ego had started playing again when I realized Karen had been gone for a really long time. Where was she? I had to tell her about my date. If I got up to look for her, we'd lose the table. The crowd had grown to standing room only. Karen had barely touched her drink. I did not want to carry around two drinks looking for her. Nor did I want to stand up the rest of the night.

So I turned my attention back to the stage and watched Hunter do his thing. For someone I'd known for such a short while, it was strange how he felt so familiar.

A warmth started small inside me and gently radiated outward. Maybe I was up for chances after all, because I suddenly realized how Persephone must have felt upon breaking free of the underworld. That first burst of sunshine after months of darkness—

"Hey, babe, how 'bout I buy you a drink?"

Babe? I glanced to my right and a short guy in a red windbreaker was leaning on the edge of the table. What kind of guy wore a red windbreaker out to a club? What kind of guy even owned a red windbreaker?

"No, thanks, I'm fine." I saw Hunter watching us. When I glanced back at Windbreaker, the guy screwed up his face like I'd spit beer at him.

I didn't want to be mean. I just wanted him to leave me alone. I didn't want to make small talk. I didn't want to flirt. I just wanted to sit here and bask in the anticipation of my date with Hunter.

Date!

As in time alone with him. Not in the hall. Not in the stairwell. He'd finally asked me out—even if it was mere hours before. He wanted to spend time with me. After nearly a week of him knowing I was a free agent and him not asking me out, I was beginning to worry he might not be interested. Tonight we'd have breakfast. Next week, we'd discuss the story.

Karen, where are you? Did you get lost? If you don't get back here soon I'm absolutely going to burst with this—this—incredibly incredible bit of news.

Please don't make me send out the search and rescue

team. Just as the Windbreaker faded into the woodwork, I spied Karen, elbowing her way through the crowd, making her way back to—What? No way.

Oh, please tell me that's not who I think it is.

Dammit, it is.

Trailing about six inches behind Karen was Jimbo Giani. If she went out and called him, I would never forgive her.

"Look who I found," Karen said when she got to the table. She reached over, picked up her beer and sat down in the seat Hunter had occupied earlier. "Jimbo, you remember Liv."

She actually *called* him Jimbo. Not Jim or Jimmy (which would be only slightly better than Jimbo, but still an improvement). I wondered if she screamed out "Jimbo" when they had sex. What a ridiculous name for a grown man. Jimbo. How could she keep a straight face?

Jimbo, baby. Oh, yes—

"Of course I remember her." Giani slapped me on the back and then took the seat next to Karen. "*Great* to see you again, Liv."

Great to see me again?

Ah-hmm. Did he not remember the last time we *saw each other?* That excruciating day he showed up with the roses, expecting to find Karen, but finding me instead?

Did the guy have no shame? No conscience? He certainly didn't have the decency to act embarrassed. And why the hell was he even here? This was a girls' night.

I shot Karen a look, but she seemed oblivious to the message I was trying to convey. Oblivious, smiling at lover boy.

"When I was coming out of the ladies' room," Karen said, more to Giani than me, "I ran into this good-looking guy."

And she was pinching his cheeks and talking baby talk to him. Uggggh. I was going to be sick.

Karen reached up and wrapped her arms around Giani's

neck, and the two of them drifted deeper into la-la land. I had to scoot my chair to the right so I could see Hunter onstage.

About twenty minutes later, Giani turned to me as if he'd just remembered I was there. "So Karen says you're writing an article about this band for the paper." He had to shout over the music. "I've written the headline for you." He swept his hand through the air in front of his face as if he were writing a mock headline. "Loud garage band, plays to classless clientele in skanky downtown club. Catchy, huh?"

He laughed at his own bad joke or should I say he made a loud wheezing sound audible over the drums and guitar. Karen watched the band, oblivious to how The Jackass was putting his hooves in his mouth. "Kare dragged me to this joint a couple of weeks ago. When she told me she was coming back tonight, I had to come out and check on her."

More like check up on her. I watched Hunter and didn't respond to Giani.

Then Giani leaned over and whispered something to Karen that prompted her to narrow her eyes and shake her head.

What? She still had a mind of her own? There might still be hope. The two engaged in what looked from my vantage point like a gridlocked discussion. I couldn't be sure because I couldn't hear what they were saying over the music, and I really wanted to watch Hunter, not them. Every once in a while Karen would steal a forlorn glance at me, then narrow her eyes at Giani and shake her head.

Finally, Giani yelled over the music, "It's just too noisy in here. Kare and I are relocating to the piano bar at the Grand Bohemian."

Excuse me?

Maybe I didn't hear him right. But I could have sworn he'd just said he was changing plans right in the middle of what was supposed to be a girls' night out, a night when, for a change, I was interested in a great guy who seemed to be returning the vibe. Everything had been perfect until Giani waltzed in uninvited and decided to change tracks in the middle of the course.

I looked at Karen, who shrugged, then leaned in to me. I leaned in, too, and met her halfway.

"Liv, I'm sorry, but I've got to go."

Giani stood. Karen stood, too, and grabbed her purse.

"You're welcome to join us," Giani said, an obvious afterthought.

I shook my head and didn't look at him. I kept my gaze pinned on Hunter. I'd be fine. In fact, I'd make a point of enjoying myself. Just me and my new attitude sitting here waiting for Hunter to finish his set.

I was getting pretty good at this solo gal thing. Really, it wasn't so bad when compared to the alternative of spending the rest of the evening watching Giani totally manipulate Karen, watching her act like an idiot.

I almost felt sorry for her.

Almost, but, naaaah, not quite. I was too pissed off to feel sorry for her.

Karen pulled away from Giani and turned back to me. "How are you going to get home, Liv?"

I kept my gaze glued on Hunter. I have two words for you, traitor: Go away. "The same way I got here."

"You can't walk home by yourself."

I slanted her a glance. "Are you going to stay and walk with me?"

"Liv, we can drop you home on the way to the Bohemian."

Oh, should I sit on your lap or drive the red Ferrari? "No, thanks."

In my peripheral vision, I could see Karen toying with her

purse strap, hesitating, obviously torn about what to do.

I hope she felt like a great big schmuck.

"Will you at least take a cab home? Please? I don't want you to walk home alone."

"Well, aren't you sweet to care."

Oh, it's just Liv.

Liv will understand.

Liv will get over it.

Well, dammit, this time Karen had gone too far, and I wouldn't ease her guilty conscience by changing my plans, by going home early like an obedient child.

I had plans. Plans I hadn't even had a chance to tell her about.

Hunter kept glancing over at us as he sang. Finally, Karen gave up and walked away.

Thanks loads, *Kare*.

The band finished its last set about half an hour later. I was doing fine on my own.

Fine. Fine. Fine.

Just fine.

True to his word, Hunter brought the rest of the band over to meet me. "Guys, this is my friend, Liv Logan."

My friend? That had a nice ring to it. It was certainly better than being his cousin.

"Liv, Jeff and KC play guitars. Bruce owns the bass and Monk bangs on the drums."

"Hi, guys." They all seemed nice enough and were very into the idea of meeting with me next week for an interview. So we agreed to get together on Tuesday at Hunter's apartment.

Hmmmmm, things were looking up. I'd just gained admission into the inner sanctum of Hunter Monahan's private life. The secret place where he hid his banjo.

See, I was doing just fine on my own.

"Where's Karen?" Hunter asked.

Karen?

Karen who?

Oh, right, I had a friend named Karen once, but I don't remember what happened to her. I think she wandered off with a strange man and I never saw her again. But that's okay because I have a new friend, named Hunter.

"Something came up," I said. "She had to go."

"Did you bring separate cars?"

"No, we walked."

Oh, God, he probably thinks we set this up, so he could take me home. *Going home with Hunter.* The thought sent a shiver of excitement through me.

"Well, good. It'll be easier this way. I mean she could have joined us, but—"

I nodded. "I'm glad she's not." Did I just say that? That was good. Smooth. Yea me!

And then my *new friend* smiled and looked at me in a way that planted a seed of hope deep down in a place I'd written off as barren and desolate, a place where I thought surely no feelings would ever take root again.

Ohmigod.

Suddenly, it was a little hard to breathe. Suddenly late-night breakfast never sounded so good.

Maybe Karen had done me a favor by leaving?

Maybe. But she wouldn't get off that easy. I'd make her suffer—because if I knew Karen she was already torturing herself. Then again, lately I didn't feel like I knew Karen. Forget Karen. I had more pressing matters to tend to, like dealing with the incredible magnetic force pulling me toward this gorgeous man and quieting the seductive voice reminding me it had been more than seven months since I'd had sex and I had a whole box of condoms in my purse. It had been even longer than seven months since I'd been so drawn to a man. The mere thought of having breakfast with him— just him and me—seemed almost erotic.

"Wait here." He touched my arm lightly, and my flesh prickled. I loved the way he made even ordinary contact feel sensual, the way he invaded my personal space and made me want to step even closer. "I just need to go take care of a couple of things and I'll be right back. Will you be okay sitting here?"

"Sure." Hey, you're talking to the new improved Liv. Super Liv, woman of amazing attitude. But not toward you.

He was gone for just a minute, then he brought me back a beer. "Don't go away."

Go away?

Not a chance.

It was midnight and the club was still packed with people, shoulder to shoulder. The recorded rock and roll music wasn't quite as loud as Altered Ego had been. I nursed my beer and tried not to make eye contact with the various men who seemed to be circling around me.

I *was* good at holding my own. Perfectly comfortable sitting by myself. The knowledge that Hunter was coming back—to me—was an added bonus. A cherry on top of the whipped cream.

And oh, the many places my mind could travel when I thought of Hunter and *whipped cream*, but for now, I'd think about breakfast. Then, who knew what possibilities lay around the corner? As I sat there on my own, holding my own, the night seemed full of possibilities.

An oily-looking, beady-eyed drunk guy sauntered, or

maybe it was more like swayed, by my table for the third time.

Why is it when a man sees a woman sitting alone in a bar he automatically assumes she wants company?

I could feel him looking at me, feel his gaze all over the v-neck of my blouse which suddenly seemed much too low-cut.

I angled my body away from him. I wasn't trying to be unsociable really, I was in a great mood. I just didn't feel like making small talk with a man I didn't know.

But he didn't quite get the hint.

What was I supposed to say when, "No, thanks, I'm waiting for someone," didn't work?

Why did I have to say anything? I didn't need to explain. But half an hour and seven no-thank-you-I-don't-want-you-to-buy-me-drinks later (three of those to Beady Eyes, who seemed determined to score), my beer was long gone, and I was still waiting for Hunter to "be right back."

The last I'd seen of him after he'd delivered my here-drink-this-and-don't-go-away beer, he was sidestepping a busty blonde in a leather bustier that let more out than it kept in.

As each minute dragged on, the breakfast seemed less and less seductive and not the least bit erotic.

Did I really say erotic half an hour ago?

Breakfast was not erotic.

And waiting here, fending off the advances of drunk men at twelve-thirty in the morning, wasn't fun anymore. Any roots of possibility had shriveled up and died from neglect.

This place was getting on my nerves—the smoke—both legal and not—the drunken partyers, the women lolling about like M&Ms in a dish waiting to be scooped up.

The story wasn't due for a week. I'd catch Hunter in between banjo gigs and interview him on Tuesday with the rest of the band.

I got up and headed outside to call a cab—it was too noisy inside to hear on my cell phone. I'd no more than cleared the door when I felt a hand on my shoulder.

Chapter Twelve

I whirled around to give whoever was touching me a piece of my mind and—

"Liv, wait." Hunter looked panic-stricken. "I'm sorry for taking so long. A rep from Vista Records grabbed us just as I was headed back to the table. I shouldn't have made you wait there by yourself, but I kept thinking he was almost finished. And—God, this is what we've been waiting for. This could be big."

He was talking ninety-to-nothing and excitement gleamed in his eyes.

And I was such a sucker.

Why was I such a sucker?

My heart resumed the rhythm it had been beating before Hunter disappeared, and I latched onto his nearness, his urgency to make me stay, and the raw excitement emanating from him.

"Vista Records?" Wow. Big time. "What did he say?"

Hunter shook his head the way people do when they don't know where to start.

"I'm starving," Hunter said. "Let's go get something to eat, and I'll tell you about it."

Awareness is a powerful aphrodisiac.

When the lines of sexual cognizance are alive and pulsing hot and fast between you and the object of your desire, you catch subtitles that usually go unnoticed.

The unspoken innuendoes in the tilt of his head, his forward posture, the intensity of his gaze, the way he watched my every move.

I found incredible sensuality in the way his lips parted when he lifted his cup to his mouth to sip the steaming coffee from the white mug as we sat across from each other in a booth in Captain Mick's All-Night Diner.

All my senses were on high alert. Smells, sounds and tastes were heightened—the sound of silverware clanking against dishes, in discord with the old Nat King Cole song playing on the jukebox; the smell of bacon and toast and freshly brewed coffee; the innocent brush of hands as we reached for the menus propped behind the napkin dispenser. The simple skin-on-skin contact made every nerve ending in my body sing.

Oh, man, I was a goner.

Should I have my notebook out on the table like I expected to interview him for this *future feature*—wink, wink, nudge, nudge. Or should I play it cool? Let him take the lead or should I?

Uggggh! I wasn't used to being the one to set things in motion. Too many hard decisions. And I was so out of practice.

Hunter ordered a big breakfast—bacon and eggs, hash browns.

I ordered toast and coffee because I was still so full from the tacos I ate for dinner.

"I'll have to make breakfast for you sometime." I intended every bit of the allusion packed into that invitation.

Was I really saying this to a guy who I had almost walked out on for making me wait?

Were these words coming out of *my* mouth?

"I'll take you up on it." His smile wrapped as much insinuation around his answer as I'd delivered with the proposal.

Suddenly, taking chances seemed the only way to go, as if we were being moved by some unseen force bent on the sole idea of moving us closer and closer until no space stood between us.

"So anyway, the guy from Vista's interested in hearing more of our original material. It's the first positive step toward a record deal. You brought us luck."

I laughed.

"No, you come to hear us play and the rep walks out of the crowd. He must have followed you in. Or maybe luck followed you into the Blue Note? I could use a little more luck in my life."

I felt breathless. And—Ohmigod. It was happening again. That tingling in the pit of my stomach. That same tingling that started small and grew until sparks of awareness exploded in my body. The same sparks I felt that night a month ago when we first met, only stronger, more certain that this might be the start of something big.

I tried to backpedal, but couldn't. Tried to take a breath, but couldn't.

Just relax.

Ride this wave.

Let the current propel me along.

Let the tide sweep me up and deposit me closer and closer to Hunter.

Oh, my God . . . Could I do this?

It felt like the course was already set. I didn't see how we could stop.

I nibbled on my toast, and he told me about his huge family that was spread all over Florida from the Panhandle to Miami.

"Irish?" I asked.

He nodded. "And damn proud of it. Hunter O'Reilly Monahan," he said with a manufactured Irish brogue. "Doesn't get much more Irish than that. You should see us celebrate St. Patrick's Day. My father and uncles have a big party in Ocala every year, which reminds me, it's almost that time of year again. What, in a little over two weeks? Maybe you can come?"

Meet his family?

The thought paralyzed me. Mentally, I shook it off. It wasn't *that* kind of *meet the family*. It was probably more of a the-more-the-merrier kind of event.

I felt a warm glow spreading across my cheeks and through my heart.

A family. A great big, boisterous family to annoy you and burden you with obligations—it sounded wonderful.

I watched his face as he talked about his dad and his four uncles, and if I had any doubt about what made this banjo-playing, rock and roller tick, I was getting an idea.

His family sounded like they were very close.

I ran my finger around the rim of my cup and tried to imagine what it would be like to be part of a big clan. But wait, I guess it wasn't a clan if they were Irish.

Clans were Scottish, weren't they?

"We've become even closer since my mother died."

I looked up. Oh, my gosh. He'd lost his mother.

"It's great you and your family have been there for each other," I said. "I know how hard it is to lose someone you love. I lost my mother, too."

He set down his mug and propped his elbows on the table.

"Sorry. How long has she been gone?"

"Eleven years. In some ways I can't believe it's been that long, seems like yesterday. But in other ways it seems like she's been gone forever."

"Is your dad still alive?"

I shrugged and stared down into my coffee cup. I couldn't believe I was telling him about this. "I haven't talked to my dad since I was seven. It was really just my mom and me all those years. We had this crazy dream that one day we'd open a bakery together."

"Why didn't you do it?"

The waitress came over and warmed up our coffee.

I didn't because . . . because. . . .

"Your food will be here in just a few minutes," she said and walked away.

He looked at me expectantly.

I shrugged. "Well, because I just didn't. You know how the real world gets in the way of the best laid dreams. Besides, I'm a writer not a baker."

I cringed at the words that had just escaped. Why did I say that? I was a fake, a poser. A writer was someone who wrote, not someone who hid behind her "Starvin' Marvin" byline and dreamed about writing words *she* owned, words I could hang my name on.

Did I say writer? I meant dreamer.

But did I even remember how to dream? I looked at Hunter. It was coming back to me.

He nodded. "A writer." The words sounded matter-of-fact, contemplative, like they had merit. "What do you write?" He sipped his coffee, and watched me over the top of the cup.

That made me squirm a little. "Oh, you know, in addition to the stuff for the paper, I write poetry here and there. And I have this book I've been working on for a while. I keep starting it and putting it away."

I realized I was wringing my hands and laid them flat out on the table. I never knew what to do with them. They were always in the way.

"What's the book about?" he asked.

I shrugged and wrinkled my nose. Ugggh, why did he ask? The story always sounded so stupid when I had to verbalize it. "It's about a chef who has a dead body turn up in his kitchen." Oh, yea. That was appetizing. Now he probably thinks I'm some sort of dark, homicidal weirdo.

"Cool."

Oh. Good. At least he was smiling.

I realized I was fidgeting with my hands again when he reached across the table and laced his fingers through mine. There was that exhilarating moment of brand-new touch. Not the accidental brushing of hands en route to separate destinations, but purposeful, *I want to get closer to you* contact.

Oh, dear God. Yes. This was good.

His thumb stroked the top of my hand. And honestly, until that very moment, I'd never had a simple touch set me on fire. I glanced up at him and our gazes meshed.

"Are you okay?" he asked.

I nodded. Oh, yes, this was more than okay. This indication that he was interested in more than just being neighbors, in more than sitting here and talking business, was what I'd hoped for—and feared—for the past month.

"I know you just ended a relationship and I don't want to push you—"

"You're not pushing me." I glanced at our hands entwined. "Really, that relationship ended a long, long time ago."

He took my hand as we walked home in the silent wee hours of the morning. My mind kept juggling thoughts, trying to sort the delusions from the possibilities. This guy could have his pick of any woman in the club, yet he chose to walk with me.

Once, I thought I wanted a nice safe life with Richard. I'd believed in Richard, trusted him. I was way off base there. What was the point of getting attached when everyone always left? My dad. My mom. Richard. Gone.

Everybody leaves eventually.

A chilly breeze made me shiver.

"Are you cold?"

"Not too bad."

He let go of my hand and slid his arm around my shoulder. And I felt warm and safe and perfectly content for the first time since . . . since I can't remember when.

Finally, we stood facing each other in the hall of our building, his door on the right, mine on the left, smack dab in the middle of a pivotal moment.

He reached up and wrapped one of my curls around his fingers.

Oh, God. I was in trouble.

If I shrank away from him, chose the safe path, it would be an effortless roll down the slippery slope to the bottom of nothing.

But I felt stiff and clumsy. Graceless.

Then as he trailed his finger down my cheekbone, to my jawline, his touch almost unbearably tender, the curl slowly unfurled and fell free.

My breath caught and a shudder of sheer longing ran in waves the length of my body.

Without saying a word, Hunter was calling me, beckoning me from my cave. Come out and "live a little."

The balance of my life hinged on the next moment. I could roll the rock and seal off the cave, hibernate away what was left of the prime of my life.

Or I could come out and live.

Roll the rock?

Rock and roll?

"This could get complicated," I whispered.

You don't know how screwed up my head is.

His finger traced my bottom lip.

"So complicate me," he said. "God knows you're already under my skin."

Ohhhhhhhhh. So much for being able to breathe. Who needed air with words like that? I think I might like it under his skin.

Standing here with this man, was I the same woman who'd once longed for the safe life?

Yep, that would be me; the one who'd lost everything despite the safety net, the one wandering this strange, exhilarating path with no idea how I'd landed here with a burning need to know this man much, much better.

His hand slid up the side of my face and his fingers tangled in my hair.

This was right where I wanted to be.

As much as the comfort of the cave called, Hunter's lips tempted me more. I leaned in and kissed him.

Just a little kiss.

Right on his bottom lip.

I gazed up at him. He smiled and looked at me for a few seconds in that smoldering way he had that cut off all common sense.

Then he pulled me close and kissed me for real.

A slow, hot kiss that possessed me and devoured me and made me want to open up my heart and let him crawl inside.

I buried my face in his neck and breathed a kiss, whispered a silent prayer of thanks—for Hunter O'Reilly Monahan, for his kiss, for him making me feel again.

Hunter O—*O?* Ohmigod!

Monica's voice echoed in my head. *I see the letter "O." Does that mean anything? Lucky girl, you've recently met your soul mate.*

My breath caught in my chest. A sudden feeling of déjà vu

washed over me, and then the sensation that I was falling or about to fall—hard—and I didn't know if it was caused by Monica's prediction or Hunter's hands in my hair and his lips on my lips, on my cheek, trailing kisses from my ear down the oh-so-sensitive spot on my neck.

Kisses that stirred the empty place in my heart into a wild spiral of wanting and longing and needing.

"Let's go inside," I whispered.

Cupping my face between his hands, he stared into my eyes. "I don't know."

What?

What did he mean he didn't know? Ohmigod.

"I mean," he said, "are you sure you're ready for this? You just got out of a serious relationship. I don't want to rush you. We don't have to—"

"What? You don't want to?"

"God, no! I mean yes." He took both my hands in his. "Jeez, yes, I want to. It's just that if we go inside, you *know* what's going to happen—"

I pulled a hand free and pressed my finger to his lips. "I *know* what's going to happen. That's exactly what I *want*."

"Are you sure?"

No, I wasn't sure. All the things I'd ever been sure of in my entire life had disintegrated into thin air. I knew making love to him was dangerous, but I didn't want to think. I wanted to feel. Feel all these wonderful emotions exploding inside me. Feel his hands on my body. Feel bare skin on bare skin. His skin on my skin. More than the innocent brush of hands. The intentional collision of two willing, wanting bodies.

I wanted this guy I barely knew. This guy I felt like I'd known all my life.

I answered him with a kiss.

223

I wanted Hunter to set fire to my bed of darkness.

Ohmigod! What the hell did I do?

I clutched the sheet under my chin and the memory of last night's three-condom reckless abandon forced my eyes wide open.

I stared at my bedroom ceiling for a few seconds before slanting a sideways glance at the pillow beside me.

A mix of instantaneous relief/horror flooded my body as I saw Hunter lying there, one sexy bare arm thrown back over his head, the other on his bare chest. The soft white sheet draped loosely over his hips and long legs.

Relief that he hadn't sneaked out before I woke up. Or was it horror that he hadn't sneaked out?

I licked my index fingers and ran them under my eyes in an attempt to wipe away any raccoonesque mascara smudges and the sleep from my eyes.

Thank God I didn't have any zits.

Ugggh, but this hair. Reached up and finger-combed it as well as I could. If you do too much to curly hair—like actually brush it—you end up with one of those seventies-era Diana Ross long 'fro dos that only look good on Diana. On me it would look more like Grandmama from *The Addams Family*.

I gently turned on my side and watched the rhythmic rise and fall of Hunter's chest.

Took full advantage of the opportunity to watch him as he slept, to study him up close, the way the mid-morning sun streamed in through the windows and played on the peaks and hollows of his cheeks.

His prominent cheekbones.

His long, dark eyelashes.

His strong, proud nose.

He was beautiful.

And an overwhelming sense of panic-laced joy spread though me like wildfire when I remembered the way our bodies had fit together last night.

Perfectly.

A new wave of desire crested, but common sense and the light of day flattened it in an instant.

God, what had I done? Had I screwed up everything?

I should have known better.

From the very first time we'd talked, this, this *thing* between us felt too strong, too important to mess up with sex. But now I'd done it. We'd done it, and there was no turning back.

He would wake up and, all of a sudden, we'd be awkward strangers who had to dodge each other in the hall, time our entrances and exits just right to avoid running into each other, and fake politeness because we were *civil* strangers who knew each other intimately without really knowing each other, without wanting to know each other.

Ugggh.

I eased back onto my pillow and stared at the ceiling.

What the hell was I thinking?

Me, the self-righteous one, who'd gotten all over Karen for sleeping with Giani on the first date. I'd managed to go one worse. I'd slept with Hunter before we'd even had a real date.

Oh, God, I just violated dating rule number four: Never sleep with a guy *before* the first date.

I had to pee and I had to make sure my mascara wasn't smudged all over my face. Ugggggh, and my breath was terrible.

I glanced at the clock. Nine-thirty. Juan was already at work. That was a relief. One less uncomfortable situation to face.

Hey, Juan, Hunter spent the night.

I glanced around the room for something to put on. A shirt, a blanket—I didn't have blankets lying around, and my clothes were strewn all over the floor.

Last night, things just kind of dropped where they fell. He'd all but torn my clothes off my body and flung them aside—thank God I'd worn my new black bra and matching panties, and no, I didn't plan it. It just . . . happened. For once I got something right and my prize was the way he'd worshipped every part of my body. Telling me over and over how beautiful I was.

With him, I felt beautiful.

And free.

Alive.

Damn this light. Why was it so bright in here?

My robe was in the bathroom, and I couldn't wrap the sheet around me because it was around Hunter.

I'd just have to brave it and walk to the bathroom.

Naked.

Gently, I eased myself up and set my feet on the Oriental rug. Holding my breath, hoping not to wake him, I stood and walked to the bathroom, purposely making myself walk slowly. With dignified purpose. In case my naked butt was the first thing he caught sight of when he opened his eyes. Scary. No, don't think scary. Think sexy.

Walk slow and sexy.

I eased open the bathroom door, taking extra care since it squeaked. Stepped inside. And shut it. Carefully.

Made it!

Hey, were these industrial-strength curls Juan set last night? I flipped on the light to get a better look in the mirror. They'd survived the night and, though they weren't salon-perfect, it was kind of fun to have that sexy, morning-after bed head look when it counted.

Oh, yea! Okay, this was *working*.

Five minutes later, I slipped on my white terry robe—Yes, the not-so-sexy one with the lame pocket. Oh, come on, he'd already seen it, and I'd be damned if I was going to walk back across the floor wearing nothing but a satisfied smile.

Uh-uh.

I tightened the belt. The robe didn't quite cover up my vulnerability. Yes, I had to admit it, I felt vulnerable and wide open. But I had to go out there and face Hunter.

I took a deep breath, opened the door.

It squeaked a little.

Hunter opened his eyes and my heart stopped.

This was it.

Nice to know you.

It was fun, and I wish we could do it again sometime, but I'm not cut out for casual sex.

"Hey," he murmured.

I stopped walking, but my heart started beating again.

"Hey, yourself."

He smiled and propped himself up on his elbow. "Want to go back to Captain Mick's for breakfast?"

We spent every spare moment together. He called me at work. And when we were both home, I cooked for him and shared parts of myself I'd never shared with anyone. My body, my writing. The corny little kitchen mystery, which he'd dubbed *Someone's in the Kitchen with Die-na*, intrigued him, and he said he wanted to read it. Ohmigod, that was worse than standing up in front of him naked. Then again, being naked and vulnerable with Hunter was almost second nature these days.

Writing was another thing we had in common. He wrote songs and was constantly working on new material for the band.

"I don't know about you," he said one Sunday afternoon as we were lying in bed, "but as a writer I just don't feel whole unless I'm writing, you know, putting my thoughts down on paper."

I kind of knew what he was saying. Although I felt like a fraud because it had been months since I'd actually worked on my book.

In fact, if you want to know how much of a goner I was, I promised him I'd write at least a page a day. Gulp. Ahhhh, and then he started after me about reading what I'd done so far.

"In good time," I said. "I need to reread it and see where I left off."

To pacify him, I shared my poetry. No one had ever read my bad poetry—which Hunter said wasn't so bad. I was so happy, I almost believed him.

"This one's really good," he said, flipping through an ancient spiral notebook. "It's like lyrics to a song."

I wanted to grab the book away from him. Please don't let him be poking fun at me.

"It is not." I tried to take the book away from him.

Why had I shown it to him?

"I'm serious," he said. "You don't believe me. I'll bet I can set it to music."

He didn't seem like he was making a joke. In fact, he seemed serious. It was the craziest, most ridiculous suggestion anyone had ever made. Even so, I let him copy it and take it with him, and I also promised to send out another round of partial manuscripts.

All because I was deliriously happy.

I hadn't felt this free since . . . since . . . Okay, I'd never felt this free.

I had to send Monica a present.

Flowers? No, might inspire an allergy attack.

A new crystal ball?

The girl deserved something for hooking me up with my soul mate. I know she didn't actually do the *hooking up,* she just had the opportunity to inform me, but somehow I felt beholden to her. You know, kind of a reverse don't shoot the messenger. More like a bestow gifts and undying gratitude on the courier.

I even walked Hunter past the old storefront where my mother and I wanted to open the bakery, before she got so sick and all my dreams started to crumble.

"If this is so important to you," he said, "you should do it."

Easier said than done. But maybe . . . just maybe.

And as the days we spent together stretched into weeks, I almost believed I could fly.

When you're flying high, it's always nice to have someone pick you up when you fall.

I was at my desk when Donna, the receptionist, buzzed that I had a visitor.

"Liv, a deputy from the sheriff's office is here to see you."

Huh?

Why?

Maybe they'd read my series of articles on up-and-coming Central Florida bands and wanted an eyewitness to underage drinking in the nightlife underworld, I contemplated, as I made my way to the lobby.

"Ms. Logan, I'm Sheri Brighton, Orange County Sheriff's

Office. Is there somewhere we can talk?"

The small blonde woman looked so serious, standing there in her gray-brown uniform, with that leather gun belt that was almost as big as she was, my mouth went dry.

"Sure. Follow me."

I led her to the conference room, the same place Giani and I had retreated that fateful day of the four dozen roses almost two months ago.

An uneasy ice-cold feeling of dread flash froze my insides.

This did not bode well.

At least she hadn't slapped on the cuffs.

But what for? I hadn't done anything.

Ohmigod, what if this was one of those cases of mistaken identity? Some kind of trumped-up charges?

A theory that proved I'd been watching way too much bad reality TV before Hunter pulled me from the ruins.

Hunter?

Oh, no, please, no. Not Hunter.

As I walked into the conference room and shut the door behind Deputy Brighton, my legs turned to jelly. Please, God, not Hunter. I forced myself to swallow the hysteria that was clawing at the back of my throat.

"Ms. Logan, do you know Richard Tanner?"

Rich?

I nodded.

Ugggggh, now what? If The Dick tried to cause problems after what he put me through—Deputy Brighton was a woman. She'd take my side.

The officer pulled out two chairs and sat in one. "Why don't we sit down?"

I didn't want to sit. I wanted to punch Rich, hurt him like he deserved to be hurt. Like he'd hurt me.

Why didn't he just go away?

He had his new life.

I had mine.

Oh, *oh*—if this is about the *When Hell Freezes Over* CD. It was mine. I'd buy him another copy, but the Don Henley–autographed liner notes were *mine*. It was my press pass that scored the—

"I'm sorry to deliver bad news, but Richard Tanner is dead."

Dead?

No! Okay, he can have the CD. Don't do this.

"Oh, my God." My knees gave way, and I dropped down onto the chair. I felt a hairline fracture zip through the new foundation on which I'd started building my life. Then my body went completely numb and everything except the deputy's words turned fuzzy around the edges.

"Why? What—What happened?" I managed to squeak.

"Car crash. On Highway Four-thirty-six."

In France? They had a Highway 436 in France? That pulled things into focus.

I shook my head.

"Wait a minute, maybe we're not talking about the same Richard Tanner. Rich is in France. He just got married about two months ago."

The deputy flipped open her notepad. "Tanner, Richard. Forty-one years old. Born July 21, 1962. Address five-twenty-one Washington Street. Social Security 428-03-2398. Emergency contact Olivia Logan. He was most definitely in Orlando."

She looked up at me.

My hand flew to my mouth.

"Ohmigod. Ohmigod."

Richard was *dead*.

I started shaking. Tears broke free and streamed down my cheeks.

And in Orlando?

What was he doing in Orlando?

"You mentioned he recently married?" The deputy's voice was soft, and it bounced off my ears as I stared at the floor, at the tiny point where four floor tiles met. As long as I concentrated on that spot it felt like I could keep it all together, not fall completely apart. If I focused—

"I don't have a record of a wife. Do you know her name and where we can reach her?"

The French Tart? Oh, God, I shouldn't call her that. "No, I don't know her name. Wasn't she with him?"

"No, he was alone."

I pressed my hands over my wet eyes and tried to stop the tears.

"I don't know who he married. I don't know when or where the ceremony was—" My words gave way to a shuddered sob and my hands fell to my lap.

I wasn't invited.

"In France. He got married in France. That's all I know. The last time we spoke was January."

Deputy Brighton scratched her head. "We got your name from a card in his wallet. He had you listed as his next of kin."

Pain squeezed my heart into a tight little ball.

What?

Why?

"No. We're not related. We had a relationship . . . once . . . but like I said he's married to someone else now."

"Any other family in town?"

I shook my head. "He's got family somewhere in Arizona, but they're estranged. I couldn't tell you who or where. He never talked about them."

My stomach clenched and heaved.

She handed me a card. "Please call me if you have any more information. I—I'm sorry, Ms. Logan."

I watched her feet as she walked to the door, out the door, closed the door.

And I was alone with the echo of my sobs.

My nose was running, and I looked around the sterile room for a tissue or a napkin, but saw nothing except cold, hard chrome, glass and tile.

Oh, dear God. Richard was *dead.*

If I looked at it rationally and compared his marrying another woman to his dying, I should have found it in my heart to forgive him.

But I hated him.

I shouldn't hate him.

And I don't know which hurt worse, that he'd chosen someone else or that he was—*gone.* Really gone.

I picked up the phone and dialed Zoe's extension.

Ring.

How could I hate a dead man? Didn't it violate one of life's natural laws?

Ring.

Wasn't there a commandment about that?

Thou shalt not call a dead man a dick, even if he did royally screw you over?

Ring.

Dammit.

Even now he was robbing me of my right to feel.

Ring.

Damn him.

Dammit, come on, Zo, pick up. Be at your desk. Don't make me walk out there in front of everyone.

Sobs racked my body.

Ring.

"Zoe Wood."

"Hey, it's Liv. I'm in the conference room. Can you bring me my purse?"

"Yeah, sure. Why? What's going on? Are you okay?"

"It's Rich—"

"Ugggh, The Dick strikes again. What's he up to now?"

I cringed at her words.

"Zo, don't call him that. He—" My voice broke. "He's dead."

Dead.

Gone.

Final.

And it was just like him.

So typical.

I should have known somehow he'd manage to have the last word and leave me behind defending him.

Chapter Thirteen

There's nothing like a bunch of wild Irish rogues celebrating St. Patty's Day to take your mind off your grief.

With all the singing and beer, and merriment and beer, and just all round good beer, who could remain immune to the levity?

Just the medicine I needed.

Hunter had been wonderful over the past five days, propping me up as I slid back and forth between despair and indignant anger at Richard.

Hunter was a calm, safe harbor.

And I hid.

If the tables were turned and Hunter were grieving the loss of *his* dead ex, would I have been so understanding?

I mean, think about it. It's human nature to glorify the dead. When someone dies, most of the bad times somehow melt away, burned off by the sunshine of glorification.

Though Rich deserved little glory, there was our history— I'd loved him and lived with him. We'd shared a life. Those memories conjured an emotional haunting that loomed, like a dark cloud, an unwelcome revenant, no matter how I tried to exorcise it.

What made the ordeal even harder was that I'd told Hunter my relationship with Richard was over, but I'd never actually confessed there was never an engagement. Maybe that was the creepy shadow I kept glimpsing out of the corner of my eye.

I should tell Hunter the truth.

Shouldn't I?

But I didn't know how. Instead, I clung to him, wishing the rest of the world would just go away.

That's why after five days of living with Richard's ghost, Hunter and I drove up to his uncle's Ocala ranch for the annual Monahan St. Patrick's Day shindig.

I was in no space to party, but it was better than the alternative of staying home with myself.

An intimate gathering, the Monahan family, all forty-seven of them, gathered under a huge white tent set in the middle of acres and acres of lawn—to enjoy corned beef and cabbage, to laugh and toast, to enjoy the serenade of a live band playing traditional Irish music.

St. Patty's Day had always been a bittersweet day, because it was my dad's birthday. I couldn't help but think about him and wonder if he was celebrating, who he was celebrating with. But enough of that. I had more important things to think about, like meeting all forty-seven members of the Monahan family.

Seemed Hunter wasn't the only musician in the family. The five-piece band was made up of cousins and uncles. Did talent flow like blood through the Monahan veins?

If not talent, then exuberance. They were an ebullient, animated bunch. I could tell just by observing. As Hunter introduced me to each one of his relatives, I soon realized they were easy to know and even easier to fall in love with.

I just couldn't help myself.

This was where Hunter got his spirit.

"You've got yourself a fine lass there, Hunter," said Quinn Monahan, Hunter's dad, as he clasped my hand in his. "Pretty, too."

What? No big girl snipes or commentary about my sturdy, suitable-for-childbearing physique?

Had all that beer blurred their vision?

Hunter slid his arm around my shoulder and slanted me a glance. "I think so."

A girl could get used to comments like that.

"You need a drink." Quinn winked at me. "What's your pleasure?"

My pleasure? Oh, if you only knew.

I felt myself blush and that seemed to make Quinn's smile grow even bigger. Hunter had his father's eyes and shades of the same half-smile.

Quinn chuckled. "Sweet."

As he walked away, a large man with silver hair danced by us, twirling a tall, slender woman to a song I actually recognized, "The Irish Rover."

Others clapped and cheered and hooted.

"That's Uncle Paddy," said Hunter. "He's the shy brother."

"A shy Monahan? Imagine that. How many brothers?"

"Five. Quinn, Paddy, Orin, Craig and Angus."

All these people from the loins of five brothers? Productive buggers. No, more like *reproductive,* 'cause there'd been a whole lot of baby-makin' going to get a family this size. By the time the current generation of Monahans had kids, exponentially they'd have people enough to populate their own small town. Monahan, U.S.A.

But Hunter had lost his mother.

I looked at the family gathered together, some eating, small children running about playing.

No dark cloud of loss looming overhead.

More like a celebration of life.

That's the way it should be, not mourning, celebrating.

If I had a drink, I'd toast to life—Hunter's gaze snagged mine—and virile Irish men.

Oh, yes, I'd definitely raise a glass to virile Irish men. A delicacy.

Hunter smiled as if he could read my thoughts and for a moment everything seemed like it would be okay.

"Hunter, good to see you." Paddy clapped Hunter on the back. His gaze landed on me and he smiled. "Mind if I cut in, my boy?"

Oh, no—

Uncle Paddy grabbed my hand, and before I could protest or Hunter could even respond, starting waltzing me around the tent.

How in the world was I supposed to dance to this fiddle music?

No problem.

Uncle Paddy steered me around the floor, twirling me and pushing me along in a Celtic sort of hoedown romp. All I had to do was hang on for dear life and stay out of my own way. At the end of the song, we stopped, breathless.

"Thank you very much." Then he actually bowed. "It is my pleasure to dance with each Monahan lass."

Monahan lass?

Me?

Whoa, Uncle Paddy. Slow down there, boy.

Don't you think you're getting a little ahead of yourself?

Ahead of Hunter and me?

But as I stood there dumbfounded, Uncle Paddy was off to the next Monahan lass, letting it all hang out and making no apologies.

As I surveyed the Monahans, I sensed the same uncomplicated, go-with-the-flow feeling that had defined Hunter's and my relationship since what felt like the beginning of time—had we really only known each other two months?

With the Monahans, what you saw was what you got. The

loving warmth that generated among them warmed me too, and sparked a vague feeling of envy.

What would happen if I tried to find my father?

The possibility terrified me.

Too many "what if's." Too many questions that I couldn't deal with right then.

I spied Hunter across the tent holding two beers, talking to a woman who had Destiny's same rich, curly auburn hair—Destiny was the only family member absent from the party. She was in New York packing and preparing to move to Orlando. Next to the auburn-haired woman, a little girl stood clinging to her leg with her right arm and holding a green helium balloon in her left hand. The child looked like a miniature version of the woman she clung to.

Ahhh, the *Monahan lass* must come in only one design, I thought, as Hunter waved me over.

The tall, thin, auburn-haired-beauty design.

"Liv, this is my sister, Shannon, and my niece, Kelly."

"Hi, Liv, nice to meet you. Hunter tells me you're a writer."

I am?

"I'm a reporter, I write for the *Orlando Daily.*"

"Oh, how interesting," she said. "What do you report?"

"I used to write the restaurant reviews, now I'm covering mostly arts and entertainment."

"She wrote a great story about Altered Ego, but don't let the modest act fool you. She's a poet and an aspiring novelist."

Not so, my heart whispered, and I didn't know what to say. That thanks to her brother issuing a post lovemaking challenge, I'd been writing pretty regularly. Hey, I was vulnerable when I'd risen to the challenge. Can you say putty in his very strong, very capable hands? Well, I had been writing regularly until Rich's accident, which pretty much threw me off course.

A cry erupted from a little boy who tripped as he ran across the grass and lost hold of his balloon. Lying on his stomach, the child wailed and pointed skyward as he watched it drift out of his grasp.

I saw Kelly tighten her grip on her balloon. "Uncle Hunter, will you tie mine on my wrist so I don't lose it?"

Hunter nodded and Kelly held out her little arm.

"Come play the next set with us, Hunter," said a middle-aged guy with dark hair, who'd been playing the fiddle in the band. "Kevin wants to take a break and we need someone to sit in on acoustic."

Hunter nodded. "Be right there."

In so many ways Hunter was like that balloon.

I'd gently held him, and the only thing that tethered him to me was the thin thread we'd woven over the last few weeks.

Would he slip away someday and drift until I couldn't reach him?

I watched his fingers tie the string in a slipknot to secure his niece's treasure.

"There you go, kiddo. Safe and sound."

If only.

Sometimes the knot held, other times it came undone, and all you could do was stand there and watch everything that mattered slip away.

At the office the next day, Deputy Brighton called to say they'd located Rich's father. "The family wants the body cremated and the ashes sent to Arizona."

Just like that. It seemed so impersonal.

No funeral in Orlando.

Well, good.

Fine.

I wouldn't have to arrange the service.

But I didn't know if that made things better or worse.

I mean, come on, it would have been up to me to arrange the funeral, the final good-bye. Unless The French Tart came crawling out of the cheese, who else was going to do it?

Richard had no other friends.

No business associates since he was the sole proprietor and lone employee of his software company.

I tapped my finger on the telephone receiver I'd just re-placed in the cradle.

Okay, that was . . . just . . . weird.

Why was it suddenly striking me how odd it was that Rich had no friends?

He was always traveling between Orlando and France, too busy to cultivate relationships. Other than ours. And he didn't even do a very good job with that one.

I'd never really thought about it.

Until now.

I stared at my blank computer screen. I was supposed to be writing the final story in the "bands on the verge of the big time" series, but I couldn't concentrate.

If I'd organized a funeral or some sort of memorial, I would've been the only one to attend.

The thought ricocheted around the dark pit inside me where I mourned Richard.

How sad to stand so alone in death.

Tears threatened, and I blinked them away.

Well, Karen would have come. So that would have been Karen and me. Maybe Hunter. Naaah. That would be asking too much of him to attend my dead ex's service.

Well, I hadn't talked to Karen since Giani dragged her out of our girls' night a month ago at the Blue Note. She'd called, left messages, apologizing for leaving, but I hadn't called her back. I'd been . . . busy. I guess I couldn't ask her to come, either. So that left just me.

My heart softened. I'd definitely give her a call. Life was too short for grudges.

I squeezed my eyes shut for a minute.

Really, Rich and I said good-bye a long time ago.

Long before he left for Paris.

I needed to get it together and get some work done.

Hushed rumors of more layoffs had heated up the office this morning. Apparently, a conglomerate was talking to paper owner McPherson about buying the *Daily*.

What would Chris VanHussen do if his father-in-law sold his future right out from under him? He'd probably just keep playing golf. Good thing, because anyone who knew business and wasn't related to Chris wouldn't hand him the wheel.

Nobody's job was safe, least of all the food critic, turned ballet critic, turned general arts and entertainment writer.

Hey, if I could write about beans, ballet and bands, I could certainly tackle basketball, ballots or business.

Don't fire me.

I'm flexible.

Moldable.

Mutable.

Miserable.

Stop that.

Think positive.

Think Hunter.

Think . . . Think about finishing your story or you will be out of a job. Then what? Hot sex with Hunter won't pay the bills.

I tried to ignore the dull, heavy ache that had weighed me down for the past week, since the Rich-bomb had exploded.

Dammit, I was sick of this uncertainty. I was sick to death of living in a perpetual state of flux. I needed normal. Safe and sure and normal. Refuge from the damn land mines of life that kept blowing up in my face.

Dear God, that was the story of my life.

I rested my face in my hands.

My life was a succession of bombs that detonated every time I thought I had my shit together.

Were there more bombs buried along the way? Or had I safely reached the other side of the minefield?

Maybe Richard's accident was the grand finale. All the crap had been blown to smithereens and the rest of my life was set for a smooth course.

I raised my head and typed the lead sentence of my article.

A safe, sure, normal course with Hunter and me at the helm of our lives. Making babies to populate Monahan, U.S.A.

I backspaced over the sentence I'd written and stared at the blank white screen.

Monahan, U.S.A., did not exist. And when you're talking about emotions and affairs of the heart, no relationship was safe or sure.

And what the hell was normal? Certainly not my life.

I tapped an anxious rhythm on the space bar.

But Hunter, surrounded by his big family, seemed so strong, so sure, as he transitioned from Disney banjo player by day to rock and roll god by night, then into the sexy philosopher who came willingly to my big bed of fire and shadows until the dawn.

The thought took my breath away.

I could get used to it.

Want him.

Need him.

Care for him . . . too much.

I could hear the insidious tick of the next bomb waiting to explode.

How much longer before it blew?

And here was Hunter. He'd suffered loss, but the Monahans rallied around each other.

Strength in numbers?

The luck of the Irish?

Sheer dogged determination?

I had to step carefully, lest I step on the next land mine waiting to blow.

If I were smart, I'd step back. Carefully retrace my steps away from him and go back the way I came in.

My intercom buzzed.

I jumped.

"Yes, Donna?"

"You have a visitor."

My stomach tightened. What now?

"Who is it?"

There was a pause before Donna's flat voice said, "Geneviève Dumond."

Who? I gritted my teeth. "From?"

"Look, Olivia, I don't have time to interview your visitors. Do you want to come out here or should I send her back?"

Oh, for God's sake. Irritation ripped through me like a shrill scream. Donna was worthless.

I pushed away from my desk without even responding to her.

In the lobby, I saw a very pretty, very pregnant, dark-haired woman waiting.

Uh-oh. Now what? My heartbeat picked up.

I tried to take a deep breath, and reminded myself I was probably just suffering shell shock from Deputy Brighton's bad news visit last week.

"Hello, may I help you?"

The woman gave me a cold, hard once-over. "Olivia Logan?"

A French accent pinched her clipped words.

I nodded.

Wait a minute. Oh, no.

"I am Geneviève Dumond. I am looking for your husband, Ree-shard."

"Excuse me? My *husband?*"

Okay, if my life was a minefield, maybe I hadn't survived the last blast and I was in some sort of strange purgatory. Or this was all simply a bad case of indigestion causing bizarre nightmares. I'd wake up any minute now and find out the past two months had, in fact, been merely one long, vivid bad dream.

"Yes." She glared at me and patted her pregnant belly. "I have something that belongs to him."

Huh? *My* husband? Whoa—

Oh, for Pete's sake, was this someone's idea of a sick joke? I darted a glance around the lobby. Only Donna, standing slack-jawed, taking it all in.

I looked at Geneviève's bulging belly.

Dead or alive, he was not *my* husband.

"I was not married to Ree-shard. He dumped me to marry some French Tar—"

French Tart? Ohmigod. Oh, shit.

My mouth went dry.

Oh, dear God, this wasn't happening.

Was this *The* French Tart? Standing in front of me, swollen stomach—

"No, no, no!" The French woman threw her hands in the air, then thrust a finger at me. "He told me he was married to *you.*"

What was going on here?

"Is Richard the dead guy?" Donna asked. "I can't keep them straight."

Geneviève's face went white. "*Mort? Qui est mort?* What does she mean? Where is my Ree-shard?"

Idiot! I shot Donna a look of death.

"Where is he?" Geneviève shouted. She took hold of my arm and shook it, tears welling and flowing. "Tell me! What have you done to him?"

Three reporters from the newsroom stood in the hall watching like it was a scene from some bent daytime talk show.

"Geneviève, it's okay." I used the most soothing voice I could conjure, and pulled out of her grasp and took hold of her hands. She gripped me back with the force of a vise. "I haven't done anything to Richard."

Her grip relaxed.

"He is fine?"

Oh, God, no, he was not fine. This was so wrong. He was dead, and if I told her here, now, she would have French screaming meemies right here in the paper's lobby.

Think.

Think fast.

Take her outside?

No. Won't work.

"He is fine?" she repeated, her voice shaking and rising three decibels on the last word. "Tell me, where is my Ree-shard?" Five decibels. And she was gripping me again.

The conference room.

Ugggh, I was beginning to hate that place.

"Let's go somewhere we can talk. *Privately.*" I gave our audience a collective dirty look that didn't seem to faze them, and all but dragged Geneviève down the hall into the conference room.

"Ree-shard? What is wrong with my Ree-shard?"

Safely inside, I shut the door and offered her a chair, but she shook her head.

"What have you done to him?"

I felt the walls closing in on me and I realized I'd been holding my breath.

I didn't want to do this.

Why did I have to do this?

"Tell me!" she screamed and started hitting me, pounding on me with her fists.

"Richard died in a car accident last week."

She stopped beating me and sucked in a breath, her mouth formed an "O," her eyes glazing over as if she were frozen.

"Geneviève, I'm sorry." I didn't know how to comfort her. So I just stood there saying, "I'm sorry. I'm so sorry."

Her face contorted and she doubled over.

"Oh! *Mon Dieu.* Please help me."

Still folded in half, one arm across her middle and the other reaching toward me, she gasped for air. "*Mon bébé.* My baby. Something is wrong."

How do you tell someone you care for that you lied to them?

I pondered the situation in the kitchen as I deboned chicken breasts for Chicken Pomodoro.

My telling Hunter I was engaged to The Dick—oops, I

promised not to call him that since he was dead, but—

Dick!

Dick!

Dick!

I stabbed at the chicken with each cathartic word.

As I was saying, my lie to Hunter wasn't an earth-shattering, I'll-never-trust-you-again-as-long-as-I-live kind of lie, but nonetheless the untruth lived in the walls of my subconscious, haunting me like Edgar Allen Poe's "The Tell Tale Heart."

I felt very hypocritical standing there hating The Dick more and more with each thump-thump of the telltale lie, for the crock of crap he'd fed Geneviève and me. And his lies were the I'm-justified-to-hate-you-as-long-as-I-live kind, a cowardly duplicity that defied reason.

Not only had The Dick lied to me about getting married to get out of our relationship, he'd used me as a convenient excuse to avoid marrying his *pregnant* girlfriend.

Geneviève said when she pressed Ree-shard to marry her and be a father to his child, he'd told her he was already married. His wife's name was *Olivia*.

Liar!

Little did she know, he'd told me the same lie with a French twist.

Lying, scumbag Dick.

Stab.

Stab.

Geneviève was in the hospital.

She'd lost the baby.

It was impossible not to blame myself for the way I'd blurted out the news about Richard's accident, but the doctor told us the miscarriage was probably due to a congenital condition rather than the shock of the news.

I couldn't imagine what she was going through, finding out the man she loved was a deceitful bastard, a *dead,* deceitful bastard, and losing her child, too.

All alone.

When I was in school I learned about Saint Geneviève, the virgin patroness of Paris, who defended the city against the depredations of thugs like Attila the Hun. Kind of symbolic, don't you think, the way she flew to the States to persecute Richard for the cad he was?

The doctor had sedated her so she could rest, and I figured I'd be doing us both a favor by coming back tomorrow.

I'd have to finish my story tonight—the story of which I hadn't even written word one today—so I could get it to Rivers before deadline. Before he fired me.

I laughed out loud.

Wouldn't that just be too ironic? To get fired on top of everything else.

Not funny.

I set the chicken on a plate and washed my hands.

But before I wrote anything, I needed to figure out how I was going to explain this three-ring circus to Hunter without lying anymore.

Something was going to give.

Telling him I didn't go to Paris and thus didn't get engaged wasn't that big of a deal, really. I'd just tell him.

That was the hard part.

Knock. Knock. Knock.

I dried my hands and answered the door.

Before I knew it, Hunter had enfolded me in a huge bear hug.

Oh, God, I needed that.

His lips found mine and he kissed me with a slow burning passion that melted me from the inside out.

The heady sensation of his lips sent warm shivers through me, deliquescing the icy, dark apprehension that had rendered me frozen most of the day.

He moved one hand down to cup my bottom and pulled me into him, and his firm *persuasiveness* was enough to make me want to forget dinner, forget the twisted tale of the day, and take him straight to my big gypsy bed for some hot, monkey sex, but—ugggh—I had to write that damn story and I had to tell Hunter the truth. Tonight.

I reveled in his strong embrace for a minute longer, until he said, "I told you you were my lucky star."

Did I mention that I was really, really crazy about this guy? I mean, who else could absolutely make the world disappear with just a kiss and—

He stepped back enough to slide a bottle of something in between us. He'd grabbed me so quickly, I hadn't even realized he was holding it.

"What's this?"

"Champagne, for my muse, for my lucky charm."

He stood there looking at me with this huge smile, like he was about to burst.

"What?"

"They called. Vista's invited Altered Ego to come out to L.A. for a showcase."

"A showcase?" As in *The Price Is Right*?

"It's where they fly us in, meet us, hear us play and decide if we're marketable enough for them to sign us to a deal."

He grabbed me in his arms again.

"Ohmigod! Oh, wow! That's fabulous." I kind of huffed out the words because he was squeezing me so tight.

After a few seconds, I stepped back into the hall and pulled him inside with me. "I'll get some glasses, let's have a toast."

Hunter went into the living room. As I reached for the

glasses, I heard the cork pop. Okay, how was this going to work? I wasn't going to be a turd in the punch bowl and ruin Hunter's celebration with true confessions of a loser's lie.

I sighed. Wow, a contract. He'd be making records. Living his dreams. Envy tugged at my heart and I wanted to slap myself silly for feeling that way.

Hunter and the band had worked hard to get to this point. He deserved this. This was about him. Not about me.

So maybe I didn't have to tell him about Geneviève—

Thump-thump.

Liar.

Thump-thump.

Well, at least not right now. When the time was right. I carried the glasses into the living room and filled them with champagne. I handed one to Hunter and sat down next to him on the couch.

He touched his glass to mine.

"To rock and roll and record deals," I said, my voice sounding very thin.

That sexy half-smile lifted the corners of his full lips and he got the most devastating look in his eyes.

A rush of emotion swirled all the way down into the pit of my stomach. Oh. My God. What was happening to me?

To us?

"I thought I was starting to care about you a little." He ran his finger over my jawline. "But then I realized no, Liv, a lot." His lips brushed mine as he spoke. "I care for you, a lot. I love—"

I pressed my lips to his as hard as I could. Don't say it. Please don't say it, because devastation always followed the "L" word. I felt dizzy and I hadn't even had a drop of champagne.

When Hunter pulled back, he had a strange look on his

face. And I was afraid he could see right through me. I smiled and lightly clinked my glass against his and sipped the bubbly.

He cleared his throat. "I have to leave tomorrow."

"That fast?"

He nodded. "Vista's president is leaving for Europe next week, and they want to slide us in before he goes. Has to be tomorrow or wait until the end of April. Gotta strike while it's hot."

It was really fast. Everything was happening so fast.

"It's only four days," he said. "It'll be over before you know it."

That's exactly what I was afraid of.

It was gloomy and rainy when I took Hunter to the airport the next morning for his nine o'clock flight to Los Angeles. How weird to watch him walk away, even weirder to know I wouldn't see him for a few days.

Wow, the first time we'd been apart in a month. I supposed it would be good for us to have a little breathing room. After the week's turn of events I was exhausted. I needed some space to process everything.

I'd been up since four o'clock working on the final article in my band series. I e-mailed it off just before we left for the airport. Then I sent Rivers a note about taking the day off. Probably not wise, given the layoff rumors, but what difference would it make if I was in the office establishing squatter's rights for my cubicle? One day off would not change the course of events at the paper.

The rain beat a gentle cadence on the roof of my car as I pulled away from the airport.

At the first stoplight on Semoran Boulevard I grabbed my cell phone and dialed Karen at the boutique.

I'd punished her enough, especially since I was sharing in that punishment. I was starting to have Karen withdrawal. I took a deep breath and prepared myself for the possibility of a luke-warm reception since I'd waited a month to return her calls. She might not want to talk to me.

The line rang twice.

"You're Putting Me On Again, this is Karen."

Hearing her voice was like coming home to an old friend—okay, I was coming home to an old friend. An old friend who just might hang up on me.

"Hey, Karen."

"Liv? Oh, my God, Liv, is that you?"

I let out the breath I'd been holding when I was bracing for the crash of a receiver in my ear.

"Hey, yeah, it's me, ohmigod, I've missed you."

We talked for twenty minutes and barely scratched the surface.

"So Monica was right about the soul mate," she said.

"I don't know about that. I mean things are great, but nothing's . . . guaranteed. You know how it is."

I stopped at a red light and tugged at my seat belt, which suddenly seemed confining.

"Oh, come on, sounds like she hit this one right on the head. See, if not for me leaving, his ship might have merely sailed right past your harbor rather than pulling in." Evil laugh. "So actually, you owe me for leaving you all alone with the God of rock and roll."

"Owe you? I owe you a kick in the ass."

We laughed.

I told her Rich was dead; about Geneviève—that I was headed to see her as we spoke; about Hunter's L.A. gig; and that I was thinking about finding my father, but I didn't know where to start.

It would take at least the four days that Hunter was gone for us to catch up. But this was so good. Oh, how I'd missed my buddy.

"So, will Giani give you leave over the next couple of nights so we can get together?"

Karen was silent for a minute.

Oh, okay, so maybe not. That was fine.

"How about tonight?" she said.

Shocked the hell out of me.

"Really? I mean, great. Fantastic. How about if I make us some dinner?"

"I'd love that. God, I've missed you."

Karen and I hung up as I pulled into the hospital parking lot.

I know I probably should have just left well enough alone, but I had to go and see Geneviève, find out how she was doing. How frightening to be all alone like this in a strange country. She'd suffered so much, so close together.

Even though I'd desperately wanted to hate *The French Tart,* I couldn't hate Geneviève.

In her, I saw a reflection of myself—a woman desperately trying to make sense out of a web of lies, a travesty with no rhyme or reason.

I hesitated in her hospital room doorway, clutching a bouquet of daisies.

Dressed in a hospital gown, partially hidden by the sheet, she was lying on the bed with her eyes closed. Her face, framed by her dark hair, looked drawn and pale.

What am I doing here?

Did I come here for her or for myself, looking for answers?

My presence would just be a reminder of all she'd lost and would probably upset her.

I'd just made up my mind to give the flowers to a nurse and had started to turn away when she opened her eyes.

"*Bonjour*, Liv. *Entrez.*"

"I didn't mean to disturb you."

She rubbed her eyes and straightened her hair.

"Please." She gestured to the chair across from her bed, and I walked in.

The paper around the flowers crinkled as I clutched it. "I brought these for you."

She reached for the flowers. "Oh! *Des marguerites. Elles sont belles.*" And sniffed them. "So bright and cheery. *Merci.*"

"How are you feeling? Are you all right?"

She nodded. "They will release me today, as soon as the doctor comes in to see me. Then I will call and see if I can change my flight to leave today."

An awkward silence stretched between us.

"If I can help—"

She shrugged.

"I am fine. I will be fine."

The curtains were open and rain beaded on the glass outside, making patterns that changed every time a drop broke free and rolled. Like jewels in a monotone kaleidoscope against the gray sky.

Or tears.

Yes, more like tears.

I glanced back at Geneviève and found her studying me, and she didn't look away.

Something in her expression said that she had just as many questions as I did. Before I could think better of it, I asked, "How did you find me?"

This time she was the one who looked out the window, staring silently for almost a minute.

"Before Ree-shard told me he was married . . . to you, I

looked through his address book and saw an entry that said 'Liv's work number.' I had no idea who this Liv was. So I copied down the number. And I called."

Now it made sense. "You would call and hang up?"

She shrugged and looked a little embarrassed.

"A woman with a name like Liv scared me. The name Liv sounded so *alive*."

Alive? Boy, did she have it wrong.

"I wanted to come and see the beautiful woman who had stolen my Ree-shard's heart."

"About two months ago, I was supposed to fly out. Rich and I were going to talk about our future." I felt foolish telling her this. But she wanted to know.

"The night before I was supposed to fly to Paris, he called and told me he'd married you."

She laughed a bitter, humorless laugh.

"He tells you he was married to me. He tells me he was married to you. *Merde alors. Ce pauvre con.*"

I wasn't sure exactly what she said, but I knew it involved a couple of choice French four-letter words.

"When Ree-shard disappeared, I decided to fly to Orlando, to expose his dirty little secret to his wife. But then I find out you are not his wife. And I have no more *bébé*."

She inhaled sharply and buried her face in her hands.

And I sat there without saying a word, without breathing, until she composed herself.

"And how long were you living with him?" she finally asked.

"Three years. And you?"

I sucked in a breath to prepare myself for details I wasn't sure I wanted to hear. But wasn't that one of the main reasons I came here?

"*Sept ans.*" She shook her head. "Seven years."

Seven—? I blinked in utter disbelief as the realization that *I* was the other woman filled me. Rich had been involved with Geneviève for four years when he met me.

The revelation knocked the wind out of me like a kick in the gut.

So it hadn't been our gradual growing apart that had forced him into the arms of another woman. *I* had always been the *other woman.*

Go figure. Me, the mistress.

Geneviève straightened the sheet and smoothed it over her flattened stomach.

You thought you knew someone only to wake up one day to realize you'd been sleeping with a stranger.

Do we ever *really* know anyone?

"Do you have any idea why he was back in Orlando?" Geneviève asked.

I shook my head and told her I hadn't spoken to Richard since the night he called and told me he was married.

"You were with him that night," I said. "I heard your voice in the background."

I told her how I'd locked my house key in the bungalow when I'd moved out. How Deputy Brighton had found Rich's family and sent his ashes to Arizona. How I'd tried so hard not to look back.

She tucked a strand of long, dark hair behind her ear and raised her chin. "I was certain the news of my pregnancy had driven him back to you."

Back to me? I had no idea why he was back in Orlando, but it wasn't because he'd come back to me.

"No, he'd probably ditched us both, then sneaked back into town to make sure I hadn't taken all the good CDs when I'd moved out."

Silently, we each pondered the possibilities.

I shrugged. "Then again, maybe he'd planned to act honorably, quietly gather his belongings and go back to Paris, to you . . . and his child."

This time the tears streamed down Geneviève's face and she shook her head violently. "No, he was not honorable. He was typical. Typical man. Faithful to no one but himself."

Dread grew and wrapped around my heart like a clinging vine as her words rang true. I got up and pulled a tissue from the box.

Men. Were they all alike?

Was Hunter like Richard?

Hunter was *not* Richard.

They were day and night.

One an artist. The other a player.

But all labels aside, they were both men.

"No man in this world can be faithful to a woman," Geneviève murmured. "It is a fact. *C'est un fait.*"

That's not true.

It can't be true.

Rich left.

My father left.

He left my mother.

He left me.

"We'll never know why Rich came back," I said quickly. "Maybe it's better that way."

We'd both been wronged.

Neither of us blamed the other.

But it was clear who Geneviève blamed.

"It's a good thing they do not give Ree-shard's ashes to me. I would flush them."

So much for the saint theory.

Chapter Fourteen

Sharing my life with a man, thinking I wanted to grow old with him, only to wake up to discover the man I thought I knew never existed, was taking its toll. Compounded with the discovery that I had been the other woman over the duration of Rich's and my relationship made me doubt my own judgment.

More than that, it made me angry.

Angry with Rich for playing me.

Angry with myself for being so clueless.

After I took Geneviève to the airport, I just didn't have it in me to cook. I called Karen and suggested we go out.

"Sure, let's try that new Thai place in Winter Park," she said. "I'll meet you there."

As I sat at a table in the corner waiting for Karen, I realized I was hurting from my four a.m. writing gig, and hoped I wouldn't nod off in my pad Thai.

A server walked by with a platter of chicken satay. The savory peanut sauce made my stomach growl.

Note to self—don't make a habit of getting up early. It sucked. But if I could stick it out a little longer, I'd probably shift into that zone where I was sure I could go the rest of my life without sleep.

The essence of curry and that sweet-spicy kind of cuminy-nutmeggy Thai aroma filled the air, and I sat back and savored the feast of scents until Karen walked in. I waved at her, and she did a double take, then floated over to the table, seemingly weightless, like only Karen could do.

"Oh, my God, look at you." She hugged me, then stepped back. "What have you done? You're so skinny."

"I already told you I forgive you. You don't need to suck up." I smiled at her. Ahhh, it was good to see her.

"Have you looked in the mirror? You've dropped like two sizes. How much have you lost?"

She slid into the booth across from me.

"I have no idea. I don't own a scale."

Had I really lost that much? Thanks to the one-size-fits-three-sizes blessing—or curse—of the Chico's Travelers, once again I was clueless. With that much expansion room, you can slide up and down the scale and remain completely oblivious. Well, that's not entirely true, I had felt leaner, lighter, but I hadn't really had time to think about it. You know me and body image. Best not to go there.

"Are you dieting?"

"No, I've just been too busy to eat. One of the consolation prizes of giving up the restaurant reviews."

Karen quirked a brow. "I've always said good sex is the best exercise."

I shrugged.

"Who needs a gym? Speaking of, how is Giani?"

I thought I saw her stiffen, but the server approached to tell us about the specials. We ordered drinks and decided to split an order of spring rolls. As we looked over the menu, I asked again, "So how's Jimbo?"

"He's fine," she said into her open menu.

"Getting plenty of *exercise?*" God, I could only say that to Karen. But she didn't laugh like I thought she would. In fact, she was practically hiding behind her menu.

I hope she didn't think I was going to go off on Giani. Really. I wanted this to be a nice night. An amiable, let's just get along, no hassle kind of night.

I put my finger on the top of her menu and pushed it down so I could see her face.

"I know I haven't been the biggest advocate of Jimbo Giani, but, honey, if he makes you happy, then I'm happy for you."

Karen folded her menu, and uh-oh, she looked miserable.

"What's wrong?" I asked.

"Nothing." Now I could clearly see the fatigue on her face and dark circles under her eyes. "Everything."

The server approached with our green tea and appetizer, took our orders and left. Karen took a spring roll out of the basket and spooned some hot mustard sauce on her plate.

"So spill it," I said. "What's wrong? Last I heard you were ready to settle down and buy into the American dream. I thought you'd have at least two point five kids, an SUV and a golden retriever by now."

Karen tried to smile, but she didn't do a very good job. "I don't know what I want. I love the idea of the family way, but I just don't know if I'm cut out for it."

Or maybe Giani wasn't cut out for her? It wasn't like I'd made that observation early on, but who's keeping score?

Stop it!

No I told you so's. I was big enough to admit I'd realized my vision of "happy" didn't necessarily have to fit hers.

"I don't know, it's been two months. The fireworks are starting to fizzle and his bad habits aren't cute anymore. In fact, they're really annoying." She rested her forehead on her hands for a second, then looked back up. "What's wrong with me? I must be really screwed up. I know nobody's perfect, but I think that's what I want."

I bit my tongue, literally, but the words still escaped. "Some men might be more perfect for you than others." Shut up, Liv, before you really put your foot in it.

261

Karen nodded. "He and I are just too different, I think. There's this side of him—this secretive, shadowy part of him I don't know. And I don't think I want to know it." She shook her head. "All I know is forever's a very long time. What if there are different men who are better for you at different stages in your life? Does that mean you get married and stay until it doesn't work anymore and then move on? And if so, what's the point of marriage?"

"The whole one man, one woman 'til-death-do-us-part quandary?" I said. "Do you realize the last time we pondered this theory was the night before I was supposed to meet Rich in Paris?"

My God, how things had changed.

Silently, we stared at each other.

"Looking at relationships from the side of the fence you're sitting on now," Karen said, "do you still believe in happily ever after? Or should we just grow up and forget the fairy tale? Enter into relationships with our eyes wide open, realize they're going to run their course, and accept it when they're over?"

What a depressing thought.

No man can be faithful. C'est un fait.

My father.

Richard.

"Don't ask me that right now."

Liv, I care for you, a lot.

C'est un fait.

The server brought our dinner, and while I ate my pad Thai, I tried to make the conversation a bit more upbeat.

When the bill came, Karen said, "Oh, I can't believe I almost forgot." She pulled an envelope out of her purse and pushed it across the table.

"What's this?"

"I have a friend, Kyle Baines, who is with the FBI. I called him this morning and asked if he could do a little investigating for us."

The FBI? What in the heck was she talking about?

"Open it."

I unfolded a fax that contained a name, address, telephone number and other personal information like birthday, March seventeenth—My blood went cold and my eyes shot back up to the name, which I hadn't really paid attention to the first time I glanced at it.

Joseph Harrison Logan.

"My father? You found my father?"

"You said you were thinking about getting in touch with him. I figured I'd help you out."

Yeah, but thinking about it was a lot easier when I had no idea where to find him. Where to even start looking. My stomach twisted like someone was wringing the water out of a wet rag. I felt bile rise into my throat. I should have sipped my water, but all I could do was stare at the page in my shaking hand.

"Liv, are you okay?"

He lived in Syracuse. I folded the paper and put it back into the envelope.

"I haven't talked to my father in twenty-five years. How did you get this?"

She wiped the corners of her mouth with her napkin.

"Kyle just entered his name and birthday into the computer and it spit this out. I don't know why, but I can always remember that your dad was born on St. Patrick's Day. Thank goodness, huh? Without that—"

Karen stopped mid-sentence, her mouth open and the color draining from her face as she stared off into the distance over my shoulder.

"What's the matter?" I turned around to see what she was

looking at and saw the hostess seating Jimbo Giani and a tall, pretty blonde.

The next morning at work, as I turned on my computer, Zoe peered around the gray fabric–covered wall that separated our cubicles.

"We're screwed," she said, a pitch lower than her usual *let's dish* tone.

"Not now, Zoe."

I shot her my best *piss off* look, then pretended to be engrossed in my planner. After watching Karen rip Giani and his little friend up one side and down the other before she finally broke up with him in the middle of the restaurant, and then listening to her rant until two o'clock in the morning, I wasn't in the mood. I was tired and grumpy, and Hunter hadn't called me last night.

I had more than I could handle.

Our first night away from each other and he didn't call. He didn't say he would, but he didn't say he wouldn't, either. And after all the shit I'd been through—even though he didn't know the half of it because I hadn't bothered to share—whatever. This just wasn't a good time for radio silence.

I was being irrational.

I knew it.

I was tired and freaked out over Rich and Geneviève and Karen and Giani.

I hated everyone right now: Giani, and especially the L.A. record company that had lured Hunter away with the bright-light promise of dreams and fame and fortune.

So screw rationality.

Screw everybody.

"Liv."

"What?!"

Zoe was standing in my cubicle now. I really thought for the first time in my life I was going to hit someone.

I whirled around. "Would you just get the fuc—"

"Gather up all your things *now*," she whispered. "Everything you want to take with you. Get it together *now*."

"What in the hell are you talking about?" I asked in a normal tone.

"Shhhhhh!"

I slammed my planner shut. "What? What are you yammering about?"

That was mean. I knew I shouldn't take it out on Zoe, even if she was annoying the crap out of me.

She glanced over her shoulder. Then she stepped closer and leaned in.

I tried to scoot away, but my chair back was pressed against the desk. If she cupped her hand and tried to whisper in my ear, I *would* hit her.

Thank God, she didn't.

The way I was acting was so wrong. I used to be such a nice person. Yeah, and that's what got me where I was today.

"Listen," she whispered. "This is serious. Gather up all your files and addresses and stuff you want to take with you and put them in your car before noon. And don't make it obvious. Because at noon we're all getting the ax. McPherson's closing the paper."

I nearly fell out of my chair. "What?"

She nodded.

Holy shit.

It was official. My life had hit rock bottom. Crashed and burned.

The only thing left to do was walk out of here and get hit by a bus.

"Why are you sticking around if you know this?" I asked. "Why not just leave?"

Standing with one skinny arm across her stomach, Zoe chewed on one of the nails on her other hand and shot me a don't-be-an-idiot look. "I want my severance pay."

Wait a minute. "How do you know this?"

I mean, did she have a bug planted in McPherson's office? Or was there a secret drainpipe in the bathroom that was connected to the office of secret shit?

"Natalie Clemmons," Zoe said.

"How does she know?"

Zoe flashed another "idiot" look. Since when did the pipsqueak develop an attitude?

"VanHussen told her. He told her everything the old man upstairs was planning to do, including closing the paper rather than selling out."

"So the Chris and Natalie rumors were true," I said. The acknowledgment made my stomach hurt. Even if Marjorie was a first-class bitch, she and VanHussen were married. They had kids. Wasn't anything sacred anymore?

Zoe raised her chin and pursed her lips. "You won't see either of them around here today, either, if you know what I mean. They're history. Together. VanHussen left the bitch. For Natalie." Zoe looked stunned but satisfied in that way some people get when they glimpse the carnage of an accident.

We heard footsteps on the linoleum behind us, and Zoe darted back into her cubicle. Only then did I realize the eerie quiet of the newsroom.

Did everyone know about the sellout but me?

Ohmigod, I was screwed.

I left Rich's photos, which I'd shoved to the back of

my bottom file drawer and never bothered to throw away, and managed to sneak out a few other things of personal value.

Computer files mostly. Those were easy to hide in my purse, and I just slipped out around ten and put them in my glove compartment. I'd planned to leave them in my purse, but Zoe managed to send me a quick SOS to be careful, they might search us.

Which they did not. And thank God they didn't, because I was still gagging to hit someone and that would have been the last straw.

So there I was, at home in the middle of the day.

Unemployed, holding a check worth three months' severance pay.

How decent of them.

At least I wasn't destitute.

No, I was three months away from indigence.

Beaten and bruised.

No idea what I wanted to do with the rest of my life except curl up in my bed and put a pillow over my head.

The phone rang and I let the machine get it.

I did not want to rehash the morning's gory events with Zoe, nor was I in the mood to listen to Karen moan about Giani. Maybe later. But right now I just needed—

"Hey, Liv, it's Hunter."

I sat bolt upright in my bed.

Wait a minute, why was he calling now? He knows I'm at work.

"I'm all messed up on time. I have no idea what time it is there right now, but I wanted to call and say hey. Let you know I'm thinking about you."

I reached for the phone, but I heard laughter in the background, then Hunter laughed and mumbled something I couldn't understand—sounded like he put his hand over the receiver.

"Anyway . . ." More laughter and hoots.

Oh, for God's sake, what was he doing?

A coil of irritation sprang free and needled every last nerve ending.

"Anyway, things are going great. Looks like they're going to sign us. So we'll come home and the lawyers will have to iron out the contract terms. God, it's going to take months before we have anything solid. Hey, but that's show biz. Listen, I'll talk to you tomorrow—Oh, I'll see you tomorrow. Yeah, that's right. God, you should be here. It's so cool, you'd love this place."

I could hear a guy's voice in the background and Hunter said, "Get out of here. Can't you see I'm on the phone? Oh, Liv, don't worry about picking me up from the airport. I'll be late. I'll share a cab with the guys."

Then he hung up.

I wished he wouldn't have called at all—calling me in the middle of the day. You knew I wouldn't be home, Hunter. Why did you call me here? Why not call my cell phone?

I got up and replayed the message, listening closer to see if I could detect any bimbo giggles in the background. There was one part of the tape that was questionable. I played it again.

And again.

Each time I felt worse and worse.

Until I shoved the telephone off the desk and sank down against the wall and cried.

Oh, God, what was wrong with me?

My life was falling apart.

I had absolutely no control over anything anymore.

I heard a pathetic howling sound like a dog being beaten

and realized it was coming from me.

So this is how it ended with Hunter. Better to end it now before that land mine exploded.

Maybe it just did.

I lay my head back on the couch pillows and cried. It was as if I were floating above my body looking down on myself.

I vaguely remembered a time when the days held so much possibility. Before the vast spaces started growing between trust and the truth.

I was sick to death of believing, trusting my life was on the upswing, because every time I did, everything blew up and sank a little lower.

I couldn't go any lower without landing in hell.

Oh, God, maybe I was already there.

Chapter Fifteen

The spell was broken, and I'd fallen back to earth with a shattering thud. Only two realities remained intact: I was jobless. And I didn't want to love a musician.

I could handle a Disney banjo player, but not a rock and roll front man.

We'd be broke.

And unstable.

He'd break my heart.

Then again, maybe I was the unstable one.

Whatever the case, I had to get the hell away from here until I was thinking straight. I wrote Juan a note: "I've gone away for a few days." Then I threw a few things in a tote bag and drove to the beach, the same place my mother and I used to go when we needed to get away. I locked myself in the hotel room and spent the better part of the next three days hashing it out with myself, writing in my journal. Though I hadn't been able to bring myself to work on the book. I'd given *Diena* an indefinite rest. Because the words just weren't flowing. Everything sounded forced and stilted.

But the journal was a help. In its pages I pondered how I couldn't come to terms with my own anonymity, so how was I supposed to live in the shadow of yet another man? Especially one on the verge of living his dreams in the spotlight.

I didn't even know if I believed in dreams anymore, because I didn't have any, except the bakery. But it wasn't really my dream. It was a hand-me-down from my mother.

I was thirty-two years old and I had no idea what I wanted. How pathetic was that?

I tossed the notebook and my pen aside and opened the sliding glass door and stepped out onto the balcony. The balmy, salty breeze wrapped around me like my mother's arms. She'd always loved the ocean, said the sound of the water cresting and falling washed away her troubles, made her feel brand-new. When I wanted to feel close to her, I'd come to the beach, because her soul lived here. I wished the surf and sand could make me whole again, but I was still broken.

A gull screeched as it flew by, its white body brilliant against the clear blue sky. If I didn't have any dreams of my own, what was wrong with borrowing my mother's? God knows she'd never used them.

The idea felt a little hollow. The bakery didn't really fit, but neither did most hand-me-downs. At least a business of my own was something substantial to hang my future on. A means to an end, so that I wouldn't have to depend on anyone but myself.

I scraped at a bubble of rusted white paint on the balcony rail. I was finished believing in others, trusting others. Because no matter how much you wanted to believe in someone else, in the end it always turned out the same.

The orange-tinged blister flaked and blew away with the wind. I mean, when Hunter was there, it was so easy to believe, but when he was gone. . . .

After my three-day hiatus, I got back into town at around two in the morning. I sat in the car for a few minutes in the sleepy, gray parking garage, listening to the silence. Hunter's truck was parked in the next row over.

Oh, Hunter.

He probably hated me. With good reason. I couldn't even be there for him, to celebrate his success, to share his joy.

What kind of a person did that make me?

A person whose world had fallen in around her, who didn't want to drag Hunter down into the depths of her despair. I was too messed up.

I got out of my car and headed upstairs.

At the beach, the only conclusion I'd come to was I needed to be by myself for a while so I could get my life back together. I needed to channel my energies into opening the bakery—that meant perfecting my mom's scone recipe, which was almost there, but not quite up to sell-it-to-the-public standards.

I was sitting in the dark living room, wired, staring out the window at the dark deserted street for half an hour, when I heard—Knock. Knock. Knock.

Someone at the door?

My heart lurched. Hunter?

Then sank. Oh, go away.

I can't talk to you right now. Go away and make it easier on both of us.

Knock. Knock. Knock.

Shit. He was going to wake Juan.

Knock. Knock. Knock.

I glanced at the clock. Three thirty-seven in the morning. Shhhhh! Just a minute.

I walked in the dark toward the door. Hunter was just going to have to understand that he couldn't do this. We were going to have to be civil and neighborly, but I needed time, space.

We used to be friends.

Could we still be friends?

Or had I ruined that, too?

Knock. Knock. Knock.

Don't beat down the door.

For a moment, the thought of his persistence lit a tiny spark of hope that cut through the muck of despair and whispered, "Maybe things will be okay." But then I pressed my eye to the peephole and saw Ron.

Not Hunter.

Ron.

I should have known. The spark fizzled like a snuffed candle. And my heart ached with an unreal intensity.

Ron started to knock again, but lost his balance and stumbled back a few steps.

Obviously drunk.

I hadn't seen him since the pantry incident a month ago. Juan broke up with him and hadn't seen hide nor hair of him.

Ewwwww. Speaking of hair, Ron's was longer and stringier. Looked like he hadn't bothered to shower or shave since the last time I saw him.

And what the hell was he wearing?

Pajamas? Whatever it was—some sort of long, white caftan—looked like Mr. GQ Cover Boy had let himself slip several notches.

I shivered and stepped back from the door. The way the peephole distorted his image made him look like some kind of miniature freaky Jesus.

Ron was certainly no Jesus.

Knock. Knock. Knock.

"What the hell is going on?" Juan padded into the hall, wearing nothing but a pair of boxers, his eyes all squinty with sleep. "And where the hell have you been?" His voice wide awake and full of anger.

Knock. Knock. Knock.

"Jesus Christ!" Juan said.

We should be so lucky. "No, it's more like the Antichrist. It's Ron."

Juan mumbled what sounded like a string of Spanish cuss words. I could honestly say this was the first time I'd ever seen Juan in a bad mood.

"I'll deal with him first," he grumbled. "Then you later, at a more civilized hour."

Uh-oh. Someone was pissed.

As I turned and made a getaway for my room, I heard Juan open the door.

"Ron, go home. I told you, it's over."

I heard the door shut. The knocking stopped. Just like that, Ron would go away and their relationship would fade into a memory of something that happened a long time ago.

There were certain people in this world with whom you just couldn't work things out. And it was best just to walk away and leave well enough alone.

Or was it?

In my room, I picked up my purse and took out my father's phone number. Then I lay down on my bed and studied it.

Maybe it was Ron's messed-up messiah look, maybe it was the general weirdness of the situation, but something reminded me of the summer when I was seven. My parents were still together and they sent me off to Oklahoma for two weeks with my dad's mom, Granny Logan, who was a staunch Baptist.

Granny Logan lived in Oklahoma so I didn't really know her. I'd never really spent any time with her since I lived in Florida and hundreds of miles separated us.

But I hoped the summer visit would change everything. We'd bake cookies. She'd let me stay up late and watch Johnny Carson and spoil me with Barbie dolls and junk food, like all my friends' grandmothers did.

As it turned out, Granny Logan didn't quite know what to do with me. She worked in her garden and read her Bible. I sat in the house all day and watched game shows and soap operas. She only got three channels, and when it rained the reception was bad, even when I moved the rabbit ears.

She bribed me with a buck for each book of the Bible I read while I was at her house. I tried, but for God's sake, I was seven years old. I'd barely mastered *See Spot run*. What was I supposed to get out of the *King James version of the Old Testament*?

I got about as far as Noah and the ark and "fifteen cubits upward did the waters prevail," before I considered it a sinking ship and went back to *As the World Turns* and *Hollywood Squares*. When the weather was too bad for TV and static took over, I played a game slipping and sliding in my sock feet down her long, polished hardwood hall pretending I was Dorothy Hamill giving a gold medal–winning Olympic performance.

One day as I watched *The Price Is Right*, the station ran a teaser for the noon news special, featuring cast members from the local production of *Jesus Christ Superstar*.

Jesus?

Heeeeey, Granny Logan liked Jesus. I liked plays. Maybe this was the bridge to common ground.

I waited until we sat down to our lunch of vegetables she'd harvested that morning then I said, "Granny Logan, can we go see the play *Jesus Christ Superstar*?"

She dropped her fork and glared at me as if I'd just blurted the F-word. My mouth went dry and she just kept staring at me.

What? What had I done wrong?

Finally, she said, "Where did you hear about such trash?"

I swallowed.

"On TV."

She pushed back her plate with such a vengeance that the

untouched ear of corn rolled onto the table. For a second I thought she was going to slap me, but instead, she ambled over to the TV, unplugged it and said if I didn't know what was wrong with calling our Lord Jesus a superstar, then I needed to spend a little more time reading the Bible rather than watching the humanistic trash on television.

I didn't know how she could call what I watched trash seeing how she was never in the room with me when I watched.

But I knew better than to argue. Trying to meet Granny Logan on common ground was kind of like trying to make a chocolate soufflé out of egg yolks and sardines, only harder.

What I didn't know until years later, was that Granny Logan had only agreed to keep me out of a martyred sense of obligation. So my parents could use the time I was away to save their marriage.

My father walked out on us a month later. I never saw him or Granny Logan again.

For years after he left, I'd wondered why my father hated me so much he would leave. I used to lie awake at night thinking if only he would've told me what was wrong, I would've changed to make him happy. So he'd come back and stay.

You'd think that after twenty-five years I would've gotten over it.

I looked at the paper and repeated his phone number out loud. All it would take was one phone call and I could ask him. After all these years.

Why did you walk out on a little girl who worshipped you?

A raw primitive grief tore at my insides. I tucked the edge of the paper with his number under the phone charger and went to bed.

★ ★ ★ ★ ★

I awoke to the sound of bells. Far off in the distance. No, wait, not bells . . .

Riiiiiing.

I sat up and blinked, looking around until it registered. I was in my room. The phone was ringing.

Hunter?

I lunged for the receiver.

"Hello?" My voice cracked.

"Where the hell have you been, Missy?"

Oh. Juan.

"I left you a note."

"You left a piece of paper saying you were going away for a few days. No address. No telephone number. No indication when you'd be back. I left about a hundred messages on your cell phone. I've been worried sick about you, 'Livia."

I rubbed my eyes.

God, what a nag. And I loved him for it.

"I'm sorry, I've had a lot—Are you at work?"

"Yes."

"Then I won't get into it now. I'll tell you later."

"My next client just canceled, and I don't have another for two hours. I'm coming home. I'll bring lunch since it's nearly noon."

By the time I'd showered and dressed, Juan was home with Cuban sandwiches, chips and giant chocolate chunk cookies. I poured us tall glasses of iced tea, and we sat at the kitchen table and ate. In between bites of crusty bread filled with ham and tender roast pork, I told him everything—about the paper closing, and how that on top of Rich's death and Geneviève's appearance and Hunter going off to L.A. was just too much.

I took the dill pickles off my sandwich and confided how

everything was compounded by the engagement lie. "And even though it's not a whopper, I don't know how I'm going to explain everything else without telling him I lied."

I crunched a potato chip and licked the salt from my lips.

"Just tell him," Juan said as he retrieved a piece of mozzarella cheese that had fallen from his sandwich onto his plate. "What's the big deal?"

"Right now everything feels like a big deal—even getting out of bed is like a big deal—"

"Talk to him. The boy's been worried sick about you. He's crazy for you, 'Livia, and if you let him get away you'll be the crazy one."

Juan's words filled me with a mixture of dread and hope. I knew Hunter was crazy for me. Because I was just as crazy for him, but . . . but he scared me to death.

He was too real. The emotions felt too big. So big I couldn't hide from them. With Rich, there'd always been a certain remoteness to our relationship, a certain part of each of our souls off-limits to the other. I pushed the pickles over to the side of my plate. The saddest part was neither Rich nor I ever even tried to excavate the emotions. We were perfectly happy leaving the depths unexplored.

But that's not how it was with Hunter. He was everywhere I breathed, in my heart, my head, my soul, under my skin, breathing life into me. When I was with him, I was alive, but dammit, when I wasn't with him, I was afraid. The deeper the emotions, the longer and harder the fall.

I picked up one of the giant chocolate chunk cookies and broke off a piece. "Since the first time I laid eyes on Hunter, I've felt like my life has been spinning and sliding out of control. My God, the psychic said he's my soul mate, Juan. What if I believe her and she's wrong? I can't take anymore right now." I bit into the cookie. A large piece of chocolate started melting on contact with my tongue.

Juan blew out a breath that sounded like, "Pooooooooh," and narrowed his eyes at me. " 'Livia, you want to spend the rest of your life running from love?"

"Of course not." That would make me just like my father. Well, maybe not *just* like him—my whole reason for running was so I wouldn't hurt Hunter like my father hurt me. And, okay, so I wouldn't open *myself* up to being hurt like that again.

Juan threw his hands in the air like he didn't know what to do with me. "You blow this chance with Hunter, you don't deserve another chance."

I blinked. My God, he was right.

Then his face softened and he smiled. "Because if you let him walk away, you'll violate dating rule number . . . *número . . . cinco? Seis?* Well, consider this *the* cardinal dating rule: Never look a soul mate in the mouth."

"What?"

Juan scratched his head. "You know, like *gee-ft horse.* Neever look a gee-ft horse in the mouth."

I laughed. "Juan, the proverb loses something in the translation."

He raised his brows and grinned. "See, you know what I mean. 'Livia, don't take love for granted, nothing is a given. Look at what happened with the *Daily.* The things that seem most stable sometimes tumble and fall. So you lose really big by playing it safe, just like you lose when you gamble. Only you don't have so much fun. 'Livia, take a chance."

Ohmigod, he was right. And I could rationalize it, but making myself believe it was another story.

"I have to get back to work. Mrs. Donneley, my pain in the ass customer is coming in at two." He rolled his eyes and massaged his temples. "I must prepare myself for her."

I stood and hugged Juan.

"You think about what I said, then you go see Hunter, okay?"

I shrugged. Juan sighed and walked to the door.

As I cleared the lunch dishes from the table, I was filled with the realization that despite the carnage caused by the exploding land mines, my life was very rich in many small, unconventional ways. Like Juan. And Karen. Maybe I just needed to clear the rubble of the past and concentrate on building anew, from the ground up. I knew right where to start sweeping.

I walked into my room and picked up the piece of paper I'd tucked under the phone last night, and stared long and hard at the name and number of the man who'd given me life.

The man whom I'd allowed to steal my life.

What the hell did I think I'd accomplish by phoning him? That we'd just pick right up where we'd left off?

I mean, what did I want from him? What did I expect him to say? So sorry? I've been meaning to call, but—

But what?

But nothing.

There was absolutely nothing he could say or do to change the past. He chose not to be a part of my life for the past twenty-five years. I was choosing to believe that trying to bring him back into my life now wouldn't solve anything.

As of this moment, *I* chose to walk away from him and maybe, just maybe, by doing this, I'd set the course for a fresh start.

With a heavy, sad heart, I tore up the piece of paper, then walked out into the living room. The early afternoon quiet was too much to bear because my thoughts were much too noisy. So I put on the new Matchbox Twenty CD. I needed to hear something bold, something with an edge. I turned up the music.

Loud.

The bass thumped through me as I walked into the kitchen, put on some coffee and took out the ingredients for my mom's cinnamon scones. I had to perfect this recipe and concoct several more originals before I could even think about opening the bakery.

Flour dust wafted up as I measured four cups for *my mom's scones.*

Four teaspoons of vanilla this time rather than three. They needed more flavor. The pungent sweetness lightened my mood a bit.

Her scones for her bakery.

A dash more ground cinnamon, too, maybe.

What did I want?

I sprinkled in the burnt-orange powder and the spiciness melded with the luscious vanilla, creating an exotic, aromatic blend that almost seemed right. But not quite. Maybe the recipe needed a little more butter.

I didn't know what I wanted.

Or did I?

I creamed extra butter in a small mixing bowl with the sugar and egg.

Is that what I'd been running from all along? Blame it all on my dad leaving, on my mom dying. . . .

I blended the dry and creamed ingredients and added the cinnamon chips, mixing the batter by hand. On the stereo, Matchbox Twenty sang about realizing too late that there were some things in life you just couldn't change.

I stopped stirring and stared at the lumps in the sticky batter.

But there were some things I could change—just like let-

281

ting go of the stale notion of reuniting with my father.

Why was I forcing myself to wear my mother's hand-me-down dreams? Again, contorting myself to do what I thought I should do, rather than reaching out to discover what *I* wanted. Maybe that's why I'd let the bakery money sit untouched in the bank all these years.

LAAAAAAAAA. LAAAAAAA. LAAAAAAA. Can't hear you. Don't go there!

Standing on the threshold of a brand-new life, did I really want to tie myself down to something my heart wasn't really into?

LAAAAAAAAA. LAAAAAAA. LAAAAAAA. Don't want to hear you. Don't want to go there right now.

My heart couldn't answer that question, but even over the mind-noise it did latch onto the feeling that I was a fool for letting go of the one true thing—or person—who wasn't a hand-me-down, the one who actually fit—Hunter.

Ohmigod. Was I an idiot?

I left the scone mess, and went across the hall and knocked on Hunter's door.

Please don't let it be too late.

I had no idea what the hell I was going to say to him. Well, yes, I did, but I didn't know where to begin.

My heart thudded and my hands shook so hard I had to clasp them in front of me.

I'd begin with the truth.

I knocked again.

And waited.

I pressed my trembling hands to my face.

Oh, God, I'd screwed up. I'd screwed up royally.

I backed across the hall toward my door and bit my lip until it throbbed to the beat of my aching heart and music I could hear drifting through my open door.

Could I blame Hunter if he didn't want to see me? I'd been living in such a panic, afraid he'd run out on me. But did I stop to think what my running out on him would do to him?

I stood on my door's threshold staring at Hunter's closed door as if I could will him to answer. The guy from Matchbox Twenty was singing about who was going to save him when all the love was gone. And I wanted to cry because his words were so true. Love never lasted. It was like a glass of fine wine that one savored until the glass was drained, leaving you thirsty for more. But there was never more. There was never enough.

I jumped at the sound of Hunter's door opening. His hair was wet, and he looked like he'd just gotten out of the shower.

That familiar overflowing sensation started in my heart.

Ohmigod, just look at him standing there. I swallowed. Why did this have to be so impossible?

He stared at me for several seconds, his brows knit, and I braced myself for him to turn around and shut the door. But instead, he walked over and hugged me.

"You're okay," he said, his cheek pressed against mine.

"I'm sorry," was all I could mutter.

Then he stepped back, frowning. "I was afraid of this."

"Afraid of what?"

"Of a total rebound experience. Liv, you just ended a relationship with a guy you were going to marry. You need time to get over it. Time to get your head together. I guess we shouldn't have taken things so fast."

I heard the elevator ding down the hall. "Can you come in here so we can talk?"

He nodded and stepped inside. We went into the living room and sat down. Again, we looked at each other for a few seconds. I knew this time it was up to me to bridge the silence.

"You know how I told you things had been over with Richard for a long time?"

He raked his hand through his damp hair and nodded.

"Well, that was only half the truth. The other half was a lie. Rich and I were never engaged. I never went to Paris. The night I met you, Rich called and told me he'd married someone else. That's why I moved in with Juan. That's why believing in you—in us—has been so hard."

He didn't say anything. He just sat there with his elbows braced on his knees and stared at me. The silence was excruciating, so I told him about losing my job and about Geneviève showing up and finding out that I'd been the other woman. Not only had Rich never gotten married, he'd lied to both Geneviève and me. "Then you flew off to L.A. ready to sign record deals and live your dreams, and it just reminded me that I have no dreams. Most of all, I saw myself wanting to love you . . . and losing you. And I just can't go through that again."

Ugggh, I was babbling and tears were threatening. And he was just sitting there looking at me with this really somber face, still saying nothing.

I held my breath so I wouldn't feel compelled to fill the silence with nonsense. Finally, he said, "Liv, I don't know what you want."

What was I supposed to say? What could I say? One minute I thought I knew what I wanted, the next I wanted to run and hide like a scared child.

"Music has always been my dream," he said. "Please don't make me choose between you and living my dream."

"I don't want you to choose."

But I don't want to lose you. If you step into the spotlight I might never see you again.

"Then you're going to have to trust me," he said.

And a tear slipped down my cheek, and I felt myself shaking my head. Trust. The thought was just too terrifying. It's not that I didn't trust him. I didn't trust the world. I didn't trust circumstance.

"Liv, then *what* do you want? Tell me what you want."

"I don't know what I want."

He stood.

"You need to figure it out. Let me know when you do."

Then he turned and walked out.

After Hunter left, the condo was closing in on me. I had to do something. I had to get out of there before I started climbing the walls.

I decided to take a long walk. To get some fresh air so that maybe I could put things in perspective.

I walked toward Lake Eloa on my usual route down Washington Street. Fuchsia, pink-and-white-studded hibiscus bushes lined the sidewalks. The tabebuia trees were in bloom. Their brilliant yellow flowers dotted the branches like canary diamonds. A sure sign spring was in the air.

Funny, they weren't in bloom before I'd left for the beach. But in true fashion, they'd popped almost overnight. The gorgeous yellow flowers would only last a short time before they fell to the ground leaving the branches bare.

So much beauty. Such a short window of opportunity to enjoy it. How ironically lifelike. You blink. You miss it. I bent and picked up one of the freshly fallen blossoms. It had not yet begun to fade, but too soon it would droop and wither. Past its prime.

I tucked it in the band of my ponytail and stepped up my pace to a jog. Eventually, I found myself at the old bakery storefront, the "For Lease" sign still taped to the window.

I really needed to call about leasing it.

Why *didn't* I call about it?

Nothing was stopping me now. Nothing stood in the way. Except the scone recipe. I had to get the scone recipe right before I could do anything.

My mother had the recipe down to a science. What was I doing wrong?

What did my mother do wrong? What stopped her from calling? She'd carried this bakery dream all those years, yet had done nothing about it. She never broke away and did what was in her heart. And she'd died young and lonely.

Unfulfilled? I couldn't say. God, I hoped not. That would've been the ultimate waste of life.

I pressed my nose against the window, just like the two of us had always done, standing right here, side by side.

My situation was different. Much different.

My breath made a fog print on the glass. I could almost feel my mother standing beside me and hear her say, "The recipe will never be right because this isn't what you should be doing. You don't have to do it for me. Take a chance, Olivia. Build dreams of your own or you'll die sad and lonely and unfulfilled."

No. . . . I stepped back, my fingertips still pressed against the glass. I watched my breath print dissipate and felt a chain slipping from my soul.

My hand fell away from the window, and all of a sudden everything crystallized.

This wasn't *mine*.

Forcing myself to wear my mother's hand-me-down dreams, I was once again contorting myself to do what I thought I *should* do, rather than reaching out to discover what *I* wanted. That's why the bakery money had sat untouched in the bank all these years. Keeping my mother's dreams alive at my expense wouldn't rewrite the past. Wouldn't change the fact that she'd allowed my father to suck the very lifeblood out of her dreams when he walked out.

Mine was waiting for me to claim it. And it was up to me to make sure my father or Rich or any other person never took my dreams from me. If I died sad and lonely and unfulfilled it was all *my* fault.

I turned away from the storefront and walked home as fast as I could.

When I stepped into the lobby, the mail carrier was stuffing envelopes into the community box. He handed me the contents of number 343.

A bunch of bills and a large Priority Mail envelope addressed to me. I glanced at the generic P.O. box return address and my heart slammed against my chest.

It was one of the partial manuscripts I'd sent out in the last round of submissions. The course Hunter had encouraged me to take a chance on.

Another rejection? Uggggh.

As I ascended the stairs, I took a deep breath and tore open the envelope. I stopped on the third-floor landing and squeezed my eyes shut before I pulled out the inch-thick stack of paper.

Here goes.

Dear Ms. Logan:

What? Not a form letter? No smudged "Dear Author" from a master copy that had been Xeroxed too many times?

My eyes scanned the page and picked up words like good premise, nice style, funny. Funny? Ohmigod. Yea! She thinks I'm funny. I hope she thinks I'm funny in the places I intended to be funny—Wait—*I'd like to see the complete manuscript when it's available.*

Ohmigod! Ohmigod! Ohmigod!

Oh, no. The book wasn't even halfway done.

My heart pounded for a very different reason now. But what the hell else did I have to do with my time except finish the damn book?

Oh, wait, there was *more*. The editor had actually taken the time to write suggestions on the body of the first three chapters.

I hugged the pages to me. To the untrained eye, this might seem insignificant. I mean, it wasn't a publishing contract— not yet. But it was an interim step. A step that confirmed I was a writer, not a baker.

How symbolic.

A sign that it was time I started writing what was in my heart. Not anonymous restaurant reviews or anything else where I hid behind a ridiculous pseudonym or anonymous byline. I had a lot of hard work ahead of me, but I was up for the challenge.

I had to tell Hunter.

After weeks of bleak, tunneling despair, I felt like I'd won the lottery. Finally, a little sunshine in my dark corner of the world, a ray that wouldn't have broken through if I hadn't taken a chance, put my former critic's butt on the line.

I pushed open the stairwell door and noticed a manila envelope leaning against my door. When I picked it up, I saw it was addressed to me. Hunter's handwriting.

Ohmigod, what was this? The mother of all rejections? Tightness gripped my chest as I unlocked the door to the condo and walked in.

I walked into the living room, and again I held my breath and opened the second envelope of the day.

I pulled out a CD and a note that simply said, "We can fix

this. And I'm not talking about what's on the CD. I'm talking about us."

Ohhhhhh. My heart did a triple-gainer. I fell back into the couch cushions for a second, then got up and popped the disc in the player and heard Hunter's voice singing my poem set to music.

Was it *really* mine? It was mine. Oh, wow. It sounded great. Hunter sounded great. I glanced at the note again, just to make sure I'd read it right.

Yep, the message was still there.

I was floored. Especially when I heard the next song on the CD, and it was called "Live a little—No, Liv, a lot."

My mind shot back to when we were toasting the night before he flew off to L.A. When he'd looked at me and said he was starting to care for me a little, then he stopped and said, "No, Liv, a lot. I care for you a lot." And how he'd almost said he loved me, but I wouldn't let him.

He loved me.

Me.

Just as I was—big girl or two sizes smaller, anonymous restaurant critic or unemployed novelist. And it was proving too easy for me to care for him, too. That's why I had to run. I didn't want him to love me, because love always led to loss, which led to me trying to reinvent myself into someone smart enough, quick enough, desirable enough to be worthy of being loved. But the more I tried to reinvent myself, the more twisted and tainted my life became.

Maybe I just needed to ride life's current for a while, because when you're on the right path, the right choices present themselves in an effortless flow. If you don't resist.

How could I resist? I was still scared to death.

But I revamped my list of affirmations to include: I graciously accept love into my life; I am lovable and deserve to be happy; love flows freely from me; and (most importantly) I know what I want.

I could almost say them without cringing. Because I finally believed I did have one or two dreams. One which I could keep alive by reporting to my muse every day (The whole French Tart/Dick episode was certainly stranger than fiction. My next book? Hmmmmmm . . .), the other dream could be revived with a knock on the door of the sexy songwriter across the hall.

My sexy songwriter.

The man who was so sure *we* would be okay. All I had to do was tell him I'd finally figured out *exactly* what I wanted.

I folded his note, put it in the drawer on top of my mother's recipe book, and marched across the hall and knocked on the door.

Well, I'd warned Hunter this could get complicated. *Hunter, my love, I'm about to complicate you like you've never been complicated before.*

Dreams were risky little buggers, but all of a sudden I had a new attitude that urged me to take a chance.

To live a little.

No, better yet, to live *a lot*.

About the Author

Nancy Robards Thompson has reinvented herself numerous times. In the process, she's worked a myriad of jobs including television show stand-in; casting extras for a movie; and several mindless jobs in public relations and the fashion industry. She earned a degree in journalism only to realize reporting "just the facts" bored her silly. Much more content to report to her muse, Nancy has found nirvana doing what she loves most—writing romantic fiction. Since hanging up her press pass, this two-time nominee for the Romance Writers of America's Golden Heart struck gold in July 2002 when she won the coveted award. Nancy lives in Florida and dreams of living the life of a bohemian writer in Paris with her husband, daughter and their three cats. *Reinventing Olivia* is her first published novel.